ALPHA ASCENDING

ALSO BY ALICIA MONTGOMERY

THE TRUE MATES SERIES

Fated Mates

Blood Moon

Romancing the Alpha

Witch's Mate

Taming the Beast

Tempted by the Wolf

THE LONE WOLF DEFENDERS SERIES

Killian's Secret

Loving Quinn

All for Connor

THE TRUE MATES STANDALONE NOVELS

Holly Jolly Lycan Christmas

A Mate for Jackson: Bad Alpha Dads

TRUE MATES GENERATIONS

A Twist of Fate

Claiming the Alpha

Alpha Ascending

A Witch in Time

THE BLACKSTONE MOUNTAIN SERIES

This is a work of fiction. Names, characters, businesses, places, events, locales, and incidents are either the products of the author's imagination or used in a fictitious manner. Any resemblance to actual persons, living or dead, or actual events is purely coincidental.

Copyright © 2019 Alicia Montgomery
Edited by LaVerne Clark
Cover by Jacqueline Sweet

All rights reserved.

ALPHA ASCENDING

TRUE MATES GENERATIONS BOOK 3

ALICIA MONTGOMERY

PROLOGUE

DETECTIVE SOFIA SELINOFOTO WAS *NOT* HAVING A good day.

When she came in for her shift that morning in New York's Midtown Precinct, the first piece of news she got was that the suspect she'd been keeping tabs on skipped town. Then at around lunchtime, the DNA results from a murder case she had been working on for six weeks had come back inconclusive. Finally, at around mid-afternoon, the lawyer of the witness in a robbery case called her and said his client had changed his mind about testifying. Months of work down the fucking drain.

They said that bad luck often came in threes, and she was really hoping that fate was done screwing her over, because she'd already reached her quota.

It didn't need repeating that she was not having a good day. But, by the look on her captain's face as he approached her, it *wasn't* going to get better.

"Selinofoto." Steve Bushnell's voice was low and gravely, containing all the brusqueness one would expect from a police captain. A former Marine, Bushnell had a reputation as a hard-ass, but he also ran a tight ship.

"Sir," she greeted, putting away a folder into her file cabinet.

"Are you headed home?"

The clock on her desk said it was already 9:00 p.m. "Yes, sir." She studied the look on his face, noting the flash of irritation in his clear blue eyes. Not at her, she could tell, but by what he was about to ask her. She liked the captain and that he didn't tolerate bullshit or the other shit people around her had put her through after *The Incident*. "What can I do for you, Captain?"

"There's been a disturbance in Midtown at some club. I need you to go check it out."

"I'm almost ready to clock out." Then, glancing around her, she realized there were no other detectives around her. She could have sworn that Rodriguez and James were right behind her just minutes ago. Their shift went until midnight, while hers should have been done three hours ago. *Of course.* Someone at dispatch probably warned them about the call and they conveniently disappeared. *Assholes.* But she was used to it, after all these months.

"I really do hate to put you out, but I'm out of options."

She let out a long, inner sigh. If she wasn't loyal to this man who had protected her and made sure she was still doing what she loved, she would have told him tough shit and to find someone else. "A disturbance at a club, huh?"

"Yeah. Probably just some kids who couldn't take their liquor." Anyone under forty was a "kid" to Bushnell. "Just take some statements and check it out." He handed her a slip of paper.

Reading it, she let out a loud, "Hmmm." She placed the paper in her pocket and then picked up her jacket. "All right, I'll head there. Want me to come back and file the report right away?"

"Do it tomorrow. Head home right after."

"Will do." She inclined her head at him and then grabbed her bag. The address the captain had given her wasn't too far, and it only took her ten minutes to drive to the place. There was already one black and white parked outside. She pulled up next to it and exited the door, then checked to make sure she was at the right place.

The sign outside the sleek black door said "Blood Moon." A strange sensation ran down the line of her back. There was something about this place ... had it always been there? She'd been working in Midtown for years, since she got out of the academy. Two years as a beat cop and then five as a detective. She must have driven down this street at least once a week, yet she never noticed the club nor recalled if she'd ever even seen it until tonight. Maybe it was new or they had renamed it, but for the life of her, she couldn't remember what stood here before.

Pushing those thoughts aside, she strolled up to the front door. There was no line of people waiting to get in, yet two burly bouncers guarded it, blocking her way. When she came closer, one of them took a step toward her.

"Easy there, boys." She flashed her detective's badge. The two men looked at each other, looking unsure. She flashed them a freezing look, not really in the mood to tolerate any chauvinistic bullshit right now. The one man backed away and even gestured to open the door for her, but she beat him to it, pushing the heavy onyx barrier with both hands and then stepped inside the club.

Most people underestimated her because of her size and the fact that she was a woman. In fact, during her first day at the academy, a group of recruits thought they could intimidate her because she had a petite stature, as well as a vagina. When she knocked their ringleader on his ass during self-defense drills, they quickly learned that Sofia Selinofoto was not someone you messed around with.

The inside of the club was much larger than it looked from the outside. It seemed like a typical club, with a large dance floor in the middle, two bars, a DJ booth and stage, plus several VIP booths scattered around. All the lights were on and it was practically empty, but she could tell that this place was probably packed all the time. Glancing around, she saw the two uniformed officers in the corner, talking to a third man.

She strode across the room and stopped short of the group of men. "Excuse me."

The uniformed officer turned around. "Well, hello, Detective." His voice was pure disdain.

Great. Just who she needed. Gabriel Martinez. "Officer." She gave him a nod, keeping her face as neutral as she could. There was no way she was going to give him the satisfaction of seeing her annoyed. So instead, she turned to the lone civilian in the group. "I'm Detective Sofia Selinofoto." She held up her badge. "And you are?"

"Zac Vrost." The handsome, blond man offered her a hand. "I'm one of the partners here."

She eyed his hand, her gaze going up his arm and then crashing into blue eyes. There was something about them that she just couldn't place, but her gut was telling her something about Zac Vrost wasn't as it seemed. "So, can you tell me what happened?"

He dropped his hand smoothly, unperturbed by her brusqueness. "I've already given my statement to the officer."

She flashed him the same look that she gave the bouncers. "Then you can give it to me again."

Zac Vrost didn't seem the least bit intimidated, and his own gaze intensified. He seemed to have a quick inner battle with himself, then began to speak. "Fine. I was inside The Lounge when—shit!"

"Shit?" Was this guy kidding?

Panic flashed for a split-second on Vrost's face. "That's not, I mean—excuse me."

When he sidestepped her like she wasn't even there, her blood began to boil. Seriously? She could take this shit from fellow police officers, but she was *not* going let a civilian get away with disrespecting her like that. She marched after him, her mind already filled with the things she wanted to say to him, when she suddenly stopped.

Zac Vrost's back was turned to her, his arm supporting someone who seemed to have trouble staying on his feet. A *half-naked* someone, dressed only in dark slacks.

"Zac," the man grumbled. "I—"

Sofia froze, feeling her heart thud against her ribcage like a jackhammer. A searing gaze bore into her, making her breath catch. Heat waves seemed to emanate from those strange eyes. Beautiful eyes, actually—one green and one blue. The force of his stare made her stagger back. Sensuous male lips parted. "Who are—"

"Mr. Vrost." She broke the gaze, snapping out of the

trance those eerie eyes cast on her. "What's going on?" There was a door behind him, and from the quick peek she got, it looked like a whole other room. Was there a secret club inside this club? What was going on in there? And why was that man half naked? It took all her strength, but she avoided looking down at his muscled chest.

Vrost mumbled something and then kicked his foot forward to shut the door. "Nothing, Detective," he said as he swung around to face her. "Just a private party."

"You're still having a party in there? After what happened?" she asked.

"Well, business is business. You know how cutthroat rent is in Manhattan. I can't afford to shut down."

True. It wasn't like it was a serious incident, probably just a couple of guys shoving each other. But something about this whole thing wasn't right. Unable to help herself, her gaze slid back to the half-naked man. Vrost had propped him up, facing away from her. Oh dear Lord, the man was sexy from behind too. That sinewy back was bunching with muscles, and all that tanned golden skin begged for a licking. *Get a fucking grip, Selinofoto.* "What's wrong with him?"

"Just a little too much to drink. It's his, er, bachelor party," he said. "You know how it is. Last days of freedom."

For some reason, her chest tightened and her stomach fell. She told herself it wasn't because of the knowledge that he was taken. Still, it was like having a bucket of ice poured all over her. "Well, then, why don't you send the groom back to the party and come and make your statement."

"No," the man slurred. "You—"

"Will do, Detective." Vrost gripped his friend tighter.

"Come along now, all your friends are waiting." He grabbed the door, opened it, then stepped inside.

She lunged forward, trying to catch the door before it closed but it was too late. It was one of those secret doors, built into the wall so no one could see it and had no latch or handle. "What the *fuck*?" Did everyone here think they were above the law? How dare he just walk away from her? There was definitely something going on around her, and she didn't like it. Vrost was definitely hiding something.

She waited there, hating that she probably looked like an idiot. Martinez and his partner were probably snickering at her, but she didn't dare give them the satisfaction of knowing she was frustrated or that Vrost had just ignored her.

When the door budged open, her body went tense, ready to tear Vrost a new asshole. But, to her surprise, someone else walked out of the secret entrance—a tall, older man. Tall was an understatement; he was probably half a foot over six feet and had broad shoulders like a mountain. He also had long blond hair tied back in a ponytail, and his loose shirt and dark pants made him look like a pirate. Or a viking. When those sea-green eyes turned on her, she found herself drawing back into a defensive stance.

"Are you Detective Selinofoto?" he asked. There was a hint of accent in his voice. She was usually good with figuring out where people came from based on their accents, but for the life of her, she couldn't tell with him.

"Yes." She made her irritation obvious in her voice. "Who are you?"

"My name is Daric Jonasson. I'm also a partner in this club," he said. "Zac wanted me to take care of you."

"Did he?" Her thoughts drew back to the other man. The groom.

"Yes, I believe I can answer all your questions. Follow me, please."

"Hold on," she said, moving away from him. "Where are you—"

He took a step toward her. Not anticipating such a bold move, she didn't have time to dodge him, and he caught her wrist, then placed his other hand in his pocket. Was he taking out a weapon?

"What the fuck! Let go or I'll have you arrested for assaulting a police officer!"

The man's eyes flashed surprise for a moment then he took a step back. He held his hands up in surrender. "I mean you no harm, Detective. I just wanted to stop you from tripping and hurting yourself."

"Tripping? On what?"

"On that." He nodded toward the floor.

She followed his gaze and noticed the empty bottle of champagne by her foot. "That wasn't there a second ago."

"Perhaps you just didn't notice it roll towards you."

"Maybe." There was definitely something going on here. "We don't have to go anywhere, Mr. Jonasson. I can take your statement right here."

"All right, Detective. Whatever you want." He cocked his head at her, the expression on his face curious. "But first, may I see your badge?"

"Fine." She held it up. "Satisfied."

"Sofia Selinofoto." The corner of his mouth quirked up. "Wisdom and moonlight in Greek."

"My family is Greek," she found herself saying, then

shook her head. Why the hell was she revealing personal information to a stranger? She shrugged. "Mr. Jonasson, just tell me where you were during the incident and what you witnessed."

"There really is no need, Detective. We don't plan on pressing charges. The disturbance happened on private property, not out on the street. Besides, the people who caused the trouble are long gone."

"But you have cameras all over the place, right?"

"Yes, but it would be a waste of resources and time—ours and your department—to track them down for a little scuffle that really hurt no one but themselves," he pointed out.

She didn't like any of this. Not the way his reasoning made sense or the way he looked at her. Like he knew everything about her with one look. But she couldn't do anything else, not unless she found evidence that there was something illegal going on. "You're right." *Unfortunately.* She took out her card and handed it to him. "But if you do change your mind—"

"I know where to find you," he finished, taking her card.

With a nod, she pivoted on her heel and walked toward the exit. She ignored Martinez's disdainful glance, despite the fact that she could feel it burning a hole in her back. Pushing at the door, she walked out onto the sidewalk.

It was one of those cold winter nights, so it wasn't surprising that she was shivering. But the cold air felt amazing on her face, and she didn't even realize that her cheeks were warm.

Despite Jonasson's reassurances, her gut was screaming at her. It was telling her something was not right at Blood Moon. Everything about the whole thing was strange.

And then the image of mismatched eyes popped into her mind. That man. He was attractive for sure. No, attractive wasn't the right word. Magnetic.

And so very taken. It was his stag party, after all, and it looked like he was trying to make the most of his last nights of freedom judging by how drunk he was. Did they also have strippers in there? Again, that strange tightening in her chest came back, but she pushed it away.

A quick glance at her watch told her that it was past ten thirty in the evening. She'd been working for over fourteen hours, and now fatigue was creeping into her body. Really, she should go home and crash. Vrost and Jonasson were doing her a favor by not adding to her caseload. This was one gift horse she shouldn't be looking in the mouth. With everything else going on, she should just walk away from Blood Moon and never come back.

CHAPTER ONE

LUCAS ANDERSON STARED OUT OF THE WINDOW OF HIS office on the sixty-eighth floor of the Fenrir Corp. building, watching the snow drifting down slowly, obscuring his view of New York in a sheet of whiteness. It was getting late, and he really wanted to leave, but he had one more appointment.

"Mr. Anderson?" The voice was hesitant, almost scared.

"Yes?" He turned around to find his new assistant, David Masters, standing by the door. Instantly, his inner wolf was on alert. *Calm down*, he said to the animal who shared his body. David was new to the job, having only been with him for a few weeks, so his wolf wasn't yet used to the human's presence. *Stop!* His wolf reached forward, trying to break through their skin, but he reined it in. It was getting harder to control his animal, but he chalked it up to the events of the past few weeks and the threat surrounding them. He reached deep inside him, trying to recall his training. *Find something to ground you. A memory. A scent.* Those from before the incident worked best. Family vacations with parents and sisters. Mama's lingering scent at the breakfast table after she left for work in the morning.

"James Turner is here, sir."

Lucas cleared his mind and focused his attention on his assistant. David looked so nervous Lucas almost wondered if the young man suspected his true nature. Humans, except for a select few, had no idea that Lycans—wolf shifters—lived among them.

"Show him inside then."

His assistant gave him a nod then took a step back, letting the door close. Lucas strode back to his large desk in the middle of the office and sat in his plush leather chair. A few seconds later, James Turner entered through the door, all smug and swagger as he walked in.

His wolf barely had time to calm down when it went on alert again. Turner's very presence and human scent sent the animal on edge, despite having known him for years. But then again, his wolf had great instincts and could probably sense that something wasn't right.

Turner was looking around the plush room, probably redecorating the space in his mind. After all, with Lucas moving up as CEO next month, the Chief Operating Officer role was up for grabs. Being one of the more senior executives, Turner was one of the leading candidates for the position. Too bad, after this meeting, he was never going to step through the doors of Fenrir Corp. ever again.

"Lucas," Turner greeted, his smile all white, shiny teeth, thanks to one of Manhattan's premiere dentists. From his perfectly-cut hair, to his bespoke Armani suit, and down to the tips of his designer shoes, James Turner reeked of money and privilege. "I can't tell you how happy I am you called me in here."

Lucas tried not to smile. Really, he shouldn't be happy about this. Except that James Turner was about to get everything he deserved. "Sit down, please."

Turner took a seat opposite him, extending his legs and crossing them at the ankle. "So, I hope everything went well in Geneva?"

"As could be expected." Lucas took a folder from the drawer under his desk, placed it on the table, then slid it toward Turner.

Turner's eyes practically glowed with glee as he took the folder and opened it. However, as his gaze scanned across the page, his expression quickly turned sour. "What is the meaning of this?"

"You can read, right?" Lucas said in a bored tone. "What does it look like?"

"I thought this was ... that you would." He dropped the folder on the table. "This is preposterous."

He knew the other man was hoping it was an offer and compensation package, not a termination letter. "If you read the rest of the papers, you'll see that we have a generous offer for you."

"But I—" His fingers shuffled through the papers, and his face turned red. "A dollar? A measly fucking dollar after all the years I worked here?"

Turner looked like he was close to blowing his top, and Lucas wanted to relish this moment. Keep it in his memory bank for those times he needed a pick-me-up. "If you read further, you'll see that Fenrir will not be going after you for the money you embezzled, nor will we take legal actions against you—don't even try denying it." His tone was now ominous and cold. "The forensic accountants I hired are the best."

The accounting firm had been thorough in their months-long investigation, and Lucas wouldn't have confronted Turner if there was a single doubt in their findings. He and his father, Grant, who was still currently the CEO of Fenrir Corp., had gone through the different scenarios of what to do with their findings. They both decided that they didn't want a scandal or any attention on the company, seeing as there was going to be a shift in power soon, so they decided to deal with the matter privately.

Turner stood up and slapped his palms on the desk. "You can't ... I'll fight this in court." Strong words, but Lucas could smell the fear from the other man.

Really, it wasn't a large amount of money, which was why they didn't detect it right away. But it wasn't the amount that mattered. It was the principle. James Turner was a thief and a liar. "Just try it," Lucas said. Maybe he let his wolf come to the surface. Just a little bit. Enough to give off a flash of Alpha power.

As a human, Turner probably didn't understand what was happening, but he most likely felt it, and it sent him slamming back down into his chair.

"Ah, looks like security is here." Lucas nodded toward the door where two burly men in uniform had entered. He had instructed David to let them in as soon as they arrived. "They will be escorting you straight to your car. Someone will pack up your office, and your personal items will be mailed to your home address." Turner opened his mouth to speak but Lucas silenced him by putting up a hand. "Don't. Don't even try it.

We have all the evidence we need. All you have to do is leave quietly and leave without a fuss. Don't even think of talking to the press; the NDA you signed is iron-clad."

Turner's face was now all shades of purple, but he gave him a curt nod.

"Take him away," he said to the guards. The scent of the human's fear and anger was offending his and his wolf's senses. He watched with satisfaction as Turner walked toward the door, flanked by the two guards.

Some might say that Turner was getting off easy. But getting justice for his white-collar crimes didn't outweigh the attention it would put on Fenrir, and in turn, the Lycan kind. They'd maintained their secret because they guarded their privacy. If the humans found out about them, well, it would bring danger to all Lycans, not just in New York but all over the world. They wouldn't be able to get any justice, but sometimes, they had to make sacrifices for the good of their kind.

"Oh, by the way," Lucas called out. Turner stopped and looked back at him. "If you think you can quickly find another job in New York or any other major city, think again. We've alerted every major corporation and headhunter in every country that Fenrir does business in. They know not to entertain your calls."

"You can't do that," Turner spat. "How am I going to live?"

"I guess you'll have to budget." This time, he couldn't hide his smile. He knew Turner was up to his eyeballs in credit card debt, not to mention, a mortgage on his Manhattan loft and a beach house in the Hamptons. The money he had in his back accounts would only cover him for a few months. "Denise sends her regards."

The man's eyes went wide then blazed with anger. "Why that little bi—" But he didn't get to finish his words as the two guards grabbed him by the arms and hauled him away. The sound of his curses and screams were like music to Lucas's ears.

In truth, Lucas had never met Denise Alderman or had known that she even worked as an intern at Fenrir had her father, Fred Alderman, not sought an official audience with Grant Anderson as his Alpha. Fred and his family were one of the three hundred Lycans living under the New York clan's protection after all, and even Grant didn't know all of them personally.

Fred had come to him, telling him that James Turner had been harassing Denise for months, sending her lewd messages and trying to get her alone in the office. Turner had finally succeeded a few weeks ago and cornered Denise while she was working late. He held her down and threatened to get her fired if she didn't let him have his way with her. If it wasn't for one of the late-night guards patrolling the office, she wouldn't have been able to get away.

Lucas's blood still boiled now, as it did the first time he heard the story. He would have been inclined to just let the man go, but Turner made one big mistake: he went after someone weaker than him *and* a Lycan to boot. He probably thought that the poor little intern whose father worked as a truck driver was easy pickings. Humans were scum, and Turner only cemented his belief.

With anger clouding his mind, his wolf snuck up on him again. "Fuck!" He grunted as he realized his hands were gripping the armrests of his chair so hard, the metal crumpled under his fingers. The wolf scratched from beneath him, claws raking under his skin. *So close.*

Ground yourself, the voice in his mind from long ago echoed. *Use the good to keep your animal in control.* But his fury at Turner was at a critical level, and none of his usual memories helped to keep his wolf at bay. So he reached deep into himself, taking a deep breath, grasping at *anything*.

Orange blossoms and olives. And eyes the color of slate.

And his wolf went still.

"Everything all right, Mr. Anderson?" came David's voice through the intercom.

"Everything is great." He straightened his tie and combed his fingers through his hair. A glance at the clock on his desk made him curse inwardly. He was going to be late. "Have the car meet me downstairs. I need to get to Brooklyn."

———

"And, with the power vested in me by the State of New York, I now pronounce you man and wife. You may kiss—oh, my."

The words hadn't even left the judge's mouth when the bride reached up and grabbed the groom's shoulders, pulling him down for a kiss. Wolf whistles and cheers rang around them as the couple continued their long, celebratory kiss. When they finally pulled away, the groom had a sheepish look on his face while his bride beamed.

Lucas smiled to himself as he watched Zac and Astrid walk down the aisle. Their wedding and reception were being held at a rooftop event space in Brooklyn, attended by close family and friends. Even though he wasn't supposed to be there, he didn't want to miss his friend's wedding.

It's not that he wasn't invited. Zac even wanted him to be best man, but understood that things were different now. Their mortal enemies, the mages, had attacked the New York clan twice now, and both times they had tried to kidnap Lucas and his twin sister, Adrianna.

They didn't know why the mages wanted them specifically, but his father and mother decided that the two of them couldn't be in the same place anymore, lest the mages struck again. He even had to move out of The Enclave, the compound where most of the New York clan lived. It was difficult not seeing his sister, since they'd hardly been apart since they were born, but he knew it was necessary for their safety.

"Sir?" His Lycan bodyguard–driver, Alfie Reyes, stood behind him, his face a mask of seriousness. "The ceremony's over, we should go now."

He knew Reyes was not comfortable defying the Alpha's order that Adrianna and Lucas not be together, but he had promised the bodyguard that he would only stay until the end of the ceremony. "All right, let's go."

Reyes walked ahead of him, his massive body blocking the narrow hallway where Lucas hid to watch the ceremony. He followed him down the emergency staircase, taking two at a time to keep up with the other Lycan. Finally, after climbing down ten stories, they reached the exit. Reyes went out first, glanced around, and then signaled for Lucas to follow him. His town car was already by the door. He ducked and entered the car, settling into the plush leather seats.

Reyes slid into the front passenger seat, next to the driver. "Shall we head home, sir?"

"Yes," he said with nod.

As the car headed back to Manhattan, Lucas stared outside, watching as the snow continued to fall. He tried to distract himself, thinking of the work he had to do, meetings to attend, and of course, the fact that he would soon be Alpha of the most powerful clan in the world. Most men would have caved under the enormous responsibilities and pressure, but not him. No, he had always known that he would be Alpha, not just because he was Grant Anderson's only son, but because he had been born for it. Knew it in his very soul, and this was the one thing he truly wanted in his life.

Yet, drifting back to the wedding, he wondered if there was more to life than just being Alpha. Zac was one of his oldest friends and also the son of the clan's Beta, Nick Vrost. Most people had thought Zac would be Beta after his father, but the younger Vrost didn't want any part of it, much to his father's consternation. Of course, Lucas had already decided who he wanted as his beta—Zac's now wife, Astrid. The half-shifter, half-witch had proven herself capable and willing to sacrifice herself for the clan. Not only that, but she also showed her mettle by not only defying him, but slowing him down when he had shifted in bloodlust when the mages tried to attack them that first time. It was at a party at Blood Moon when—

Orange blossoms and olives. Gray eyes with a tinge of azure.

The memory kept popping into his head, intruding on his thoughts. As he battled for control of his body with his wolf, he found himself grasping for that memory.

It was the only thing keeping him sane these past few weeks. His damn wolf was always sniffing the air, looking for traces of it, which is why he couldn't simply brush it off as a dream or hallucination. It was real, he really did smell and see that. But when?

"Reyes," he called.

"Sir?"

"Change of plans. We're not going home."

"Where to?"

"Blood Moon."

If the bodyguard had any reservations, he didn't show it. He simply mumbled something to the driver, who nodded. When they crossed over to Manhattan, the car headed toward Midtown, instead of the Upper West Side.

"Stay with the car, Reyes," he instructed.

"Sir, I can't—"

"This is Blood Moon. I'll be safe in there. You know it." Blood Moon was a club for shifters and magical people, and in fact, Fenrir Corp. partly owned it along with a few private Lycan investors. It had always been a safe place for Lycans, and since its inception over thirty years ago, it was protected with powerful spells so that humans would ignore its existence, just like The Enclave. Since the attack on the club, the magic had been reinforced by several powerful witches and warlocks.

Reyes nodded. "I'll wait for your call when you want to leave."

With a nod of thanks, Lucas exited and headed straight for the club. The two bouncers—Lycans—immediately recognized him and bowed their heads in respect as they opened the door to let him in.

The music was pulsing, filling the club with energy as people gyrated on the packed dance floor. It had always surprised him how full Blood Moon was, but then again, there were few places that catered exclusively to Lycans and witches and those few humans who knew about their existence. Despite the hum of the music and the mixed scents around him, in here, he felt at ease. He was just about to head to the bar for a drink when he felt a hand on his shoulder. His wolf went on alert again and he whipped around, a snarl on his lips.

"Jesus Christ, it's just me, Lucas."

"Bastian." Lucas felt his body relax and his wolf back down, recognizing the other Lycan.

Bastian Creed grinned at him, his handsome face turning almost boyish. With his thick ruddy beard and tattoos that snaked past his collar and cuffs, he looked more like a biker than a self-made tech billionaire. "Remind me never to creep up on you," he laughed. "Where're you going?"

"I was going to get a drink."

The other Lycan chuckled. "At the bar? Why? Come on." He gestured at Lucas with his hand. "I have a VIP table."

"It's fine, I—"

"Lucas, your family owns most of this club," Bastian pointed out. "You can enjoy some of the benefits. Besides, it's been too long. Why don't we catch up?"

"Fine," he relented.

Bastian flashed him another grin, then led him across the dance floor, stopping at the largest VIP table in the cordoned off in the club. When he saw the table, he nearly turned around.

"Who are these people?" he huffed. There were more than a dozen men and women hanging around the large, semi-circular booth, drinking and chatting. There were all dressed to the nines, and as far as he could tell, all human.

"Friends of mine." He sent a stunning redhead a dazzling smile, who returned it with a sultry gaze. "We just hopped off my plane after partying in London, so I thought I'd take them here."

"Human friends?" he asked in a disdainful tone. "You know this is a Lycan club, right?"

"It's not a secret or anything." Bastian winked at him. "There are some humans in here. Those few immune to the spells."

That was true. Magic wasn't absolute, but it did help keep out most non-Lycans and non-magical people. The bouncers did their best to discourage humans from coming in, but business was business.

Still, he preferred that the humans stayed in their human clubs and leave Blood Moon for the Lycans. "Thanks for the offer of a drink, Bastian," he said. "But I should go."

Bastian's face suddenly turned serious. "Hey, look." He placed a hand on Lucas's shoulder. "We don't have to go to my table. Let's go somewhere more private and have a drink, okay?"

He considered saying no, but Bastian was already dragging him to a different VIP table, one that was thankfully empty. The bouncer removed the cord to let them through and they slid into the booth.

"Two whiskeys," he said to the waitress who approached them. "Neat and make them doubles."

"Of course, Mr. Creed," she said, her eyes looking at him invitingly. "I'll be right back."

"Thanks, sweetheart," he replied and gave her a wink.

"Do you sleep with anything that moves, Creed?" he asked wryly.

Bastian shrugged. "Hey, it's not like I promise them commitment or any of that shit. There's so many women and so little time." It was well known that the playboy billionaire changed his bed partners more often than his shirts. "Not all of us can live like monks."

"Contrary to popular belief, I'm not celibate," Lucas said. "I'm just choosy."

"You prefer Lycan women." Bastian raised his hands in defense. "Hey, I'm not knocking your preference. We all have our likes and dislikes." He nodded at a group of women on the other side of the room, then towards three females dancing by themselves on the dance floor, "Don't you love that human women come in all shapes and sizes? But, you gotta live a little, right? Why not sample the endless buffet humankind has to offer?"

Because humans are despicable. But Lucas didn't vocalize that out loud. Bastian wouldn't understand. No one did, not even Adrianna. Humans had hurt him and Adrianna. And they hurt their kind.

"Don't tell me you've never slept with a human before?" Bastian asked.

"Of course I have." A few times, in fact. Human women were good for fucking and nothing else. His wolf barely tolerated them, and he always left after the act was completed. Besides, it wasn't like he could ever marry a human, so why bother forming any relationship? He would need a strong mate, someone who could handle being Lupa of the largest Lycan clan in the world. But he was only thirty-one, and there was time yet to think of mates and producing heirs.

Thankfully, the waitress came back with their drinks. He took a sip, watching as Bastian whispered in the young woman's ear and her face lit up.

Lucas downed the whiskey in one motion. "Thanks for the drink." He placed the glass on the table. "I'll see you around."

"Hey." Bastian placed a hand on his arm. "If you need to talk, you have my number."

Though he appreciated the thought, he wasn't about to pour his heart out to Bastian. An Alpha had to be strong and show no weakness. "I will," he lied, then let himself out of the VIP area.

He was already taking his phone out of his pocket to call Reyes when he stopped. His wolf on the other hand perked up.

Orange blossoms and olives.

Before he could stop it, his wolf's head swung around, nose in the air. Searching for the source of the faint scent. His wolf scratched at him in desperation, willing him to follow the trail before it went cold. It was strange how in the sea of scents inside the club, he could pick out that one singular smell. He crossed the dance floor, pushing bodies aside so he could follow it. When he reached the bar, he ran smack into what seemed like a wall of orange blossoms and olives.

Hair like a mahogany waterfall flipped around and he found himself staring into slate-colored eyes. Against pale skin and framed with dark hair, they looked hauntingly luminous. They flashed with something—recognition?—before settling on his face. He knew she was staring at his eyes; most people did. The heterochromia he inherited from his mother made one blue and one green, and it startled many who saw it for the first time.

"Oh." Lush, pink lips pursed together, and he had to pull back the urge to sink his teeth into them.

"Have we met?" He cocked his head, breathing in more of her delicious scent. Yes, that definitely was her. Lycan scents were unique, and he was sure he would have remembered smelling her before.

A frown crossed her pretty face, and she narrowed her gaze at him as if waiting for something. When all he did was stare back, she straightened her shoulders. "I have to say, I've heard lots of lines, but that's a new one." She grinned. "Why don't you just buy me a drink and we can skip the bullshit?"

His wolf growled in appreciation. That was certainly new. Normally quiet around females, this one had his wolf's complete attention. "What would you like?"

She turned to the bartender and raised her hand. The man nodded, finished up an order, then walked over to them. "What'll it be, Sof?" His grin was a mile wide. "The usual?"

"You bet, Hal." She nodded at Lucas. "He's buying."

Lucas did not like how the bartender spoke to her with such familiarity, and neither did his wolf.

"And what are you having—" Hal's eyes widened in recognition. Though Lucas had never met him before, the bartender obviously knew who he was. "Mr. Anderson," he said, lowering his gaze. "What can I get you?"

"Whiskey. Neat."

"Right away, sir." He backed away slowly, putting a good distance between them before he turned around to get their drinks.

Satisfied the other man was far away enough, he turned to her. "Sof, was it?"

She neither admitted nor denied anything. "And you are?"

"Lucas." He sidled closer to her, wanting to take in more of that scent. "You seem to come here often enough."

"More often than most."

Her non-answers were driving him crazy. She seemed direct enough earlier, asking him for a drink, but ignored his questions about her. "The bartender recognized you."

"Hal seemed to know you, too. He called you Mr. Anderson. And acted like he was scared of you or something."

It seemed nothing escaped her. "I'm not a regular here, but the staff know me." He eyed her again, trying to think of where they'd met before. He didn't know every single Lycan in New York and New Jersey, and he would have remembered if they'd met at some function. He would never forget that face, or that body. She was on the slender, athletic side, but that conservative black dress she wore gave the promise of sensuous curves underneath.

"Ah, I see."

She didn't seem to recognize him. Usually, when eligible Lycan women realized who he was, they were all over him. Maybe she wasn't eligible. The thought rankled him, but he didn't know why. No ring on her finger, so not engaged or married. A boyfriend? That usually didn't stop some from trying. Who was this woman?

"Here you go." Hal placed two glasses in front of them. "On the house."

"Thank you." Lucas handed the glass to her, but not before giving it a sniff. "Bourbon, huh?"

She took it from him. "Of course. I hope you don't think I'm one of those froo-froo drinkers."

"Froo-froo?"

"You know, mixed drinks with lots of sugar and cream and umbrellas?" Her eyes closed as she put the glass to her lips, took a sniff, then sipped.

His eyes followed the way her lips wrapped around the rim of the glass. "No, you definitely don't seem like a froo-froo drinker."

Slowly, she opened her eyes then gazed up at him. Their color seemed to shift, now more lighter blue than gray. "It's getting really hot and crowded around here."

"I know a place where we can get some air."

She cocked her head slightly. "Let's go then."

Anticipation crawled up his veins. His wolf was eager to get her alone too, away from all these people, especially the males around them. Sliding a hand to the small of her back, he guided her away from the bar, using just the lightest touch. She allowed him to lead her to the back of the club, toward the private elevator that would lead them to the outdoor deck. It wasn't very high up, but it had a great view of the lights in Times Square.

The snow had stopped, but it was still chilly. She walked ahead, stopping by the ledge and placing her glass on it. "Wow, this is amazing. You'd never know this place existed from the street."

He followed her, leaning his forearms on the ledge, his own glass gripped in his fingers. "Yeah, it's positioned perfectly so you can't see it from the street, but it still has a view." But he wasn't really looking at the view. Instead, he found himself staring at her face. Out here, he could really see her. Her skin was like alabaster, and some might say her features were too strong, but he liked them. The high cheekbones, strong jaw and chin, those plush lips. And those huge eyes, framed by dark, sooty lashes. He could get lost just looking at her.

She shivered, and he found himself removing his jacket and wrapping it around her. "Better?"

"Yes." She lowered her lashes. "Thank you."

Unable to take another moment of torture, he reached out to brush a stray lock of hair from her cheek. It was an excuse to touch her, and a shock of electricity jolted up his fingertips when it made contact with her skin, but he didn't jerk back. He traced his finger down to her chin and their gazes clashed. Her eyes seemed to flash to a light blue for a moment, and he wondered if she had felt it too.

"Are you visiting New York? Which clan are you from?" he asked.

His words must have broken the spell between them because she frowned at his question. "Visiting? I'm from New York. And what do you mean, clan?"

He double-blinked, letting her words sink into him. Glancing down at his coat around her, he realized that her body didn't adjust to the cold like his did. And when he tried to reach out to her and search for her wolf ... he found none.

Human.

He was so sure she was a Lycan. She smelled like one, for God's sake. Maybe she had a parent who was a Lycan. But no, she didn't even recognize him or known what a clan was. If she was from the New York clan, she would know who the Alpha was, and who Lucas was.

"Lucas? Is something the matter?"

Her voice jolted him back. "No." *Yes. You're human.* Still, that didn't mean anything. He wasn't going to get down on one knee and propose to her. He could always take a page from Bastian's book. She was obviously interested in him, or else she wouldn't have come up here. "So, you're from New York?"

"Queens, born and bred." She took a sip of her bourbon, her eyes never leaving his. "And you? Where did you grow up?"

"Manhattan."

"Ah, true city boy." Her laugh was like tinkling bells, and her smile—it made her entire face light up.

"Guilty," he replied. He wanted to shuffle away from her, but he found himself doing the opposite, moving closer so their forearms touched. His wolf whined happiness as her scent tickled his nose, now mingled with his own because she was wearing his coat. What the heck was wrong with his animal?

She wrinkled her nose. "You're not one of those snooty Manhattanites who think the boroughs aren't New York, are you?" Despite her serious tone, there was a slight tugging at the corner of her lips.

"Hey, I've gone as far as Brooklyn."

"Ah, hipster, then are you?"

"Please," he said. "Do I look like a hipster?"

"This suit jacket that probably cost more than I make in a month says no." She rubbed her cheek against the lapel. "And your shirt."

"What about it?"

"Tailor-made?"

"Guilty," he chuckled. "Specially made just for me. I like shirts that fit well."

Her gaze lingered on his shoulders and his chest. "You're probably one of those hedge fund guys, aren't you? Or lawyer?"

He shook his head. "Far from it. I'm not that ruthless."

"Then what do you do?"

"I'm in business," he said. "Family corporation."

"Interesting. Which one?"

He opened his mouth, then shut it again. Somehow, this human woman got him to drop his defenses. Why did this feel like an interrogation?

"Why don't you answer some of my questions first?" He leaned down closer to her. "Like what's your full name?"

She turned her head to him, tilting her chin up slightly. "Does it matter? You didn't invite me up here for my name."

His hand snaked up to reach behind her neck, moving so fast she gasped. He played with the soft, delicate skin there, and he heard her heartbeat spike up. Moving his thumb under her ear, he could feel the thrum of her pulse and the tinge of her arousal mixing in with their combined scents.

Her lips parted invitingly, and he leaned down closer until he was only a hair's breadth away from her.

No.

She was a human. Nothing would change that. Shock. Betrayal. Loathing. All the emotions churned inside him like a maelstrom.

He pulled away, disgust creeping in him. His wolf protested, snarling at him, but he pushed back. "I should go."

Her gasp was sharp, the sound striking him like a knife in

his chest. "Of course. You go ahead. I'm enjoying the fresh air here."

If he looked at her now, at those eyes, he would never leave. So he avoided her gaze and instead, turned his back to her. "Have a great evening." He strode toward the exit. Instead of going to the elevators, he went to the staircase. The door hadn't even closed behind him as he descended the stairs, taking them two at a time, trying to get away as quickly as possible.

His wolf was scratching at him, its claws digging into him, wanting to surface. This time, he wasn't distracted so he pulled it back. *She's human,* he reminded it. *Just like those men who hurt us, hurt Adrianna.* Like the one who hurt *Caroline.*

His wolf quieted down at the mention of the name. The tightness in his chest he didn't even realize was there eased. When he reached the bottom of the stairs, he tore across the club, needing to get out of there as her scent still seemed to linger in the air. He flew out the door and into the street, letting the cold air wash over him and clean his senses.

He took his phone out of his pants pocket and dialed Reyes's number. "I'm here," he said. "Come pick me up. I need to go. Now."

"Right away, sir."

Though he fought with every instinct he had, he couldn't help but look up. The deck wasn't visible from here, but he wondered if she was still there. Still standing by the edge, wrapped up in his coat, looking out into the city. He huffed. It didn't matter. He would never see her again.

CHAPTER TWO

"ROUGH NIGHT?" DETECTIVE FLEETWOOD SNICKERED AS Sofia passed by the group of detectives hanging around the water cooler.

"I'm sure she doesn't mind it rough," Sergeant Benito stage-whispered. It was followed by more sniggering and chuckles.

She didn't say a word nor act like she heard them. A few months ago, she might have told Fleetwood to mind his own Goddamn business, which would have gained her some respect. But now if she had said that, she would be labeled a whiny, sensitive bitch. Of course, ignoring them would make them call her an *uppity* bitch, so she couldn't win either way. Damned if you do, damned if you don't. *The story of my life.*

Plonking down on her desk, she booted up her computer and stared at the screen as it slowly came to life. Her vision blurred and she found her thoughts drifting to last night.

She shouldn't have done it. Her actions could have been misconstrued as police harassment. There were no pending charges, no crime committed. But her instincts were screaming at her. Something was not right in Blood Moon. And so, for the past few weeks, she found herself going to the club every couple of nights. She was hoping to catch something illegal going on. Or maybe find some answers to her questions. Every night, she stood by the bar, waiting. Waiting ... for what?

For him? The man with the mismatched eyes.

It was a fluke. He hadn't shown up there in all those weeks and then last night, he was there. Came right up to her. His presence was overwhelming, and it wasn't just his over six-feet frame and broad shoulders. It was his strange aftershave; she couldn't get it out of her mind. Ocean sea breeze. It wasn't unpleasant, in fact, it was amazing. She told herself that he might have the answers she was looking for, which is why she kept talking to him. Let him guide her to the rooftop so they could be alone. Allowed him to come close to her.

And then he pulled away.

Maybe it was just her imagination. That only she felt the attraction sizzling in the air, the tension between them. His touch was, for lack of a better word, magical. And she was sure he was going to kiss her. But he drew back, away from her.

Of course he did. He's fucking *engaged*.

That made her groan and bury her face in her hands. She was a Goddamn idiot, almost kissing a nearly married man. His poor fiancée. Did she know he went to clubs and bought strange women drinks? Maybe it wasn't a habit. Maybe he was just looking for a one-night fling before the ring, then got cold feet.

Good, she thought. Though she didn't know his fiancée, she should be glad he got attacked by his conscience. She wondered how the poor woman was coping. Or who she was. It would be easy enough to find out ...

She shook her head. *No way.* Sure, she could easily look him up. She even knew his name, though she didn't dare speak it, even in her mind. One little web search. Or hell, she had police records at her fingertips. But she was *not* going to go there.

"You okay, Detective?"

She shot straight up. "I'm fine, Sergeant."

Sergeant Alice Winters cocked her head. "You look pale. Didja sleep at all last night?"

Of course not. She'd tossed and turned, her mind wide awake, thinking of blue and green eyes and the scent of the ocean. He even left his jacket with her. She told herself that she would toss it away, but it was still in her closet. This morning, when she got up to get dressed, she found herself breathing in that scent. Later, she told herself, later she would throw it out.

"I got a lot of cases on my mind." She liked Winters a lot. The young sergeant was spunky and didn't have that hard edge most cops had. Not yet, anyway. Winters was also one of the few people in the precinct who still spoke to her in public, not caring about her reputation.

"Didn't anyone tell you not to bring work home?" she said wryly.

"Just give yourself a few years. Once you get your detective's badge, you'll see how the real world works."

Winters chuckled. "Right." Her face became concerned again. "If you need anything ..."

"I'll be fine," she insisted.

With a final wave, Winters strode away from her desk.

Sofia turned to her computer, checking her emails and trying to concentrate on the case file currently sitting on top of her inbox. But, try as she might, her mind kept drifting. She opened her top drawer, staring at the contents. Inside was a photo of a woman wearing a complete police uniform, her smile wide.

I miss you, Mom.

Normally, she had her mother's portrait on her desk, but lately, she was afraid something would happen to it. A couple weeks ago, she found it lying face down on her desk. Despite the many times she would prop it back up, she would come to work with the frame disturbed. She knew what that gesture meant. That even her own mother would be ashamed to look at her. Which was ironic.

Always do what's right. Even if the whole world is against you.

She would never forget her mother's words, and she would be damned if she lost her integrity at this job.

With a deep breath, she straightened her shoulders and went to work. Finally, it was the end of the day, and she could go home. She walked into the empty locker room so she could get changed before heading to the gym.

"Motherfucker!" She exclaimed when she opened her locker. Inside was a dead rat, lying on top of her running shoes. "Goddammit!"

Really, she should have been used to it by now. Months and months of disdainful looks, anger, and even the small "pranks" like leaving dead pigeons in her desk drawer. But she refused to back down, even ignoring pleas from her family. In her heart, she did the right thing. And she was still paying for it.

TGIFF.

Thank God It's Fucking Friday.

Though Sofia didn't sleep any better last night, she was at least looking forward to the weekend. Her dad and grandfather would be expecting her to come home, so she would at least be able to relax, eat something other than instant ramen or takeout, and maybe even visit Mom's grave.

At around ten o'clock, she was heading out to get a cup of coffee when her phone rang. "Selinofoto," she answered.

"Detective, this is dispatch," the businesslike voice said on the other end. "We need you on a scene. Homicide."

"Send me the details, and I'll be right there." Hanging up the phone without another word, she grabbed her keys and headed for her car. She checked her phone for the address and after making a quick mental note, drove to the scene. With midtown traffic, it took her a good twenty minutes to get there.

The address that dispatch gave her was right at the edge of their jurisdiction. It looked like a couple of cops from the neighboring district had been called in, because she didn't recognize the uniformed officers guarding the yellow tape draped across the alley. She approached the officers and held up her badge.

"Detective," one of them greeted as he lifted the tape for her.

"One of you come with me," she said as she crossed under the tape. They hesitated, but then the younger officer followed her into the crime scene.

It was a standard alley between two buildings, wide

enough for only a sidewalk and a one-way street to fit through. The other side had also been secured with yellow tape, and a black and white was parked to block the entrance. It was mostly empty, except for the lump on the ground right in the middle of the sidewalk. Dead Body. Or *D.B.* for short.

The smell was the first thing she noticed as she drew closer to the body. It shouldn't have stunk, seeing as it was winter, but it wasn't the usual smell of a rotting corpse. Piss and shit. *Huh.* And when she was standing next to the body, she realized the source of the stench. A colostomy bag lay next to the body, its contents oozing out.

She'd been around her share of dead bodies before, so it didn't bother her too much. The young officer, however, looked a little pale. "First D.B.?" she asked.

"Y-yes ma'am."

Probably fresh out of the academy. She remembered what it was like. "What's your name?"

"Chen, ma'am. Barry Chen."

"Breathe through your mouth, Officer Chen. Can you tell me what happened?"

The officer opened his mouth to take in a deep breath. "A delivery guy found the body and then called 911. We got here about twenty minutes ago, confirmed that he was dead, and then secured the scene."

"Did you find anything unusual? Anyone hanging around?"

"Had a couple of looky-loos, but we shooed them away."

"Good." She kneeled down to get a closer look at the body. "Jesus," she muttered under her breath. The man's face was bloody and beaten, the features unrecognizable. The front of his coat was open, and his shirt was covered in blood.

There was a sizable dent on his skull where blood and bits of gray matter had oozed out.

"Looks like he was beaten to death," Chen said. "We searched, but didn't find any weapons nearby."

The crime lab would be able to confirm how and when the guy died, but this couldn't have been an accident. She put on a pair of gloves, then checked his pockets and took out a sealed plastic bag. "Huh." Unzipping the bag, she took out a wallet, some keys, and a hundred-dollar bill. The wallet contained a driver's license. "Thomas Dixon. From New York. Seventy-six years old. Huh." She held out the license. "License expired almost twenty years ago." The wallet too was worn and old, but the hundred-dollar bill was crisp and new. "Well, look at that."

"Detective?" Chen asked. "What is it?"

"I think our victim just got out of jail. The hundred-dollar bill was probably what he had in his prison inmate account, and the rest of the personal effects were what they confiscated when he was booked."

"Oh, right."

She looked over her shoulder and saw the tech lab guys entering the scene. "Thanks for your help, Officer. Let's give the crime lab guys space to do their work."

———

After the coroner took the body away, Sofia headed back to the police station to do more digging on Thomas Dixon. Sure enough, he came up in the police database. He went to prison twenty years ago for kidnapping, assault, and aggravated murder, but he'd already had a rap sheet a mile long before then. Shoplifting when he was a minor, robbery, drug possession, domestic battery ... it went on and on. He'd been in and out of jail, but didn't do anything for more than a year until the kidnapping case.

Apparently, he and a bunch of other guys kidnapped two rich kids as they were leaving their private school. They shot the kids' bodyguard, then took the children. A private security firm had discovered them hours later. The kids were unharmed but the kidnappers had all been seriously injured in some kind of car crash, leaving most of them injured.

Huh.

No wonder Dixon had a colostomy bag. The records came with a couple of photos of the guys after they had been brought to the hospital. *Jesus Christ.* They looked like they had been shredded to ribbons. Dixon himself had a nasty scar down the front of his face and had lost an eye.

Hmmm. It was strange how the two children escaped with no injuries. When she tried to access the files from the case, she found herself locked out. Probably sealed from public access. Not an unusual thing with minors. Being a part of law enforcement, she could easily access the files. She tapped in her password and waited for the records to download to her computer.

A few minutes later, the case file was on her hard drive. Clicking on the folder, she opened the document, scanned the names and—

Motherfucker.

CHAPTER THREE

"I THOUGHT WE TALKED ABOUT YOU NOT BRINGING YOUR work home." Sergeant Winters gave her a reproachful look.

Sofia barely glanced at her. "I didn't."

"No?"

"That's because I didn't go home."

"You what?" Winters walked around, then looked down at her desk. "Detective, are you all right? What are you doing with all those files?"

Piles and piles of folders and envelopes littered her desk. Since every inch of space was taken up, so she put some of them on the floor. "Working. What does it look like?"

"And you haven't gone home yet?"

She thought for moment. "I did. I think it was around two in the morning on Saturday when I went home to shower and change." She sniffed at her shirt. It was still okay, but she should probably change it today.

"Saturday? But it's Monday morning!"

She checked her desk calendar. "So it is."

"What's going on, Detective?" The sergeant had her hands on her hips.

Sofia sighed and leaned back in her chair. "It's this case I'm working on." She rubbed her eyes with her fingers.

"The D.B. from last Friday?" Winters frowned. "From what I heard, the guy's a scumbag."

"Yeah, but that doesn't mean he doesn't deserve justice." The more she read about Dixon, the more she hated him, but he was still the victim of a crime.

"But still, why all this fuss?" Winters asked.

Why indeed. This whole thing was like a fucking Pandora's box. The moment she opened those records, more and more things came out. Things that didn't make sense. "I'm still working on it," she said.

Winters shrugged. "All right. But you should know, the captain wants to see you."

"Huh?"

She jerked her thumb toward Bushnell's office. "Yeah. He wants you to come to his office. Now."

Sofia blew a tendril of hair that had come loose from her messy bun. "All right." She stood up. "I'll head over there now." A pain in her neck made her wince and she stretched out, feeling her muscles protest. How long had she been sitting there? She fell asleep sometime after midnight last night and took a quick nap in the break room. It had still been dark when she sat down at her desk.

"Sir?" she said as she poked her head into Bushnell's office. "You wanted to see me sir?"

He looked up at her from where he was sitting behind his desk. "Detective." He gestured to the seat in front of him.

"Will this take long, sir?"

"It might." He cleared his throat. "Two things. The first one, you already know about."

Ah. Maybe he had heard about the rat. She made sure to get rid of the evidence before anyone saw it, but people here were fucking nosy. "All right." She sat down on the chair.

"Let me cut to the chase, Selinofoto." He clasped his meaty hands on top of the desk. "We have a court date for the Bianchi case."

Her entire body went rigid. "Good to know. When?"

"Seven weeks. I want to make sure you're still testifying."

"Yes," she said quickly. "Of course. Why wouldn't I?"

His eyes briefly darted behind her, probably scanning the bullpen. "I know no one's made it easy for you here for the past couple of months. Hell, I haven't done anything to help you out."

"I wasn't expecting you to coddle me, sir," she said.

"Still, I know things have been tough. Plus, I still can't find anyone who wants to take you on as a partner."

"That's fine, sir." Her cases were piling up, but she had managed them. "Wait, are you trying to convince me not to testify?"

"What?" His eyes narrowed at her. "Of course not. I mean, not if that's what you want. Listen." He got to his feet and walked around his desk, sitting on the chair next to hers. "I really admire what you did. It takes guts to take down a corrupt police officer. Especially since Derek was your partner."

The words were like ice shards, hitting her in the chest. And the way Bushnell looked at her with that soul-piercing blue gaze, it was obvious he knew they had been *more* than just partners.

"Bad cops make all of us look bad," he said. "They deserve worse punishments than even regular criminals."

Yeah, well, she wished everyone in the station saw it that way. But no, the only thing they cared about was that she turned on one of their own. That she had been the one to report him to Internal Affairs and cuffed him during that sting operation. Unfortunately for her, IAB wanted Derek so bad that they didn't warn her that breaking the blue wall of silence had dire consequences.

When she didn't say anything, he continued. "The heat's gonna be on you, Selinofoto. You know how Bianchi operates. I can have a couple of the officers escort you—"

"With all due respect, sir, I don't need any babysitters or bodyguards." Her fingernails dug into her palms. "I'll be fine."

The captain's bushy eyebrows drew together, his clear blue eyes narrowing. "Anthony Bianchi isn't someone you mess around with lightly. Your testimony is going to be the final nail in his coffin. He's gonna go down."

As he should. "I can't do my job properly if I'm being guarded all the time."

"I'm not talking a protective detail, just someone to make sure you get home okay."

The thought of anyone following her around made her uncomfortable. "I respectfully decline, sir. But," she began when Bushnell looked like he wanted to protest. "I'll check in via phone with the desk sergeant every night when I get home."

That seemed to mollify him. "All right. I'll have a couple of patrol cars drive by your building as well."

She supposed she could live with that. "You said there were two things you wanted to discuss."

He harrumphed and got to his feet, and walked back behind his desk. "Yes. I got an interesting call this morning about you. From 1PP."

One Police Plaza. The NYPD's headquarters. "Is it the chief?" God, she hoped she wasn't getting into more shit because of the Bianchi case.

"Er, no. From the commissioner."

"Commissioner Foster?" She frowned. Why would the head of the entire police force of New York City call Bushnell about her? How would he even know her name? "If this is about me testifying—"

"It's not." He lowered his voice. "It wasn't an official call or anything. He said he wanted to know why one of my detectives was opening sealed files all weekend."

"Oh." *Fuck.* "It's for a case, sir."

"And you've been working all weekend?"

"Yes. Is he asking me to stop looking into old case files?"

"Not really." He scratched his chin. "It was a strange call actually."

"Strange?" Her curiosity was piqued.

"Yes. First of all, the fact that he called me directly ... I've been working for the NYPD for thirty years, ten as captain. I've never gotten a call directly from the Police Commissioner of New York."

"Really?" Interesting.

"Yes. And the fact that he said this was a non-official chat ... I mean, we access case files all the time, it's part of our job. But all the ones you opened seemed to have gotten his attention."

"Is that so?"

"Care to enlighten me on what you're doing?"

Could she trust Bushnell? Did she have a choice? "Sir, I've been investigating a murder."

"The D.B. from the alley."

"Yes." She took a deep breath. "And the more I dig into it, well, the weirder it becomes."

"Weird? How?"

She told him about Thomas Dixon and how she arrived at the scene. "Then I got here and started digging into his records. First of all, he just got out of Sing Sing a week ago. Based on the crime lab's findings, he was murdered a day after he got out."

"Old enemies, maybe?"

"Could be. But he's been in prison for twenty years. He's got no family or no known contacts in New York City. He kept to himself in prison, and if anything ... he was a model inmate, according to the warden." She had called up the jail on Friday to get the skinny on Dixon. Warden Ellis had been shocked to find out Dixon had been murdered. He didn't rat on anyone, didn't join any gangs, nor did he have any known associates who visited him. If anything, he had seemed content to do his time.

"Was he mugged?"

She shook her head. "He still had all his personal effects. And the way he was beaten ... well, it seemed highly personal. The suspect or suspects would have had to be up close."

"What's weird about that?"

Her heart hammered into her chest and she hesitated. "I don't want to sound like a crazy conspiracy theorist, sir."

Bushnell flashed her a look of impatience. "Just spit it out, Selinofoto."

Here goes nothing. "Dixon was sentenced to twenty years in prison for the attempted kidnapping of two children. Their dad is Grant Anderson."

"Who?"

"He's the CEO of Fenrir Corporation."

"Oh. The billionaire." Everyone knew about Fenrir, of course. They owned most of New York City and had their hand in almost every type of business from real estate to healthcare.

"Yes, sir." She cleared her throat. "The children were unharmed, but the kidnappers were severely injured."

"Did Anderson report the kidnapping?"

"No, not until they were found. A security contractor that works for Fenrir—Creed Security—plus Anderson's own team found them first, then turned them over to the NYPD."

"Maybe they didn't want the attention."

"Well, I thought it was convenient that all the kidnappers were hurt when their van crashed, but the children were fine. Or at least, we think they are because they were never brought to any hospital. Plus, the children were kidnapped at around three in the afternoon and were found twelve hours later. What were they doing during all that time? Driving around Manhattan? Why wouldn't they stash the kids somewhere until they contacted the parents for a ransom?"

"Maybe moving around helped them stay undetected for a couple of hours. So what happened?"

"Once the kidnappers recovered, they all went on trial and were convicted. It was quick too. The trial dates were all pushed up, ahead of even older cases, and all six men were convicted within a year."

"You think Anderson may have used his influence?"

"Could be. It's not illegal, I mean, if he didn't bribe the judge. But here's the thing: none of the kidnappers could definitively recall what happened during the time they were with the children. They all had wildly different stories, too. Some of them said they drove around for hours, others said they stashed them in an abandoned building. One of the suspects even told the DA the story of a beast attacking them. But, all of them confessed to planning the kidnapping, taking the children. The same thing with the witnesses at the school. The kids were taken in broad daylight, but none of the other nannies or parents or children could definitively recount the events."

"Witnesses can be unreliable. Although that is strange that kidnappers themselves couldn't recall anything. Could it be possible head injuries caused them to have different stories?"

"Some. But all?" she reasoned. "And well, because of that, I started digging into Anderson and Fenrir Corp. At all cases somehow connected to them over the years. Some of it was inconsequential really, though a few stood out. For example, have you heard of the Fenrir building explosion from a couple decades ago?"

"Of course," he said. "I was a beat cop then. Everyone heard about that accident. An entire floor of the building blew up, right? Everyone thought it was a terror attack." His brows drew together.

"Yes, sir. No one recalls anything, and the whole thing was chalked up to a leaky gas pipe."

"It happens, I suppose." His gaze narrowed at her. "What else?"

"There was also a case a few years ago at a bar in the Village. Someone reported an explosion of some kind. When the fire department got there, the bar was perfectly fine, except that everyone inside was unconscious. They all woke up on their own, but no one could remember what happened. The fire department concluded it was probably a gas leak. No one was charged."

"If no one was hurt, that makes sense. What's the connection to Fenrir?"

"Well, it's not a solid connection, but the bar was partly-owned by Gunnar Jonasson, whose mother works for Fenrir." Her gut told her he was probably related to Daric Jonasson, though for some reason, she couldn't find any info on the older man. He sounded foreign, so maybe that's why he didn't have any domestic records. But she would be keeping that to herself for now, as she didn't want to reveal her visits to Blood Moon.

She continued. "The other owner is Sebastian Creed Jr., whose mother also works for Fenrir. His father, on the other hand, owns Creed Security." The name popped up when, after an exhaustive search for anything connected to Fenrir or Grant Anderson, she started looking into Creed Security, the only other figure that was connected to the kidnapping, and that's when the younger Creed's name popped up.

"Sounds like a lot of leaky gas pipes and forgetful witnesses. Still, Detective, none of those prove any criminal activity. Or a direct connection to your victim. Did you find anything useful?"

She cleared her throat. "It's not so much what I found as what I didn't find."

"What you didn't find?" he echoed.

"Yes, sir." Where to begin? From the beginning, she supposed. "I found another case that might be related. This one circles right back to Dixon. Or rather, the kids he tried to kidnap. The boy's name only popped up one other time. He was seventeen, about to graduate from his prep school. A couple of students from his class had some party in a lake cabin upstate. Someone called 911 and the EMTs found two boys that were severely injured. Kevin Hall and Jeffrey Smith. Hall died later, but the other, Smith, he's in a wheelchair."

"And no one could remember anything?" It was a statement, not a question.

She nodded. "Over twenty kids and no one could recall what happened. In fact, the official police report from the local station seemed to have gotten lost."

"Lost? Then how did you know about this incident?"

"The two boys' parents filed a suit in civil court as soon as Anderson's boy turned eighteen a few months after the incident. The suit alleges that he beat up the two other boys. He and one of the boys had fought over some girl at the party. Anyway, the case was settled out of court for an undisclosed amount. I tried contacting the parents of both boys, but they refused to talk to me."

"And the girl?"

"I'm still working on finding her contact info. It's like she just disappeared off the face of the earth. I have a couple of guys working on it." In the meantime, she'd tracked down the girl's social media sites, and looking through them was one of the things on her growing to-do list.

"You've had all weekend to think about this." The captain's face turned grave. "So, what's your hunch?"

"I can't draw any final conclusions yet, sir. But you have to admit, it's hard to put all these connections aside as a coincidence."

"Fenrir is a big corporation," he began. "They have hundreds of employees in New York, so it's not impossible that their name could be connected to any number of incidents."

"True. But what about the connection with Dixon?"

"What about it?" He narrowed his gaze at her. "You obviously have some theories about Dixon."

She swallowed the lump in her throat. "I think ... well, this is just an early thought, but what if the son found out about Dixon getting out and decided to get some revenge?"

"Twenty years later?"

"We don't know what happened during those twelve hours they were kidnapped, sir." Her flesh crawled, thinking of the possibilities. Those men ... at least one of them had a rap sheet that made her want to vomit. "And who knows if that car accident was a coincidence or something else." If it had been one occurrence, she wouldn't have thought anything of it. But after looking at all those cases, her instincts were telling her *something* was going on.

"And Anderson's son?"

"If the accusations in the civil suit are true, then he has a history of violence. Maybe his father covered it up, and who knows what else over the years? It could be he found out about Dixon getting out and then decided that he could finally get revenge." Mismatched blue and green eyes flashed in her mind. Had she been staring into the eyes of a killer?

Bushnell leaned back and folded his hands over his middle. "These are grave accusations, Detective."

"I don't have any solid evidence, sir. I'm just trying to connect the dots with what I do have."

"Then maybe you need to get more evidence. Start from the beginning. With Dixon. And then if anything happens with the investigation ..."

Bushnell's keen eyes bore into her. It was as if some silent agreement passed between them, and she knew what he was trying to say. Keep looking into the Dixon murder and then see if Grant Anderson or anyone from Fenrir tried to interfere. "Of course, sir." She stood up. "I'll get to work."

"Go see the son."

She wasn't sure she heard him right. "What?"

"Interview him. Shake him up. Ask him what he was doing the night of the murder. See if you can get a reaction."

"I—" *Fuck.* "Isn't it too soon? We don't want to tip them off."

"He's your only suspect, right?"

"So far."

"A solid alibi could eliminate him, then you can look at other possibilities."

"And if he doesn't have one?"

"Well, if your suspicions about his father are correct, then we'll see for ourselves if they are tampering with witnesses."

Shit. She couldn't deny that was a good plan. The only plan she had right now. She just wished it didn't involve having to confront *him* so soon. "All right."

"And we'll keep this between us for now. For now, he's

only a person of interest. Give him the old 'we need to eliminate you from the suspect list' chat."

"Of course. I'll get on it right away, sir." She spun around and headed for the door. As soon as she was out, she let out a sigh of relief.

Bushnell believed her! Well, at least he knew there was something suspicious about all these connections.

And now the inevitable was here. When his name first popped up in that police report for Dixon, her instincts went ballistic. As she dug deeper, there was that sinking feeling in her stomach that she'd been trying to ignore. She hoped it wouldn't come to this, but now it was here. She was going to have to face Lucas Anderson.

———

The Fenrir Corporation building on Madison Avenue was a prominent fixture on the Manhattan skyline. The onyx, obelisk-like building had been in the same spot for decades and was one of the tallest buildings in New York. Sofia herself had been there a handful of times, as the lower floors were mostly retail shops, cafes, and restaurants. The upper floors, however, were restricted to Fenrir employees only, and as far as she could tell, was locked up tighter than Fort Knox.

"Did you have an appointment today, ma'am?" the stern-looking uniformed guard asked when she approached the security desk.

"No." She held out her badge. "But I'm here on official business. I need to speak with Mr. Lucas Anderson."

The guard's body went rigid at the sight of her badge, but

he straightened his shoulders. "I'm sorry, Detective, I'm going to have to call this in to my supervisor."

"Go ahead."

She watched the man as he got up from his desk and disappeared into a back room. Technically, Fenrir was a private building, and they didn't have to let her in, at least not without a warrant. However, she had flashed her badge many times before, and nine times out of ten it was enough to scare anyone into letting her get away with almost anything. Based on her experience though, she knew there was small chance they'd let her in, at least not if the head of security was well-paid. Still, she had a few more tricks up her sleeve. Mentioning the word murder investigation, for example, could make most people cooperate.

A prickle went up the back of her neck. It was like someone was watching her. Glancing up, she saw the security camera overhead and knew that was true. But who could be watching her?

A few minutes later, the same security guard came out. Sofia was already preparing for a battle.

"Someone will be right down to escort you, Detective."

That was quicker than she expected. "Escort me? Off the premises?"

The guard shook his head. "Uh, no, ma'am. You can't just go to the executive floor without authorization, so someone's coming down so you can access the elevators."

"Huh." She hoped she didn't sound too surprised.

"Would you like—oh." The guard nodded toward a man approaching them from behind the security gates. "Looks like your escort's here."

She turned her head toward the figure approaching her.

The man was older, with white hair, and a tall and lean frame. The expression on his handsome face was curious. "You must be Detective Selinofoto."

"I am," she said with a flash of her badge. "And you are?"

"My name is Jared Patrick," he said with a curt nod. "I'm the Head Executive Assistant of Fenrir Corporation. This way, please." He pivoted on his heel and gestured for her to follow him.

"Mr. Patrick—"

"Jared."

"What?"

He turned. "Just call me Jared. Everyone does."

"Right. Jared." She picked up her steps, trying to keep up with him. "Where are we going?"

"To the executive floor. Mr. Anderson said to bring you to his office."

Her heart skipped at the name. He knew she was here. Did he realize who she was, that they had met before? Or did he want to meet her because she was with the NYPD? Not that it mattered now. She was about to see him again.

She followed Jared into the elevator, trying not to think about what would happen when they did meet face to face. He led her into the last set of elevators, all the way in the back of the lobby. Inside, there was no panel to indicate the floor, but, as soon as his palm planted on the wall, numbers lit up and he tapped on the *P*. Biometrics elevators. The security around here was top-notch.

The sleek, shiny elevator car began to move so smoothly, but for the fact of the story level announced on the panel, she wouldn't have noticed it. The doors slid open moments later, and Jared lifted a palm, indicating that she should get out first.

As she glanced around, she couldn't help but feel a little underdressed in her slacks and blouse. The office was plush and modern, all black and metal and shiny surfaces. There was a hushed silence as they walked down to the end of the hallway, in front of a set of large wooden doors. There was a table by the door, and a young man stood up as they approached.

"David," Jared greeted.

"Mr. Anderson said to let her in as soon as she got here," the young man said.

Jared turned to Sofia and nodded at the door. "Go ahead."

"Thank you, Jared."

"Most welcome, Detective."

She stepped up to the front of the doors, then took a deep breath before taking hold of the handles. *Now or never.* She pushed the doors open and stepped in.

The inside of the office was even more intimidating than the outside. Of course, she hardly noticed it because her gaze immediately went to the man sitting at the large desk by the window. His head was bent, staring at something on the desk. Part of her was irritated that he didn't even look up when she entered. He wasn't alone either; there was a woman standing next to him, her head also bent down. She was the first to notice Sofia, her face lifting up to meet hers. Light amber eyes, the color of bourbon, clashed with hers, and she nudged the man next to her.

Sofia felt like her feet were suddenly encased in cement as those mismatched eyes met hers. One green, one blue.

This was the third time she'd seen them, but it had the same damn effect on her. Despite her heart slamming into her chest, she pushed forward, walking closer to him.

"Detective." His voice was like molten honey, warm and thick. This close, she could feel the full impact of him. His handsome maleness, from the arrogant slash of this eyebrows, down to his patrician nose and high cheekbones, all the way to his sensuously molded mouth. It took all her strength to speak.

"Mr. Anderson." She showed him her badge, holding it like a shield. "I'm Detective Selinofoto."

His gaze never left hers. "So I was told. Please, have a seat."

She couldn't help but follow his instructions, annoyed with herself at how easily she obeyed. "Thank you for agreeing to see me. I'd like to ask you a few questions about an active case." As she settled into the soft leather chair, she glanced at his companion. "Could we have a few minutes alone, please?"

"Whatever you have to say, you can say in front of Astrid."

When she glanced up at the young woman, an ache in her chest bloomed. The woman next to him was gorgeous, and by the way she stood so close to him, she could only guess this was his lovely fiancée. She looked at Sofia curiously, though her amber gaze was intense. Perhaps they didn't keep *any* secrets from each other. "If that's what you want."

"It is. Now, tell me what this is about."

"Thomas Dixon."

His gaze narrowed. "Should I know that name?"

"You should. He kidnapped you and your sister twenty years ago."

If he was affected by the name, he didn't show it. The man must have ice in his veins. "I don't really concern myself with the past."

"He was murdered a few nights ago," she said. "Found in an alley, beaten to death."

"And?" He leaned back in his chair. "Why don't you cut to the chase and tell me why I should care?"

"Where were you last Thursday, between nine p.m. and midnight?"

"At home."

She glanced at Astrid. "Where you with him?"

The young woman's eyes went wide. "Excuse me?" Her head snapped to Lucas. "What's going on?"

"I wish I knew." He raised a brow at her. "No, Detective, I was alone."

Fuck. If he had a solid alibi, she could be on her way. Part of her wanted that, so she could put this whole thing behind her. That and she'd never have to see him again. "That's unfortunate."

His eyes turned hard. "You think I murdered this man? What's his name?"

"Thomas Dixon."

"It seems to me that he's already done his time. Why would I go after him, twenty years after he kidnapped us?"

There was no way she was going to tell him about everything she knew, of course. She was here to judge his reaction. "This is just a preliminary, informational interview," she said. "Just to narrow down the list of suspects. If you have someone who can confirm that you were at home, then I'll be on my way."

His voice turned frosty. "If I'm not a suspect, then I don't owe you any explanation. I could refer you to my lawyer. I'm sure they could be persuasive."

God, she hated it when these rich guys pulled that crap. He probably had the best lawyers in the city at his beck and call. "Do they persuade everyone on your behalf, Mr. Anderson? Like the witnesses that seem to *forget* about what they've seen whenever there's a case involving your family or Fenrir?" *Fuck.* She didn't mean to say those words, but they just came out.

The two dark slashes of his eyebrows drew together as his freezing gaze bore into her. The air in the room suddenly became thick, like his anger had somehow manifested, threatening to choke her. But she refused to back down. *Cat's out of the bag.* If he was half as smart as she thought he was, he knew she had suspicions. Hopefully, this gamble would pay off.

Before Lucas could say anything, the door behind them opened. Astrid frowned, then suddenly, her face lit up. "Zac!" She stepped around the table and quickly strode toward the door.

The atmosphere went back to normal and Sofia glanced behind her at the newcomer. "Mr. Vrost?" What was *he* doing here? And why was Lucas Anderson's fiancée wrapping her arms around—*oh.* Now they were kissing.

"Miss me, sweetheart?" Vrost said to Astrid.

"Always." Her smile was wide, her eyes staring up at him as if he were the only person in the room.

Sofia glanced back at Lucas, as if asking for an explanation. He didn't give any, but again his gaze never left her. His face was completely passive, but there was a burning hatred in his eyes. She had obviously gotten under this skin. *Good.*

"So, who are you—" Vrost stopped when he saw Sofia. "Detective ... Selinofoto?"

"Mr. Vrost." She glanced at Astrid, who was tucked into his side. "Care to explain why you're here?"

"I came to pick up my wife for lunch."

"Your wife?"

"She works here," he explained, nodding at Astrid.

Works here? So, Astrid wasn't Lucas's fiancée? *Fuck. That was embarrassing.* "I see."

"How do you know the Detective, Zac?" Lucas asked, his voice edgy.

"She came to investigate the disturbance at Blood Moon. That night there was a fight, remember?"

"At your bachelor party," she added.

"My *what*?" That finally seemed to get a reaction from him.

"Mr. Vrost told me that you were having a party at the private room in Blood Moon," she began. "That's why you were drunk and half-naked."

He cocked his head at her. "We've met ... before?"

And she knew he meant before the *other night*, of course. "You weren't sober, and we weren't introduced."

"Lucas." Zac walked over to him. "It was a crazy night, so I'm sure you don't remember everything that happened." He looked back at her, a strange look on his face. "And you, Detective? You remember everything? And you're here to find out more about that night?"

"Of course I remember." He seemed confused by that.

"And I'm not here about that night. Your partner, Mr. Jonasson, made it very clear that you wouldn't be pursuing any charges. I'm here about another matter." She turned to Lucas. "So, are you sure no one else can confirm your location Thursday night?"

"Are you going to arrest me?"

She bit her lip. "Like I said, this is only a preliminary interview."

"So you have other suspects?"

She gave a non-committal sound, hoping not to give away too much. "I should be on my way." She got to her feet. "Thank you for your time, Mr. Anderson."

"You're welcome, Detective."

"I'll see myself out." She pivoted on her heel and strode toward the door. The hairs on her neck prickled, and she knew he had his eyes on her. She straightened her shoulders, her spine stiff as steel as she walked out. She kept her posture rigid even as she left the office and made her way to the elevator. It was only when she was out in the street that the tension drained from her body.

She closed her eyes, ignoring the people around her. It didn't go as bad as she imagined. Initially, she thought she'd be embarrassed if he brought up the roof deck incident. After all, she had practically offered herself up to him, allowing him to buy her a drink and take her somewhere private. But he didn't give any indication that he even remembered her. Maybe he was drunk that night too and didn't recall. Or he bought lots of girls drinks and almost kissed them that she didn't even stand out.

This made things simpler. For one thing, she thought she'd have to pass the case on to someone else if it came out that she'd met him before. Of course, him not having an alibi made things complicated, too. Not only would he stay on her suspects list, but now she would have to look into all those other cases as well. Vrost seemed to think she wouldn't remember that first night at Blood Moon. Was someone supposed to make her forget? How? Bribing an officer was a serious crime. Could it be that Fenrir was not only tampering with witnesses, but buying off cops too?

She took one more glance at the Fenrir building, straining her neck to look at the top floor. The sun blinded her for a moment, and she shielded her eyes with her hand. She didn't mean to give them so much information about her suspicions. But her instincts were telling her something was not right and that there was more to this than meets the eye.

The idea of unraveling this mystery both thrilled and terrified her.

CHAPTER FOUR

LUCAS WAS PRETTY SURE MINUTES HAD PASSED SINCE the detective left, but he was still staring at the door. Part of him still couldn't believe what had happened. That after days of being haunted and tortured by slate gray eyes, orange blossoms and olives, and smooth skin under his fingertips, she had walked right into his office. His wolf whined as soon as she disappeared, its head sniffing around, trying to soak in as much of her scent as possible.

Stop it, he commanded his wolf. What the hell was wrong with his animal? Couldn't it sense that Detective Selinofoto was the enemy? That she had dared to threaten him? And the clan?

"Uh, Lucas?"

Astrid's voice broke him out of his trance. He glanced up at the couple, his gaze zeroing in on Zac. "Bachelor party, really?"

"You stumbled out, half-naked and delirious while I was talking to the detective," he explained. "I didn't know what else to say. She wanted to go inside, and I couldn't let her see what the mages had done."

He supposed that made sense. "Why didn't you say it was your party? You're the one who just got married."

"I wasn't exactly with Astrid then," he reminded him. "And I was playing the part of the owner, remember?"

"Hold on." Astrid held up a hand. "Can someone please explain to me what's going on? You've met this detective before?" she asked her husband.

"Remember Deedee's party, when the mages attacked The Lounge?" he said, referring to the private area in the back of Blood Moon. "We had to clear the main club and some cops came. Detective Selinofoto was there, and she got a little too nosy." He gestured toward Lucas. "She saw Lucas after he shifted."

In bloodlust. He could almost hear the unspoken words. That's why he couldn't recall much. His jaw tensed. They'd met before—even before the night on the roof deck—but he didn't remember. But why didn't she say anything? "I thought we took care of all the witnesses?"

"Me too." He looked at Astrid. "Your father gave her the forgetting potion."

"Huh." She tapped a finger on her chin. "Maybe it didn't work on her or he didn't use a strong enough batch."

"But what was she doing here today then?" Zac asked.

"A security officer called up here and told us that a detective wanted to talk to Lucas."

"And you let her up?" he asked Lucas. "What did she want?"

When he saw her in the security cameras, he had been so shocked that he immediately told them to let her upstairs.

That, and his curiosity was piqued. What was she doing here?

"She seems to think Lucas was involved in a murder," Astrid said.

Zac looked at them incredulously. "Okay, you both are going to have to explain this one to me."

This time, it was Astrid who brought Zac up to date, starting from when the detective asked Lucas about Thomas Dixon. "... and then you walked in," she finished. "Frankly, it was ballsy of her to just come in here and accuse him of murder."

"Ridiculous," Zac said. "Why don't you ask your father to pay the detective a visit? Surely he can formulate a potion that will work on her? That way, she won't remember any of this ever happened and she'll forget about Lucas."

His wolf made its displeasure known with an angry growl, the deep rumble vibrating in his chest. He didn't have to guess that the wolf didn't like Zac's words.

"Magic doesn't work that way," Astrid said. "At least, not the forgetting potion. It can only erase recent memories. She might forget she ever came here today, but she won't forget that night. Though, I have heard it's possible ..." She drifted off, her brows wrinkling. "Magic like that, something that would strip the memory of an entire event or person, it's extremely difficult."

Relief poured through him, knowing her memory couldn't be totally erased. "Making her forget seems a bit drastic," he said, his voice controlled.

"That's why we have the police commissioner in the know," Zac said.

The New York Lycans had connections everywhere,

including the highest law enforcement offices in the city. It was necessary to keep their existence a secret.

"We can always ask him to put pressure on the detective," Astrid continued. "Then she'll back off Lucas."

"Let's not use our connections yet," Lucas said. "Besides, we won't know what she knows."

"What do you mean?" Zac asked.

"You heard what she said. She seems to know that we do something to make sure no human ever remembers us." She practically egged him on, telling him that she knew about witnesses conveniently forgetting anything that had to do with them. His gut was telling him she was hiding more.

"I wonder if this so-called murder is just the tip of the iceberg," Astrid said. "She knew about when you and Adrianna were kidnapped. I'm sure my dad had to give the potion to people who saw you get kidnapped outside your school."

"I bet she's been digging into other cases involving us." And *him*. What else could she have found out? Did she uncover what happened when he was a teenager? With Caroline? Anger surged through him at the thought. When he glanced at Zac, the worried look on his face told him he was thinking of that night, too. After all, he and Adrianna had been there.

What was Selinofoto's end game, anyway? Did she think she could bring him down? She was a human, despite what his nose was telling him, and no match for him. If she was getting her kicks trying to dig up the past, he'd show her *exactly* what it was like to go up against a Lycan.

"I have to agree with Lucas," Astrid said. "I think she was hoping to gauge your reaction, Lucas. Maybe she knows more but needed to confirm something else. Something bigger."

Zac frowned. "Don't you have someone who could alibi you for that night?"

"Of course," Lucas admitted. "The security team saw me go into the house, and I didn't leave until morning."

"Then why didn't you tell her that?" Zac asked in an exasperated voice. "You could have gotten rid of her right away."

"She said I wasn't under arrest. I don't owe human authorities an explanation for my whereabouts." He was going to be Alpha of New York, the most powerful Lycan clan in the world. "And my connection to her murder victim is thin." True, while he wasn't sad that one of his kidnappers was dead, that didn't mean he had a motive. Any good lawyer would have shredded the detective's circumstantial evidence, and Fenrir kept the best on retainer. He decided he would actually enjoy watching his lawyers tear into her investigation.

"So, what are you going to do now?"

"If she knows something, we can't let her keep digging. She already knows too much and connected too many dots." He turned to Astrid. "I want to know everything about this detective. Have Mika pull up everything we can about her. Then, make sure someone keeps an eye on her."

"Are you sure that's smart?" Zac asked. "If she finds out we're watching her, she might not take it well. And she'll be even more suspicious of you and she won't let go."

A small part of him was hoping that she wouldn't, and that she would keep coming back to see him. He wanted to watch her try, and play right into his hands. She thought she had the advantage, but she'd soon find out that he always came out on top. From out of nowhere, an image popped into his head of him on top. Of her. Naked and thrusting into—

"Just do it," he barked at Astrid forcefully. He heard a growl coming from Zac. Understandable, seeing as she was his mate and carried their pup. But she was also going to be his Beta and better be prepared to obey his orders. Still, he'd never seen Zac look at him with a murderous look in his eyes before. "Please," he added in a gentler tone, which seemed to mollify his friend.

"Will do. Zac, let's go get lunch, yeah?" She ran a hand down his arm, trying to soothe him. "I'll see you later, Lucas."

As he watched them leave together, he felt a pang of envy. Astrid and Zac were True Mates, an unusual pairing that meant they were fated to be together, and now they were about to have their first child. Lycan children were rare, and only two of their kind could produce a pup. If a Lycan were to mate with a human, they would have human children, if at all. The one exception was True Mates.

He brushed that envy aside, as well as other emotions clouding his judgement and focused on the detective. What were her motives? Did she suspect anything about the existence of Lycans? That only meant that they would need to keep a closer eye on her.

This was a dangerous game he was playing with Sofia Selinofoto, and this would take all his attention. Because there was no way he was going to lose.

CHAPTER FIVE

SOFIA DIDN'T KNOW HOW LONG THOSE MEN HAD BEEN following her or who sent them, but she had two guesses on the latter. Bianchi or Lucas Anderson. She didn't know which one she wanted it to be.

After she left Fenrir Corp. yesterday, she went back to the station. Despite how the meeting with Lucas Anderson ended, she was still able to gather good information. But to process it all, she needed to step back. Plus, there were other cases on her plate, not to mention with her testimony in the Bianchi case coming up in a few weeks, she needed to brush up. The rest of the afternoon was spent trying to follow up on leads, tying up loose ends, and going back to old case files. She was exhausted by the time she went home, though she did remember to check in with the desk sergeant as she promised Bushnell.

That morning, as she was entering the station, she felt like someone was watching her. But before she could turn around, her cellphone rang. It was an important call, from a lead on a robbery case so she ran to her desk to take down notes.

By mid-afternoon, she needed a dose of caffeine. There was a local coffee shop she frequented that was just a few blocks from the station. It was when she was heading there that she caught the dark sedan from the corner of her eye. This was not the first time she had seen it, she realized. Last night when she was going home, it was waiting a block from her apartment building. This morning, when she stopped at a light, it was two cars behind her. When she went out to grab lunch, she passed by the sedan as she crossed the street.

And now, there it was again, crawling along the street beside her. She saw an opportunity when she spied a delivery van stopped up ahead. Picking up her pace, she walked past the van, leaving the sedan behind. She circled around the front of the van, then reappeared on the other side, heading straight for the driver's side.

"Hey!" She rapped her knuckles on the glass. Though it was tinted, this close she could make out two figures inside. The driver started, his head jerking toward her, then looked at the man next to him. She shoved her badge against the window and lifted her jacket to show them she was packing. "Open up! NYPD."

It seemed like they were contemplating what to do, but with the van in front of them, there was no escape. The window rolled down.

"Are you following me?" she asked. "Who are you working for?"

The driver and his passenger remained silent, but the guilty looks on their faces was a definite yes to her first question while the expensive matching suits they were wearing answered the second. Bianchi's men were usually lowlifes and thugs, not guys who looked like they stepped out of a *GQ* magazine cover. Just to be certain, she snatched the driver's phone from his hands.

"Hey!" he protested. "You can't do that!"

She held a hand up. "I can have you arrested for harassing an officer of the law." The phone was locked, but she dialed the emergency contact number, then waited for an answer.

"Fenrir Corporation, Security Department. How may I direct your call?"

That was all she needed. "Tell your boss to stay away from me." She tossed the phone back at him and marched away before she did something stupid.

Adrenaline pumped in her veins, making her forget about the need for a caffeine boost. She walked back to the station, hoping the exercise would make her anger dissipate. However, as she seethed, it only made the fury worse.

That arrogant bastard! It had barely been twenty-four hours, and he already had his goons following her. If she had any doubt that he was hiding something, they were all gone now. Her visit shook him up, and now he was having his people tail her, and God knows what else. Probably look into her background. Not that she had had anything to hide. It wasn't like she had any weaknesses. Although ...

Dad. And Pappoús.

She sat up straighter. Surely Lucas Anderson wouldn't try to harm two old men. But she didn't know him at all, and who knew how ruthless he could be? With all his money and power, surely he could crush anyone he thought beneath him. The fact that families and loved ones were always vulnerable to retaliation was like a shadow that hung over detectives and other law enforcement agents. They could be easy prey to people who would want to put pressure on police officers.

She made a decision. A stupid one maybe, but if she didn't nip this in the bud, she might regret it later. Hesitation and waiting on the sidelines had gotten her in trouble. Now she would face the lion and show him she wasn't afraid.

Just as Sofia had thought, Lucas Anderson didn't leave the office until hours after most normal people went home. It was just after nine o'clock when she spotted his familiar, tall form exiting the Fenrir Corporation building, heading toward the sleek black town car waiting by the door. She had been waiting in her car, parked across the street from the building. Sliding out of the driver's seat, she made a beeline for him.

He was reaching for the door when she approached him. The look he gave her was one of complete surprise. "Detective? What—"

"Don't play dumb," she warned. "You know why I'm here."

That cold mask slipped back on. "I do?"

"You think you can have me followed and I wouldn't notice it?" she seethed. "Did you look into my background too?"

He didn't even deny it. "What would you have done in my place?"

"I'm an officer of the law."

"And you thought to threaten me without a warrant or any real evidence." His hand snaked out to grab her wrist in a movement so fast she barely saw it. She was too distracted by those eyes, she decided. His palms were warm and much rougher than she would have thought for a man who spent his days in an office. She was average height, but he seemed to tower over her, his presence overwhelming. There was also that electric shock that shot up her arm, but she didn't want to give him the satisfaction of seeing her struggle so she remained still. At least, that's what she told herself.

"I wasn't threatening you." She turned her face away, wanting to escape that gaze.

"Weren't you?" A finger tipped her chin, forcing her to face those mesmerizing eyes again. "You were trying to shake me up. See if I would react. Did I perform to your satisfaction, Detective?"

Much to her horror, she felt a warm surge of desire in the pit of her stomach and her core clenched as an image came to her mind of the many ways he could *perform to her satisfaction*. When his nostrils flared, she thought for a moment that he had peeked into her head. *Ridiculous.* "I could have you arrested for assaulting an officer."

He let go of her wrist. "Apologies."

"You will stop having me followed by your lackeys."

"And you will stop looking into things that don't concern you."

"Are you telling me to stop doing my job?" Would he offer her some type of bribe now?

"Of course not," he said. "But why do you insist on pursuing this? Thomas Dixon was a lowlife ex-con."

"Thomas Dixon may have been the scum of the earth, but he didn't deserve to die like that." This was one of the few times she truly hated her job. "He still deserves justice."

He gritted his teeth, but said, "And I hope you find it. But I'm telling you; I didn't murder him."

"And what about Kevin Hall?"

His face darkened, and once again, the air around her seem to contract, making it difficult to breathe. "Stick to your job, Detective." His voice had turned Arctic. "And I'll leave you alone. But if you keep digging up the past in an attempt to harm me or those close to me, you *will* regret it."

It didn't sound like a threat. No, it was a promise.

CHAPTER SIX

THE BLOOD IN HIS VEINS TURNED TO ICE AT THE mention of that name, but as soon as the words left his mouth, he regretted it. His wolf snarled at him, the animal making its displeasure known.

An unknown pride surged through him when she didn't react. She didn't back away, flinch, or even blink. No, Sofia Selinofoto was not affected by his words. She was strong as steel, beautiful as a blade. He was disappointed, however, that the arousal he detected earlier no longer tinged her delicious scent.

"Mr. Anderson?"

They both turned toward the source of the voice. Reyes had appeared behind them and looked at them with his intense eyes. "I'm sorry it took me longer to check on that other matter." His gaze flickered at Sofia. "Is everything all right, sir?"

Even a perceived threat to Lucas could set him off and Sofia wouldn't be a match for the Lycan's strength and speed.

"It's fine, Reyes." He looked back at Sofia. "The detective was just leaving."

Her slate gray gaze intensified at the dismissal, but she didn't say anything. She pivoted on her heel and walked away, heading straight to her vehicle. Whether it was on purpose or not, she moved with a sensuality he had never seen in other women. Even dressed in a shapeless blouse and slacks that did nothing to flatter her body, he couldn't stop looking at her. It wasn't until she drove off that he turned to Reyes. "Let's go back to the townhouse."

"Yes, sir."

He slid into the back seat of the town car, sinking into the soft, buttery leather seats. As the car drove through the streets of Manhattan, he found himself thinking of that name he hadn't heard in a long time.

Kevin Hall.

So, the detective *had* looked into his past. Grant Anderson had used all his powers and cashed in every favor to make sure no one knew the truth. But, that damn civil suit hit them out of nowhere, and though they were able to settle out of court before there were any hearings, there was no way to remove the knowledge from public record.

Only he, Zac, and Adrianna still knew the truth of what happened that night, but if anyone were to ask him, Kevin Hall and Jeffrey Smith both deserved it. For what they did to Caroline.

His wolf reared up again, the fog of anger clouding his mind and had him releasing the tight control he usually held. A growl ripped from his throat. *No!* When he looked down, he saw the leather seats had ripped to shreds underneath his claws.

Shock made him startle. The wolf had gotten close to the surface again, closer than it had ever gotten, and he didn't even realize it this time. A pain ripped in his head.

Ground yourself. Use the good, Lucas. Keep him in control.

"Sir? We're here." Reyes looked back at him his face inscrutable.

The battle between himself and his wolf ended. For now, at least.

"Thank you, Reyes." He opened the door and slid out of the car, then headed inside the dark, empty townhouse.

———

Damn his wolf. Damn it to hell.

Last night, it had been testing his patience and control. The fact it had gotten close enough to the surface to make itself physically known should have made him angry enough. But, no. Now the damned animal wanted to control his thoughts too. Making him think of orange blossoms and olives. Of sensuous curves moving with a cat-like grace. Of claiming sultry lips made for kissing and a body shaped for making love.

Making love?

His wolf really was going mad. Lucas never made love. No. He had sex. He *fucked*. But never, *ever*, made love.

"Lucas? Lucas! Are you all right?"

He'd been so consumed by his inner battle that he didn't see or hear his younger sister enter his office. "Julianna," he greeted, getting up from his chair. "How've you been? How's Jersey?"

She stepped into his open arms, and he breathed in her familiar scent as they embraced. Crisp, cool ocean breeze. Similar to his, and their father's. His family were the only people he would let in this close, whom he would let himself be so vulnerable with. And that's why he fiercely guarded them and would do anything to protect them.

"Are you okay?" She stepped back and glanced up with him, her mismatched eyes just like his except mirrored. Most people said she looked more like a female version of their father than their mother, with her stubborn chin and angular face made even more prominent by her severe, chin-length haircut. His middle sister always had this seriousness about her, and right now, she was gazing up at him like a concerned grandmother.

"I'm fine," he assured her. "To what do I owe this visit? I thought you'd be staying in Jersey for the time being?" His twin sister, Adrianna, had moved there over the weekend to begin taking her place as future Alpha of the territory to replace their mother, and Julianna went with her to help along with the transition.

"You know all about what's happening over there."

His jaw clenched. "I do." And it had pained him not to help out his twin sister, but he knew better than to get in her and Mama's way, or worse, act like some white knight coming in to rescue them. "I don't like that she and Mama may have enemies we don't know anything about."

"Did she tell you that one of *them* has been assigned to be her bodyguard?"

"What?" That he didn't know. "What happened?"

Julianna relayed to him the story of how Anatoli Corvinus had somehow convinced Mama to take on his nephew,

Darius, as a bodyguard for Adrianna. "And now he's around all the time."

"Do you think he's going to hurt her in some way?" His wolf surfaced again, this time, out of concern for its twin.

"He wouldn't dare," Julianna said. "But I don't like the way he's always staring at her when he thinks she's not looking. Besides, you know I can take care of her."

"I know you can." His sister had been part of the Lycan Security Force for years. It was an unusual position for the daughter of two Alphas, but he knew how it suited her and how much she loved it, especially with her fiercely protective nature. "I'm glad she has you with her."

"And you?" Julianna's sharp gaze turned to him. "Who's going to watch out for you?"

"I can take care of myself. I'm not alone here."

"If I could rip myself in two, I'd be watching out for both you and Adrianna."

That made him smile. "I'm the future Alpha of New York, I have lots of people protecting me."

"But not family." She stressed the last word.

"You're not the only member of our family here."

"And what? Isabelle's supposed to protect you?" She rolled her eyes at the mention of their youngest sibling. "What would she do if a mage attacked you? Throw one of her Louboutin heels at them? Whack them with her Chanel purse?"

"Julianna," he warned. Most people thought Isabelle Anderson was about as deep as a wading pool, but Lucas saw in his sister something no one else did. An intelligence she hid behind that vapid facade and a kind heart she masked with vanity. Why she preferred people see the surface was a mystery to him.

His thoughts turned to another person who was like a puzzle he couldn't solve. Sofia Selinofoto was an enigma that both angered and frustrated him. His reaction to her was disturbing. One moment, he wanted to crush her under his heel like a bug for daring to threaten him and the next, he wanted to bite those lush lips and have her under him, naked and writhing with pleasure.

"Will you tell me what's wrong?"

The question caught him off guard. "Why do you say something's wrong?"

Julianna looked at him wryly. "I've never been able to sneak up on you, and yet you didn't notice me coming in here. And now, it's like you just ... left. Your body's here, but your head's someplace else."

"I have a lot on my mind."

"What?" She placed a hand on his arm. "You can tell me."

"It's nothing." He flinched away from her touch, and he didn't miss the hurt in her eyes. "Julianna, I swear I'm fine."

She let out a sigh. "If you won't talk to me, will you at least talk to Adrianna? She's your twin, so I know there are things you'd rather talk to her about." She held up a hand when he tried to protest. "No, it's fine. I understand. You guys have this special bond. I just ... I care about you, you know that, right?"

"I do. And I'll talk to Adrianna."

That seemed to satisfy her. "Good. I have to go see Mika and Aunt Alynna and report to them. I couldn't come here and not say hi to my favorite brother."

"I'm your only brother," he reminded her, getting a chuckle from her, and it seemed all was right with them again.

She leaned up and kissed him on the cheek. "I'll see you around, Lucas."

"Take care, Julianna."

As his sister left his office, he walked back around to his desk. Julianna was too perceptive for her own good, which is why she was so well-suited to being part of the Special Investigations unit of the Lycan Security Team. He knew she had good intentions, but this was something he had to deal with himself.

He raised his hands, turning them over to examine his palms and fingers, imagining them tipped with razor-sharp claws. His wolf was getting bolder, possibly stronger. It was all these memories and the past coming back to haunt him. Thomas Dixon. Kevin Hall. Caroline.

And it was Sofia dredging this all up. Turning his animal against him. If she really knew what he was, she would stop digging into his past. Because if he lost full control, there would be consequences.

CHAPTER SEVEN

JULIANNA MUST HAVE RETURNED TO NEW JERSEY THAT same day, because that was the only explanation as to the numerous missed calls and messages he got from Adrianna. He hated to ignore her, but he told himself it was for the best. Adrianna had her own problems to deal with. With her naturally nurturing nature, she would put all her worries aside to help him.

But, if he were to be truly honest with himself, he didn't want to face her because he knew that she could read him like a book. They shared a womb, after all, and all his twin had to do was look at him to know what was bothering him. And frankly, he wouldn't be able to lie to her.

So, he did his best to ignore her calls and messages. After all, he was busy with running a worldwide conglomerate. His father was still technically CEO and Alpha, but with the title coming to him soon, Lucas had already assumed many of the responsibilities of both positions. His father was traveling currently, trying to go to the various offices and partners around the world to give his final goodbyes and soothe any worries with the upcoming transition.

He thought he could continue to brush off his sister, but then her last message hit a nerve.

Mike's Diner, 6 p.m. Be there or not, I'll be waiting.

The words made him flinch. Adrianna was taking out the big guns. She was apparently concerned enough that she would not only defy their parent's orders that they not be in the same place together, but she would choose a place that meant something to both of them.

He had no choice but to go there and see her. But, if any of the Lycan Security Team found out where he was going, they'd report him to Nick Vrost or his father. They were under strict orders to guard him at all times. How could he possibly get away from his shadows?

———

The solution to his problem came in the form of his future Beta and his best friend. Zac was the one person who understood why he couldn't just ignore his sister. He was trying to help him find a way to go there without alerting anyone when Astrid walked in and asked what they were doing. Zac, of course, couldn't lie to his wife.

"We'll take you," Astrid offered.

"We will?" Zac frowned.

"Of course," Astrid said matter-of-factly. "It's the only way. We can tell Nick that Lucas wants to have dinner with us in private regarding clan and Fenrir matters. The team is already working double shifts, having to protect the Alpha while he's abroad, the Lupa while she's going back and forth from Jersey, and trying to figure out where the mages are hiding." As Beta-in-training, Astrid was privy to all this information. "Reyes can go home to his wife and kids, and Lucas can go see Adrianna."

Lucas thought it was a brilliant plan. "Excellent solution. Make it happen."

He had to admit he'd made the right choice in picking Astrid as his Beta. He meant what he said before, about her being the best person for the job because she wasn't afraid to go against him if necessary; after all, an Alpha needed someone to balance him out, someone who would help him look at things objectively and not be afraid to do the necessary work to protect the clan. But now he saw Astrid's craftiness and intelligence in action. He had no doubt she would be a great second-in-command in the next couple of decades.

At five that afternoon, he met them in Fenrir's basement parking lot. He had one of his personal cars taken out and insisted on driving them, since he didn't usually drive himself around. Besides, it was a tradition of sorts for him to drive to Mike's Diner. When he and Adrianna first got their licenses, they had driven to Jersey by themselves and stopped at this rest stop in the middle of nowhere, the diner the only place to get a bite. The food was terrible, but it was the memory of that first time they stopped there that made them keep coming back each time they drove to Jersey. Adrianna had chosen the place because of its meaning to them, and because she knew he wouldn't be able to say no to her.

With traffic, it took them thirty minutes to arrive. He pulled into the closest parking spot and then turned to Zac who sat in the front passenger seat. "Coming?"

"Eww, no." Astrid piped in from the back. She was

frowning as she looked at the screen of her smart phone. "Reviewers gave this place a one-point-oh rating. And that sounded generous, based on the pictures. I know I'm pretty much indestructible, but I have doubts whether the True Mate pregnancy powers can withstand those mashed potatoes." She gave an exaggerated shudder then took out a paper bag from her purse. "Good thing I brought snacks."

"We'll stay here," Zac chuckled. "You go and see Adrianna."

"And tell her we said hi," Astrid murmured through a mouthful of what appeared to be a brownie.

"I will." He slipped out of the car and headed inside. It was exactly six o'clock when he entered and spotted the back of Adrianna's head as she sat at their usual table. She was not alone, though. Seated across from her was a silver-haired man. At first, he thought it was some old timer keeping his sister company, but as he drew closer, Lucas realized that he was not much older than him. He was glancing around, as if assessing the place for danger.

"Adrianna?" He stood right beside her when she looked up.

Adrianna's face lit up as soon as their eyes met and she quickly got to her feet to embrace him. He breathed in her scent—like freshly-baked pastries Nonna used to make—and wrapped his arms around her.

"You came." There was doubt in her voice and he hated himself for making her think he wouldn't.

"Of course." He pasted a smirk on his face. "You didn't give me much of a choice. Though I'm glad I did. It's nice to see you." He looked over to her companion, who was now peering up at him with cobalt blue eyes. His wolf went on defense, sensing the other Lycan's animal. He could feel it, its hackles raised as well, but there was something about it that was strangely familiar. Like finding a kindred spirit. "Who's this?"

"Oh." His sister's voice was breathy. "This is Darius."

He didn't need the introduction of course, as who else would be here with her.

The other man gave him a curt but respectful bow. "It is an honor to meet you."

"Darius Corvinus, right? Julianna's told me all about you." He waited to see if the man reacted, but he didn't even flinch. "She said you were keeping a close eye on Adrianna," he continued. "Thank you."

"It is my duty to serve my Alpha. If you'll excuse me, I'll give you some privacy. I shall be waiting right outside the door." Darius bowed his head again, then strode out the door. But Lucas didn't miss that flicker of wanting in his eyes as his gaze passed over Adrianna. It was like a spark; small, but strong enough to turn into a blaze.

"Interesting guy." Very interesting. He turned to his sister, raising a brow at her as if to ask, *what is up with him?*

She ignored his non-verbal question. "Sit."

And so he did, taking his usual seat. "So, are we having greasy, cold burgers or soggy, salty fries?"

She laughed. "How about the usual?"

He called the waitress over and gave her their order—a vanilla milkshake for him, chocolate for Adrianna, and a plate of onion rings to share. When the waitress left, he turned back to his sister. "So, why did you want to meet me here?"

"Why have you been ignoring my calls and my messages?"

"I'm not ignoring you." But he knew she would see right through that lie.

"Yes, you have," she insisted. "What's wrong?" She was trying to look him in the eye, and he suddenly found the dried crust of ketchup on the edge of the table interesting. But Adrianna continued her assault. "Tell me. You know I'll find out one way or another."

He couldn't keep ignoring her, so he looked at her. Those eyes so much like his own were full of concern. "Lucas? Please. Tell me what's the matter."

"It's nothing." He picked up the menu, pretending to peruse it, though the words just blurred on the page and made no sense.

Adrianna's gaze felt like a laser beam, zeroing in on him even as he tried to deflect her. He wasn't sure if it was the twin bond they shared or if it was because no other person on the planet knew him as well as his sister. The words that came out of her mouth were almost prescient.

"What's her name?"

His head snapped up, and he knew he couldn't lie to her. So he decided to just not say it. "No one you would know." Technically, the truth.

"And why wouldn't I know her?"

"Because she's human."

Her emotions were so transparent on her face. Shock. Surprise. "Oh."

"And she's investigating me for a murder."

The same emotions on her face magnified. "Oh." She collected herself. "What are you going to do?"

"I don't know." And that was the one truth he couldn't deny. Sofia had gotten under his skin, and he didn't know how to get her out. Or if he even wanted her out. He glanced toward the door and saw the shadow of Adrianna's new bodyguard. "What about you? What's the deal with that Darius guy?"

Her face went all red. She too, couldn't lie to him. "Huh? What about him?"

She always answered a question with a question when she didn't want him pestering her. "Don't play innocent with me, Adrianna. No bodyguard looks at their client that way. Or the other way around."

"This isn't fair. It's nothing."

Oh, he had seen the interest in her eyes, enough to make him uncomfortable because he didn't want to think of her—or any of his sisters—that way. But the way she blushed harder confirmed his suspicions. And that concerned him.

"He's part of The Family, right?" he said, mentioning the name of the organized crime group that had taken residence in Jersey. "Those people causing trouble for Mama?"

"We've taken care of it," she said defensively.

"It's your territory and your business." He placed a hand on hers. "I know the women in our family are capable and strong. None of you would stand for me and Papa coming in like white knights, but promise me you'll tread carefully. Especially around that one."

"I—yes, I promise!" she said in a petulant tone. "But you have to promise me that you won't ignore me again. That really hurt, Lucas."

That stabbed through him like a knife. "I'm sorry, Adrianna." He squeezed her hand. "I swear I won't do that to you again."

"Good."

Their waitress's arrival seemed to have broken the tension, and they switched their topic of conversation to more mundane subjects. They seemed to have come to a silent agreement—or perhaps an impasse—neither wanting to get into the other's business for fear that they would have to talk about sensitive subjects.

Surprisingly, he found himself having a good time. Or not surprisingly, actually. Adrianna always had this way of soothing and calming him. And this place reminded him of the good memories from the past, not just the bad ones that had been swirling in his mind.

When the waitress came with their check, she insisted on paying and he let her. "Did you drive by yourself here?" she asked as the cashier handed her her change.

"No, but I had Zac with me, so we didn't have to get anyone on the Lycan Security Team to come and follow me. He's waiting outside."

"He is?" She frowned. "Why didn't he come in with you?"

"Don't worry, Astrid's with him," he explained. "He couldn't lie to her and then she insisted on coming. Besides, she took one look at the reviews of this place and gave a hard no. Do you want to say hello?"

"It's okay." She gave him a dismissive wave. "You guys should go before anyone suspects anything."

He pulled her into a hug, taking in her familiar, comforting scent. "This was nice, Adrianna. I really needed this." He meant every word. "Thanks for telling me to come here. I knew your bossiness would come in handy someday."

"Ha! *Now* you admit I'm the boss because I'm older."

"By one minute," he relented. "I'll talk to Mama and

Papa, and we can figure something out. It's ridiculous that we can't even be in the same room together." It really was unreasonable; they couldn't expect them to stay apart indefinitely.

"I know. Have a safe drive back. And call me if you need to talk. About anything," she said with genuine concern.

He shoved his hands into his pockets. "I will." Heading toward the door, he exited the diner. Darius was there, and their eyes met, and a kind of silent truce–agreement passed between them as their wolves assessed each other. He would stay out of their business for now, but if he hurt Adrianna, there would be hell to pay.

He strode back to his car, opened the door and got in. "Hey—fucking hell, really?"

The seat beside him was empty, as Zac was in the back. At least, he assumed it was Zac that Astrid was straddling, with his hand up the back of her shirt.

"Oops." She giggled and scrambled off her husband's lap.

"Sorry," Zac said, though the grin on his face told Lucas he wasn't sorry at all.

He sighed. "C'mon, lovebirds, let's go back to Manhattan. Ugh. It stinks in here." It smelled like desire and passion.

"I'll pay to get it cleaned," Zac said as he entered the front seat.

"You should just buy this car from me," he grumbled.

"Maybe I will," his friend countered. "Those seats in the back are nice."

"Really nice," Astrid purred.

"Shut up, both of you," he groaned. He was just glad he had gotten there before they actually started having sex. He put the car into gear and pulled out of the parking lot. As he was waiting for his turn to exit into the street, his phone beeped. There was a message from Adrianna.

Darius says you're being followed. Watch out for a dark sedan. Want us to follow you back? He typed a quick reply telling her he would take care of the matter.

Lucas didn't need two guesses to figure out who was following them. Sofia Selinofoto was bold. And she was great at maintaining a tail without being detected.

"Lucas? The road's been clear for about ten seconds." Zac frowned. "What's wrong?"

"We have a tail."

Astrid turned around. "Where? Who?"

"Who do you think?" Zac asked. "I told you she wouldn't like it if you went after her."

He didn't even know the half of it. "I'll take care of her." He drove out from the driveway, his senses on alert as they pulled onto the highway. If it wasn't for shifter eyesight, he wouldn't have seen the dark sedan a few cars behind them. The driver was definitely a woman.

Yes, she was good. But he was better.

CHAPTER EIGHT

SOFIA PRIDED HERSELF ON KEEPING HER COOL IN ANY situation. But last night shook her up more than she cared to admit. And she hated being rattled because that meant she did stupid things. Like, following Lucas Anderson.

Last night she had undoubtedly crossed a line. Obviously, she had struck a nerve when she mentioned Kevin Hall's name. Did she really have anything to fear from him? If she didn't, surely, she did now.

Still, here she was, following him. *Like he had me followed.* She used a different vehicle from the precinct pool. It was unmarked and would blend in. She had arrived at the Fenrir Corp. building just after five, so she was surprised to see Lucas in the driver's seat of the green Aston Martin that was coming out of the garage.

When it headed toward Midtown and into the Lincoln tunnel, she frowned. *New Jersey?* She tailed him for a good thirty minutes until he pulled off the parkway and into a large truck stop. He parked the car by the lone diner, and she had kept going, circling around the back once before making a U-turn, heading back into the parking lot. She picked the space at the end of the lot and turned off the engine. And so, here she was, thinking about her next steps while kicking herself for the poor choices she made when it came to Lucas Anderson.

Why couldn't she just let it go? Well, for one thing, there really was no other leads in the Dixon case. The one or two possibilities she had didn't pan out. A former cellmate who supposedly had a beef with him died in prison a decade before. All other known associates were dead or so old themselves that there was no way any of them could have committed such a violent murder. His other accomplices were still in prison. He didn't even have any family. Dixon was abandoned as a child, grew up in the system, and was left to fend for himself the moment he turned eighteen. It was like he was a ghost outside prison.

Speaking of ghosts, whoever their killer was seemed like one too. The crime lab didn't find any traces of DNA on the body, which was highly unusual for such a violent murder. No footprints, or vehicle tracks either. It was like whoever did this magically appeared in the alley, beat the shit out of Dixon, and then just disappeared into thin air. Which made her think it could be a professional hit, and Lucas Anderson was certainly rich enough to hire someone. But then again, a killer for hire would use something clean, like a gun or poison.

It was all too much, too many coincidences and she was far too invested in this thing to let it go. She would have to see this through. Decision made, she exited the car, pulling her coat closer to her body. There was no way she could enter there without anyone noticing her. It was far too empty and her suit would stand out amongst what she could imagine the clientele was like.

She waited, and an hour later, he emerged and walked to his car. Much to her surprise, someone emerged from the back seat and slipped in the front. Huh. She didn't even notice anyone was in the car. She watched him drive out of the parking lot before starting her engine and turning toward the direction where the Aston Martin went. The road wasn't too busy, so she had to make sure she stayed behind. There were more cars on the highway, so it was easier to follow him while staying far enough away.

She thought they'd be heading back to Manhattan, but to her surprise, he took the next exit into an industrial zone. Her alarm bells went up. Maybe she was right to follow him. Why would the soon-to-be CEO of one of the biggest corporations in the world be sneaking off into the middle of nowhere in Jersey? Surely he had lackeys to do his dirty business. Unless this was personal business.

The road was taking them deeper and deeper into the area that housed many of the factories and refineries in the Garden State. She trailed behind, but there were fewer vehicles as they went further, and soon it would be obvious she was tailing them. And, he must have realized it, because there was a roar of an engine and then taillights ahead of her disappeared down the road.

"Fuck!" She stepped on the brakes and slammed her palms on the wheel. There was no way she could keep up with a sports car, not at that speed. It's not like she was in her jurisdiction either, and if she attempted to stop him for speeding, it would definitely look like harrasment. She supposed she could keep going, but she had no idea if Lucas had kept going straight or turned off into one of the many facilities in the area.

From this point on, she could only go back to Manhattan. However, before she could turn around, a pair of headlights appeared in the distance, growing larger as it drew close. The green Aston Martin was unmistakable, even in the dark. It slowed down as it passed by her car and even though she couldn't see the driver, she could feel him looking straight at her.

She tried to contain a shudder. He knew, the bastard. Knew it was her following him.

CHAPTER NINE

THOUGHTS OF THE CONSEQUENCES OF HER ACTIONS coming to bite her in the ass kept her up that night. However, she didn't think it would happen quite so soon. Like, the moment she walked into the precinct.

"*Detective.*"

She turned her head toward the hissed whisper. "What's up, Winters?"

Sergeant Winters's lips were pursed together. "Captain wants to see you."

"Okay." The look on the other woman's face told her there was more. "And?"

"And he's not alone. Deputy Commissioner Aarons is there with him."

Now that raised alarms. "The deputy commissioner?"

"Yes." Winters's eyes darted around. "And someone else. Some business-type guy in a suit."

Fuck. She hoped it wasn't who she thought it was, but her luck wasn't that good. When she glanced over at the captain's office, the blinds were drawn closed. *Dammit.*

With a deep breath, she strode to her desk and deposited her purse, then headed into the office. A sharp, "Come in," followed her knock. As she entered the office, she kept her gaze on Captain Bushnell, who was seated behind his desk, while ignoring the other occupants of the room who sat on the chairs across from him. But she didn't need to look at the dark-haired man to know who it was.

"You wanted to speak to me, Captain?"

Bushnell's face was impassive, not revealing an ounce of emotion, not even in his blue eyes. "You know Deputy Aarons, Detective."

"Sir," she said with a slight incline of her head. Though she had never talked to him face to face, she recognized him from his photos. Aarons was a large man, though he had a slight paunch, probably from sitting behind a desk for years. His head was completely bald and his eyes small and beady.

"And of course, you've already met Mr. Anderson."

Though she turned to him, she focused on a spot just above his shoulder. "Mr. Anderson."

"Detective."

Her head snapped back to the captain and her stance became rigid. "What can I do for you, sir?"

"Actually—"

"The commissioner himself sent me here," Aarons interrupted. "He asked that I meet with you, your captain, and Mr. Anderson," he said, his tone impatient. "So, it seems Mr. Anderson is a person of interest in your case."

"Yes. Sir," she added quickly.

"And could you explain how he's connected to a murder of this ex-con?"

"I followed proper procedure, sir," she said.

"I didn't ask if you followed it or not." Aarons voice was tight.

"It's an active case." Her gaze flickered to Lucas. "I can't just discuss the details."

"And I'm the deputy police commissioner of New York."

Bushnell cleared his throat. "Just explain to the commissioner, Detective Selinofoto."

"As I said, I followed procedure." She refused to look at Lucas, even though she could feel his gaze on her. "I investigated all the leads. Mr. Anderson just happened to be one of them, and I went to interview him to eliminate him from the suspects list."

"And did you?" Aarons shot back. She hesitated, and he continued. "Mr. Anderson asked to come here to offer his cooperation on all matters in this case, by the way."

"He has?" She couldn't stop herself nor hide the surprise in her voice, and she cursed at herself silently.

"Yes, it seems he also forgot to mention one important detail when you went to interview him—which he reminded me, he did voluntarily at your request." His beady eyes quickly glanced at Lucas. "He assures me and Commissioner Foster he wasn't being untruthful, just forgetful."

"You have to understand," Lucas began. "I'm in and out of the city and the country all the time. When you asked about that night and I said I was alone, I must have mistaken it for another night."

Her chest tightened and she knew things were about to go bad for her. But she pressed on. "So, you weren't alone that night, like you told me?" She had no choice but to look at him now, because she needed to see his face. It was the only way she would be able to tell if he was lying.

"I was." He met her gaze full-on. "But I have bodyguards on me twenty-four hours ever since we had a security issue during a family event a couple weeks ago. I have at least one bodyguard in the house with me at night. I'm sure I can ask our head of security for the name of the guard and he would be happy to speak with you."

She swallowed hard, and her entire face felt like a three-alarm fire. It was hard to breathe, but she managed a small gulp. "I see." Her case against him was crumbling before her very eyes—correction, it had crumbled—and nothing was left but ash.

"What have you got to say for yourself, Detective?" Aarons's voice was trembling with a quiet rage.

"I was only doing my job, sir."

"If you had done your job, we wouldn't be here," he spat.

The full impact of his words hit her like a jackhammer, and she visibly flinched. Curling her fingernails into her palm, she focused on the pain, because there was no way she would let them see her cry.

"Selinofoto is a good detective, sir," Bushnell said, but Aarons only huffed. "And she followed protocol every step of the way."

"I'm sure she did," Aarons sneered. "I've also heard other things about her—"

"You are dismissed, Detective." Bushnell's voice thundered with force, but she knew it wasn't directed toward her. Relief poured through her, and she nodded, then pivoted and went out the door.

The numbness began to spread, but she still felt eyes on her as she left the captain's office. Everyone knew something was going on, of course. This fucking precinct! Didn't they have anything to do other than stick their Goddamn noses in everyone else's business?

She made a beeline for the women's bathroom, the one place that would be empty this time of day. It was, thankfully, and she threw the door open and headed to the nearest sink. Her eyes were shiny with tears, but none had fallen. Brushing them aside with her knuckles, she took a deep breath.

Before she could even begin trying to make sense of the situation, the door flew open, making her startle. "You!"

He was the last person she wanted to see right this moment, but of course, Mr. High and Mighty Lucas Anderson shows up at the worst possible moment.

"Are—"

"You're not supposed to be in here." Did he come here to gloat? Well, she wouldn't give him the satisfaction of watching her cry.

"Sofia." He took a tentative step forward. "I didn't—"

"Get out."

"Please—"

Rage boiled in her veins. "I said get out."

"Let me explain—"

"Explain?" Her head jerked towards him. "Explain what? That you've been toying with me all this time, you vindictive bastard?"

"I haven't—"

"You could have told me about your bodyguard—don't

even try to give me that crap about you forgetting—but instead, you withheld that information for the sole purpose of exerting your power and influence and then humiliating me in front of my superiors!"

The guilt on his face and his silence confirmed her suspicions. But before she could continue her tirade, the door flew open, crashing against the wall.

"Sir, you're not supposed to be here," warned the stern voice. "This is strictly for female officers and detectives."

Winters!

Lucas took a step back. "Pardon me, I got lost."

Winters raised a brow, obviously smelling his bullshit. "I'm going to have to escort you out."

Lucas shook his head. "No need, Officer."

"I have to insist." She gave him a sweet smile. "I wouldn't want you to get 'lost' again. The precinct can be quite tricky." Opening the door, she gestured for him to leave first.

"All right, Officer," he relented. He gave Sofia a last glance before walking out. Winters gave her a sympathetic look before following Lucas, the door closing behind her with a soft thud.

The tension began to drain out of her body, and she slumped forward, bracing herself on the sink. God, what a fucking mess she was. She'd never been this emotional, not even when the shit with Derek went down. But Goddamn Lucas Anderson was turning her into a wreck.

Maybe this was how rich people acted; they thought everyone was beneath them and they could just move them around like puppets. Or that they were dancing bears for amusement. And to think that night at Blood Moon, she almost kissed him.

Looking up, she stared at her reflection in the mirror. *Time to move on, Sofia.* Really, her career and her ego couldn't possibly suffer any more, so maybe from here, the only place to go was up. And now that Lucas Anderson had had his fun with her, he could move on to his next victim. Because if she saw him again, it would certainly be too soon.

CHAPTER TEN

When he arrived at the station this morning, Lucas only thought of the satisfaction he would feel once he put Detective Selinofoto in her place. He already knew that he would win this game, and there was no way she was going to come out on top.

But his victory felt empty.

She never flinched or wavered the other times they verbally sparred. He threatened her when she confronted him, and she stood her ground. He even made her chase him down a deserted highway, but she remained cool as a cucumber.

But today, when he wounded her pride by implying her incompetence at her job and humiliated her in front of her superiors, he saw something that would haunt him for a long time.

Hurt.

And, Goddammit, he should have known better. Sofia was a woman in a male-dominated field. She probably had to work twice as hard as any man in the job to get half as far. He knew this because he'd seen it in his own mother. Frankie Anderson was not only a business woman but also a female Alpha in her own right, and she was constantly being underestimated. Hell, his twin was about to embark on the same path, and Julianna and Isabelle would always have people discounting their skills because of their sex. If any of them found out about what he did to Sofia, they would kick his sorry ass.

This whole damn situation wasn't even his doing. Nick Vrost, who was still Beta and head of security for Fenrir, had somehow found out about Sofia and insisted they nip it in the bud by calling the commissioner. Frankly, he thought it was an overreaction, and if he had known what would happen, he never would have agreed to it.

He was a fucking bastard. And for once since he'd met her, his own wolf was in agreement. It ripped him from the inside, and he had no choice but to follow her because the animal was growling at him. Her rage cut into him like a blade, every word twisting it into his gut. She was right, and he was man enough to admit it.

"Here you go, sir," the young female officer's tone was sickly sweet and condescending at the same time. "I know this big precinct is *sooo* confusing and it's easy to get lost and many of the signs here have big words like, 'authorized personnel only' so it might be difficult to understand." She pointed to the sign above the door leading out to the street. "There's a simple one for you: *Exit*."

"Thank you," he said, feeling thoroughly reprimanded. The officer smirked at him, then turned around and walked away.

His town car was already waiting for him at the curb.

Reyes was standing next to it and he opened the door when he spotted Lucas. He was about to slip inside when he stopped and turned to the burly bodyguard.

"Reyes, I need to ask you something."

"Sir?"

"You're former military right?"

"Yes," he answered. "I took early retirement when Mr. Vrost contacted me and offered me a position."

"Do you have any contacts in New York?"

"Contacts?"

"I just need someone to keep tabs on Detective Selinofoto."

"Sure." Reyes scratched his chin. "But we have people on the Lycan Security Team who could do that."

"You mean, those two pups who couldn't tail her for more than a day before being discovered?" he said.

"Ah." He thought for a moment. "I know a guy. Do you just want surveillance or—"

"Just watch her. I want to know where she is at all times and if she does anything unusual." He lowered his voice. "And be discreet. This can't be traced back to me, or Fenrir, or the clan."

He nodded. "Yes, sir."

As he got into the car, Lucas knew he was being an idiot. The smart thing to do was to put this behind him and forget about Sofia Selinofoto. He had already won the game. But his wolf wouldn't let him rest. It seethed with anger, which was directed at him.

And her face. Her Goddamn beautiful face filled with hurt. Whenever he thought of it, his gut twisted with agony. He would give her some time, but he would have to find a way to approach her, so they could talk. Maybe in a few days she would cool down, and he could actually get close enough to talk to her and apologize. His wolf seemed appeased for now, and he only hoped he could find a way to keep it under control.

———

Reyes's contact was good. No, he was excellent. He went to work right away that same day, and he was getting reports every few hours on her location. Not that there was anything to report. She went home, then went to work the next day. She went out for coffee, then lunch, then drove to a crime scene, then went home. The following day was Saturday, and she didn't leave her apartment until late afternoon when she walked to the nearest Subway station. Thirty minutes later, he got the next report as he was sitting in his home office, going through some emails.

"Queens?" he said aloud as he read the text message. "What the hell is she doing in Queens?"

He promised himself he would give her a few days to cool off, but he didn't think he could last any longer. What had transpired two days ago at the precinct haunted him, and each time he closed his eyes, all he could see was her face. Guilt and his angry inner wolf made him want to break his promise.

Grabbing his coat, he headed out to the hallway and then ran into Reyes, who was making his usual rounds around the townhouse.

He glanced at the coat in his hands. "Are we going somewhere, sir?"

"Yes," he answered. "Queens."

"I'll get the car."

And so soon, they were on their way. Reyes got in touch with his contact to get the exact location where Sofia went. Traffic was light, and eventually they reached their destination, the car stopping in front of a restaurant on Ditmars Boulevard in Astoria. The blue awning that wrapped around the corner said "Giorgios's Taverna."

"Is this the place?"

"That's what he said," Reyes answered.

What was she doing here? He supposed she could be having dinner, but there were lots of restaurants in Manhattan. *She could be on a date*, a dark voice in his head said.

"Was she alone?"

"As far as he could tell."

Maybe she met up with her date here. A first date, maybe? That's one reason why she would want to go somewhere far from her house. Maybe she didn't know this guy. Perhaps they met on some hookup app. A growl ripped from his throat, and he didn't realize how loud it was until Reyes's head snapped back toward him.

"Sir?" His expression was cautious.

"Wait here," he told Reyes as he exited the car. On the outside wall was a painted mural depicting white stone buildings topped with blue domes on a hillside overlooking the sea. He walked around to the side where the entrance was covered by an enclosed makeshift patio. There was a line of people outside, huddled under the heat lamps. Sofia wasn't out there, and he ignored their annoyed looks when he headed inside.

The interior was surprisingly spacious with white walls

and wooden beams. One wall featured a similar mural, while the rest had various photos and newspapers clipping. The one right by the entrance featured a young man in a chef's hat next to a very famous American actress. He recalled some story about her having an affair with a Greek billionaire and living on his yacht before the paparazzi discovered them. It was a huge scandal because the billionaire divorced his wife to marry her.

"Can I help you?"

He turned his head and saw an old man carrying a large tray filled with dirty dishes. "I'm looking for someone."

"We're very busy right now," he said impatiently. "Do you have a reservation?"

Glancing around, he saw that all the tables were full, and two waitresses were running around, filling glasses as the diners looked around annoyingly. If he hadn't worked in his mother's family's restaurant, Muccino's, for three summers straight, he wouldn't have recognized how frantic and tense the atmosphere was inside. In a dining room this size on a Saturday night, there should be at least four wait staff serving, and they only had two. They were obviously having a bad night. "I don't want to take up your time. I just—"

He stopped short when he saw a flash of dark hair and cat-like graceful movements from the corner of his eye. When he realized who it was, he mentally slapped himself on the forehead for not recognizing her immediately.

Sofia looked different tonight, with her mahogany hair pulled up into a sleek high ponytail, plus she was wearing more makeup. Instead of her usual dark suit jacket and trousers, she was wearing a crisp white shirt and a black skirt that showed off her slim calves. Truly, the outfit shouldn't have affected him, but seeing her in something so different arrested him. She was carrying a tray laden with food and was placing plates on a table with four diners. What the hell was she doing working here? Surely she made enough money as a detective?

"Hey!" The old man slammed the tray on the hostess's station, the dishes inside clattering loudly. "If you don't have a reservation, then you can wait outside or find somewhere else to go."

"I'm sorry, I just need to talk to Sofia."

A bushy white brow raised. "Sofia? She's busy. We. Are. All. Busy." He emphasized his words by slamming the tray up and down.

He felt a familiar presence behind him and turned his head.

"*Pappoús*? What's going on—you!" Sofia hissed when their eyes met. "What the hell are you doing here?"

"Is this your friend, Sofia? He says he wants to talk to you."

"*Friend?*" She glared at Lucas. "Not at all, *Pappoús*."

"Then what is he doing here?"

"Leaving," she declared.

"Sofia, please," he began.

"It's one thing for you to gloat when I'm at the precinct, but I won't allow it here." Anger blazed in her eyes, and fucking hell, she looked even more beautiful. Like an avenging Goddess coming down from heaven.

"I'm not here to gloat."

"Then why are you here?" she shot back.

"I'm here to apologize."

That seemed to shock her into silence.

"Sofia, I—"

"Papa! Sofia!" another voice called frantically. "What's going on out there?" A man's head was peeking through the small window from the kitchen where food was passed to the waitstaff. "Stop dawdling, the food's getting cold, and the dishes are piling up!"

"Sorry, Dad!" Sofia called back, then turned back to Lucas. "Leave. Just leave and never come here again! I don't want your apologies."

"But—"

The man who was obviously Sofia's grandfather turned to him with a stern look. "Young man, unless you're planning to help in the kitchen, I demand you leave right now."

"Fine." He wrestled the tray from him. "Which way?"

The older man looked confused. "Which way to where?"

Lucas hauled the tray up. "To the kitchen."

"What?" Sofia exclaimed. "What the fuck—get out of here!"

"Papa! Sofia!" the man in the kitchen bellowed. "Come on now!"

"Fine," the old man said. "Come with me."

"*Pappoús!*"

But Sofia's cries of indignation were ignored as he followed the old man to the kitchen area. The old man pushed the swinging door to let him inside. As soon as he was in, he glanced around, trying to assess the situation. Sofia's father was by the stove, watching over the pots and pans on the industrial-sized burners. There was only one other person there, a short, middle-aged Hispanic man crouched over the counter as he chopped onions with rapid speed without missing a beat.

"This is your crew?" he asked, surprised. "It's Saturday night. And you're fully booked."

"Tell me about it." The old man handed him an apron. "One server, a line cook, and my busboy–dishwasher all call out sick! Some bug going around. Then, it's like the whole neighborhood decided they were fed up with cooking at home and decided to eat out tonight! Madness, I tell you."

"Who is this man?" Sofia's father pointed a wooden spoon at Lucas like it was a sword.

The old man scratched his head. "Eh, who are you again?"

"Lucas. Lucas Anderson."

"Giorgios Selinofoto," he introduced. "And that's my son, George. George, this is Lucas. Sofia's, uh—he came here to see Sofia."

George Selinofoto's piercing gaze bore straight into him. "Then why are you in my kitchen?"

"He wanted to help."

Slate gray eyes looked him up and down. They were the only feature on his face that marked him as Sofia's dad. "All right then. *Help.*" He turned back to the stove.

"Load those," Giorgios pointed his chin at the tray of dirty dishes, "into the dishwasher. I'll be out front, helping Nicki and Sofia."

"Yes, sir."

Lucas walked over to the large commercial dishwasher in the back. Placing the tray down on the sink, he began to systematically scrape the food from the dishes and load them into the dishwasher. By the time he was done, Giorgios had already placed a second tray by his feet. He made quick work of that as well, then started the machine.

"What else can I do?" he asked George.

"What do you know how to do?" the other man challenged.

Lucas looked around. "I can help with the prep."

"Ernesto," he called to the Hispanic man who was now slicing bell peppers. "Tell the boy what needs to be prepped then get on the grill."

Lucas felt the corner of his lips tug up. He hadn't been a boy in ages, but he wasn't about to argue with a man in his own kitchen. He'd learned that lesson the hard way from Uncle Dante.

Using a mixture of pantomime and broken English, Ernesto told him which of the ingredients needed to be chopped and how.

"*Gracias*," he said. "*Yo me encargaré de ello.*"

"*Hablas Español?*" The man looked bewildered.

He chuckled. "*Un poco.*" He'd only learned enough Spanish to work with the staff at Muccino's. And most of them probably not words he would say in polite company. Grabbing the chef's knife, he turned his attention to the tomatoes, thinking about the last time he was in a kitchen like this.

When he and Adrianna were young, his parents insisted they both learn everything about the family business—both Fenrir Corp. and his mother's family's successful chain of fine dining Italian restaurants—by working from the bottom. And so the summer they were sixteen, they both worked in the Fenrir Corp. mailroom and the Muccino kitchens on alternating days. Lucas had to admit, he much preferred the hot kitchen to the cool, climate-controlled environment of the mailroom. The heat and the frantic energy seemed exciting to him and he realized why his uncle Dante and now his cousin Gio loved it in there.

As the night progressed, he did almost every single job in the kitchen, except the cooking itself. George took a quick break, at which point his father took over. Giorgios must have been in his seventies, but he still moved with the speed of a man half his age. When George came back, he handed a plate to Lucas, then told him to take a break. He gobbled down the grilled squid and potatoes, not because he was in a hurry, but because it was delicious. The squid was cooked perfectly, not rubbery at all, and the potatoes were crisp on the outside and soft on the inside.

Giorgios came up to Lucas to put in another load of dirty dishes. "You don't even look tired."

He grinned. "I work out." Not that he could tell the old man that he was a Lycan, and therefore he had a lot more stamina and strength than normal humans. A couple of hours in the kitchen would hardly take the wind out of him.

The old man patted him on the shoulder. "We're almost done."

An hour later, sometime after midnight, Lucas was dragging the mop from the broom closet when Ernesto grabbed it from him.

"No," he said. "I take care."

He smiled. "Thank you. *Gracias.*"

"You go to boss." He pointed to the dining room, and he walked out of the kitchen. The dining room was empty, the tablecloths and centerpieces taken away and tabletops wiped clean. He saw Sofia and the other waitress standing by the bar counting out tips and headed their way.

"No, no, Nicki," Sofia said, shaking her head. "Take it all. You deserve it."

The younger woman's eyes went wide. "I can't! You worked the shift with me."

"And you're still in school. Besides, I only came because all those people called out sick and Dad and *Pappoús* needed the extra hand." She pushed the bills away. "Go on. Use it for text books or a nice night out after your exams."

"Thanks, cuz!" she cried, gathering the bills and tucking them into her purse. When she looked up, her gaze landed on Lucas. "Is this your friend, Sof? The one *Pappoús* said was helping out in the kitchen?"

Sofia whirled around, her lips tightening as he drew closer.

"Miss me?"

"No," she snapped back. "I barely noticed you were around."

He folded his arms over his chest. "Of course not." *Liar.* He was pretty sure she peeked inside the kitchen throughout the night. Once or twice, he caught her face through the window and knew she was looking at him.

"Hello," he said, turning to the younger woman. "I'm Lucas."

"I'm Nicki. Sofia's my cousin," she explained. "Where did you meet Sofia?"

"I was her suspect in a murder investigation," he offered cheerfully.

Sofia glared at him, but Nicki giggled. "Ha ha, right." She leaned over to her cousin and stage-whispered, "He's cute. Don't scare this one too much, okay?"

"What?" Sofia managed to squeak.

"Nice to meet you, Lucas. I'll see you soon, cuz." Nicki was already waving goodbye and walking out the door.

"Is that what you do? Scare boys away?"

Sofia's hand fisted at her side and she shot daggers at him with her eyes. "What are you doing here?"

"I helped out in the kitchen," he said.

"That's not what I mean!" She threw her hands up. "And what was that all about? How the hell do you know how to do kitchen work?"

"Ah, so you *were* watching me?"

Her face went red, and she opened her mouth but stopped when Giorgios interrupted them. "Sofia! Lucas!" He clapped one hand on his shoulder and the other one wrapped around Sofia's upper arm. "We're done for the day, thank goodness! Come, come, we have wine at our best table."

They didn't have much choice as the old man dragged them over to the middle table on the right side of the dining room, flush against the wall. George was already sitting down, a bottle of wine and four glasses in front of him.

"Thank you," he said to Giorgios.

"No, no, thank *you*." The older man smiled warmly as he took his seat next to his son.

Sofia had already taken the seat against the wall and so Lucas slid in beside her. He flashed her a grin, but she remained stony-faced.

"You really did save our bacon, tonight." George wiped his face with the towel slung over his shoulder. "We were deep in the weeds when you came."

"And he didn't need our help at all!" Giorgios exclaimed. "Look at this one, eh? So comfortable in the kitchen. From your expensive shoes and shirt, I thought you were one of those big shot Wall Street guys. But, no, you've worked in a restaurant before, right? It's very obvious."

"I did, when I was much younger." He nodded gratefully as George pushed a glass of red wine toward him, then took a sip. *Huh.* "This is excellent."

"I know the guy who supplies all the fancy restaurants in Manhattan," the older man winked at him. "He says he gives me the best price while charging those high-end places like Le Cirque and Muccino's twice as much as we pay."

Lucas choked and slapped a hand over his mouth to stop himself from spitting wine all over Giorgios's face. The alcohol burned as it went down the wrong pipe.

"Are you all right?" Giorgios offered him a handkerchief.

"I'm fine. Thanks." He cleared his throat, making a mental note to have a talk with Uncle Dante about his wine supplier. Beside him, Sofia huffed and took a sip of her own wine. This evening made her even more of a puzzle, and he was determined to find out more about her. "So, did you start this restaurant, Mr. Selinofoto?"

"Please, call me Giorgios. Everyone does. And yes, young man, I did. Came here to America when my kids were still toddlers and I had been widowed for two years. The Greek community here is very close, and with a lot of help, I was able to open this restaurant more than thirty years ago."

"Don't be modest, *Pappoús.*" Sofia said. "You wouldn't have stayed in business if the food wasn't so good."

"And if you didn't have a famous client." George cocked his head to the photo by the entrance.

"Her?" *Huh.* Now that he thought of it, that young man in the photo did look a lot like Giorgios. "You cooked for her? On her yacht?"

"On *the* yacht." Giorgios wiggled his eyebrows.

"Papa was half in love with her," George said, but his voice was teasing. "He named our signature dessert after her."

"Bah, half the world was in love with her! I heard a king offered to marry her and make her his queen. But, no, she only had eyes for the billionaire." He chuckled. "Too bad he was married *and* was keeping that opera star as a mistress."

"The things we do for love." As George sipped on his wine, his eyes darted up, toward one of the photos hanging on the wall above them. It was a portrait of a woman dressed in a full formal police uniform, smiling at the camera.

Lucas did a double-take, then looked at Sofia. "That's your mom, right? She looks like you."

"Yes," Giorgios answered for her. "Our dear Nadia."

"She's very beautiful," he commented.

"She was." Sofia took a sip of her wine and then looked ahead, a blank look on her face.

"Oh." He tried to meet her gaze, but she refused to look at him. "I'm sorry." He wanted to hold her hand or do something to comfort her.

"Sofia was just thirteen years old when Nadia passed away," George began, his voice somber. "She worked as a beat cop and died while on duty."

"It was very sad," Giorgios said quietly. "She was like my own daughter. And she was very brave. Sofia looked up to her a lot."

At that moment, Lucas wanted to kick his own ass. It was obvious she loved being a cop and took pride in her work because her mom had been one. He felt like a real bastard, and he would understand if Sofia never forgave him for the part he played in her humiliation.

"So"—George narrowed his eyes at Lucas—"how do you know my daughter again?"

"I was one of her suspects in a case," he said. That seemed to jolt Sofia out of her trance, and she jerked her head to him, the look on her face incredulous. "What? I'm not going to lie to your father and grandfather."

"Is this true, Sofia?" Giorgios eyed Lucas warily.

She took a big gulp of wine. "Former suspect. He's been eliminated from the list." Placing the glass on the table, she stood up. "It's late, and you know how the subway service is at this time of night. I should get going."

"You can stay over, Sofia," George offered. "Your bedroom is always ready for you."

"I know, Papa." She smiled fondly at him. "But I have stuff to do tomorrow, and if I stay tonight, I'll end up staying all day tomorrow and I'll never leave."

"You be careful on the subway," Giorgios said. "You know how dangerous it is at night."

"I'll be fine," she assured him.

"I can take you home," Lucas offered. "My car's waiting outside." As some point when he'd started working in the kitchen, he sent off a quick message to Reyes to tell him to park the car and get his own dinner.

"No. No way," she said in a vehement tone. "I'd rather walk."

"What?" Giorgios exclaimed in a baffled tone. "It's late, and this gallant young man is offering you a ride in his car."

"You'll be home in twenty minutes," her father assured

her. Then he turned to Lucas with a dark glint in his eyes. "Right? You'll take her straight home?"

"I promise." He placed his hand over his heart. "On my grandmother's grave."

"See? And we know he is a good, hardworking boy," Giorgios said. "He'll drive you straight home."

Sofia shot him a murderous look. "Fine," she relented. "Just a ride home."

"Just a ride home," he echoed.

They all said their goodbyes and grabbed their coats. The two older men stayed inside to lock up and do some last-minute checks and urged the two of them to head outside.

Lucas opened the door and gestured for her to go first. The car was already outside on the curb and Reyes stepped out of the driver's side and opened the door.

"I thought you were driving," she said, eyeing Reyes.

"Disappointed? I know you've seen some of my driving skills."

She ignored his comment and went inside the car. He instructed Reyes to drop off Sofia at her home plus one other thing, then stepped into the car. It didn't escape his notice that she had squeezed herself all the way to the other end of the backseat.

"Do you need my address?" she asked, turning to him.

"No."

"Of course not," she said grimly, then crossed her arms over her chest.

Throughout the ride, Sofia seemed determined to look anywhere else—outside, the roof of the car, even the back of Reyes's head—except at him. Which suited Lucas just fine because that meant he could stare at her.

Seated against the window, her ankles crossed and hands on her lap with only the streetlights outside lighting her figure, Sofia looked like a serene goddess. He realized that although he knew more about her now, she still remained a mystery to him. However, he did like that they both had such similar backgrounds: immigrant grandparents who were restaurant owners. He bet she'd probably worked at Giorgios's Taverna since she was a teenager, which showed in her confident and efficient movements around the dining room. Obviously, she was hardworking and competent, and he thought of his own mother. She would probably love Sofia, being so much like herself. Not that Frankie Anderson would even get a chance to meet her, he told himself.

They finally crossed the bridge into Manhattan, and the car headed to the Lower East side, then after winding down through the deserted streets of Midtown, slowed down to a stop in front of a brick building on Fifth Street in the East Village.

"Thanks for the ride." She reached for the handle and pulled. The door didn't open, so she tried it again. After doing it a third time, she turned to him. "There's something wrong with your car door."

"No, there isn't." Aside from giving him Sofia's address earlier, he had also instructed Reyes to turn on the automatic child lock.

It took her only half a second to realize what was going on. "You did this on purpose?" She jiggled the door handle again. "You asshole! Let me out! This is kidnapping." She turned her rage at Reyes. "Open this door now! Or I'll have you arrested." He answered by raising the barrier between the front and back seats which only enraged her more.

"We're here outside your building," he reminded her gently. "And I promise to let you out, after we talk."

She slumped back in her seat, scowling like a petulant child. "Do I have a choice?"

"No."

After a brief silence, she whipped her head toward him. "Fine. Talk."

Again, she was looking at a spot above his shoulder which irritated him because short of forcing her eyeballs to move, he couldn't make her meet his gaze. He sighed. "Sofia, I need to apologize for what happened in your captain's office. It wasn't my intention to humiliate you."

"Oh yeah? If coming into my boss's office with *his* boss, telling him you had an alibi all this time and then making me look like an idiot wasn't your intention, what was?"

He wasn't sure himself. After all this time, he should have come up with a better excuse. "You're right," he admitted. "I wanted to put you in your place. And I'm very sorry for my actions and that they hurt you." Swallowing his pride, he continued. "But I didn't think Aarons would take it so far. I just wanted you to back off and stop digging into my past."

"Did you hurt Kevin Hall?"

The question was meant to put him on the defensive, he knew that. But he would not respond to that, because the answer was too complicated. He supposed they could stay here all night staring at each other, but he decided to break the impasse. "Look, Sofia, I'll answer any other question you have about me—except about Kevin Hall."

She hesitated but then spoke, "Where's your fiancée?"

His—oh right. Damn Zac. "I don't have one. I'm not engaged and I never was."

Her lips pursed together. "Then why did Vrost lie?"

"To protect me and the company." That was mostly true. "I'm about to take over for my father as CEO of a multi-billion-dollar company. He couldn't let it out that I was, uh, partying in a nightclub in such a state. He didn't want any official report on the incident. As you've probably guessed, my family and I are very private. We hate publicity."

She seemed to contemplate his answer. "I guess that makes sense."

Her question made him even more curious. "Now it's my turn." He slid closer to her, and her incredible scent filled his nostrils. She went still but didn't try to move away. A good sign, and so he decided to address the other thing that went unacknowledged between the two of them, before all this business with Thomas Dixon. "Why did you keep coming back to Blood Moon after that night? No, don't deny it—the bartenders knew who you were and that you didn't seem like the typical clientele there." She was *human*, something he seemed to have forgotten tonight.

Surprise flashed on her face, but she didn't say anything, so he continued, "And why did you come with me to the roof deck at Blood Moon?"

She inhaled a sharp breath. "I was curious."

"Curious about what?" Did she suspect anything about the existence of his kind?

"About ... you." Her shoulders tensed, then she turned her face away. "I wanted to see you again. To know if I imag-ined you or not."

The confession struck him down like a hammer to the head. She wanted to see *him*. She came to Blood Moon for *him*. A primal part of him rose up, and all he could think about was her delicious scent, which was now wrapping around him like an embrace.

"Sofia. *Sofia*, look at me." When she didn't, he reached over to tip her chin towards him, and that familiar sizzle of electricity shot up his arm. "I thought I imagined you too."

Slate gray eyes peered up at him. She was finally looking at him. "You did?"

"It was driving me crazy. Your perfume. Your eyes. I thought it was a dream." He'd been half mad the entire time, but the smell of orange blossoms and olives had grounded him. "And when I saw you that next time, I knew I just had to have you."

"Lucas."

His name on her lips was like a siren's call he couldn't resist. He didn't wait for her to react or protest as he snaked a hand around her slim waist and pulled her close, his mouth landing on hers. She shivered when their lips touched but yielded to him without hesitation.

When his tongue swiped across the seam of her mouth, she opened to him. Her taste was even better than her scent, and he craved more of her. To devour her. Possess her. Pulling her onto his lap, he made her straddle him. Her skirt rode up her thighs, and he slid his hands down to her pert ass, pushing her hips down so he could feel the heat of her against his growing erection. When she brushed against his hard-on, he moaned, and she pushed her own tongue into his mouth, sweeping inside and tasting him.

Fucking hell, she was magnificent. Her scent bloomed, filling his senses. He moved his hands up her waist to cup her breasts through her shirt. He normally went for curvy girls, but her tits were more than enough for him. He wanted to know what color her nipples were, though he already knew they would taste delicious. His fingers deftly undid the top buttons of her shirt and slid down under her padded bra. Damn, her nipples were already hard, and he rolled a tight bud between his thumb and forefinger making her gasp and pull back. When he tried to capture her mouth again, she evaded him and scrambled off his lap.

"No," she said, shaking her head when he tried to reach out. "Why?"

"What kind of question was that? You know why."

Her face was scarlet. "We can't."

He took hold of the anger rising in his chest. "What do you mean we can't?"

"I'm a detective," she said. "This is unprofessional. I shouldn't have ... gone back to Blood Moon."

"I'm not a suspect anymore. And we're two consenting adults." She more than consented; he could still smell her arousal. "We can do what we want."

"We just can't, okay?" she bit out.

"Give me one good reason why not?" He raised his voice, but couldn't help it. Even his wolf was mad, and he could feel it urging him on to make her theirs. It should have surprised him, since his wolf never cared about his other women before, but he was too frustrated, too angry to care.

"I ..." She bit her lip and turned away. "We just shouldn't."

Then it dawned on him, the real reason why she pulled away. She still thought he was capable of cold-blooded murder. Maybe not Thomas Dixon, but her question earlier about Kevin Hall pretty much confirmed it. He was a fool for acting on his attraction to her. She was human, he reminded himself. She would never understand.

"Lucas—"

This time, his name from her mouth was like a dagger slicing through him. He leaned forward and rapped his hand on the barrier, signaling to Reyes to disengage the locks.

"It's unlocked." He didn't look at her, only hearing her sharp intake of a breath before the door opened. When it slammed shut, he remained still. When the scent of orange blossoms and olives began to fade, he gave a second rap on the barrier.

"Sir?" Reyes asked as the barrier began to lower.

"Home." His throat felt tight as he tried to control the rage of his wolf. His fingers gripped the seats, and though he heard the sound of claws ripping into the leather, he ignored it.

As they drove back to his townhouse, he vowed to forget about Sofia Selinofoto. He'd acted on impulse tonight, and no matter how sweet her taste or soft her body, he wasn't going to go near her. But he only hoped she wouldn't cross him again, because if she insisted on digging up the past, he wouldn't be able to control his actions or his wolf next time.

CHAPTER ELEVEN

No matter what Sofia did, she couldn't keep her mind off what had transpired Saturday night. When she trudged up to her apartment, it felt like she was in a dream—or nightmare. The full force of what happened didn't hit her until she was inside her apartment. Her lips burned at the memory of his mouth on hers.

What had possessed her to do that? To confess to him what had been in the back of her mind all this time? Lucas acted so differently that night, and she had to begrudgingly admit that a small part of her admired him for literally getting his hands dirty to help out her dad and grandfather at the restaurant. He didn't complain or think any job was beneath him—a far cry from the rich boy she thought he was.

She didn't want to ride home with him, but at the same time, she *did*. To be alone with him, in that small space, breathing in his aftershave that reminded her of summers spent at the shore. And God, his kisses and his hands—they were like a drug. Strong enough to make her forget reality—

that even though he wasn't a suspect in Dixon's murder, there was still the question of what happened to Kevin Hall.

Sure, it would have been easy to just forget it. But she couldn't. Her mother's words came back to her. A year before her tragic death, she told her mother that she wanted to be a cop like her. Sergeant Nadia Selinofoto had beamed at her and told her to remember one thing: *Always do what's right. Even if the whole world is against you.*

And she was doing the right thing. That's why she helped arrest Derek, and that's why she wasn't going to get involved with Lucas.

By the time Monday rolled around, she was exhausted and miserable from lack of sleep. She was so distracted, she didn't even notice her phone ringing and completely missed the call. When she picked up her cell, she glanced at the number and frowned, then dialed it. "Hello? I missed a call from this number. This is Detective Sofia Selinofoto."

"Detective, this is Morales from the Tech Division," the voice on the other line replied.

"What can I do for you?"

"I have that contact you were looking for. A Miss Caroline Devereaux."

It took her a second before she recognized the name. The girl Kevin Hall and Lucas fought over. "You did?"

"Yep. It took a while because she moved to France when she was eighteen. Then she got married a few years ago and changed her name, but I have her number and address for you in Nice."

"Can you email it to me?" She rattled off her email address, then thanked Morales for his help.

Caroline Devereaux. It felt like it had been ages since she started this case, but really it had only been over a week. With everything that was happening, she had even forgotten to check the other information she dug up on Devereaux.

Swiveling her chair around, she faced her computer screen and clicked her mouse cursor on the bookmark she saved. She had found an old social media profile for Caroline, but the last update was years ago.

The profile photo showed a gorgeous, blonde, and green-eyed teenager. Her smile was wide and her face shone with the vibrance of youth. Caroline Devereaux was stunning. It was no wonder two boys fought over her.

Lucas fought Kevin Hall over her.

A twinge of jealousy made her stomach clench. That was a long time ago. Did Lucas still hold any feelings for her?

Not liking the direction of her thoughts, she clicked through the rest of her photos. It was the usual stuff a teenage girl might post—selfies with her friends, studying in the library, vacations with her family. After a few clicks, she stumbled upon a selfie of her and a boy about her age, their faces pressed together, and a cartoon heart drawn around them. "KH + CD 4EVER" proclaimed the caption. Kevin Hall. She clicked again. More photos. Them at the school cafeteria. At a diner sharing a milkshake. Wearing formal clothes at prom.

Something she didn't find, however, was Lucas Anderson. In fact, he didn't have any social media profiles. He was maybe only a few years older than her, so she knew he wasn't some old fuddy-duddy who didn't like technology; in fact, Sofia had a profile herself, though she didn't really post anything. It was strange, really. He didn't have a social media presence and there weren't a lot of articles about him or his family. *He did say they were private.* And she thought back to the kidnapping—if she or any of her future kids had been kidnapped, she'd be afraid of what info was out there on the Internet.

Aside from having no recent postings, there was nothing odd about Caroline Devereaux's profile. There really was nothing odd about it, except that there had been nothing posted in years. The last post was a picture of a cabin surrounded by pine trees and the caption, "Grad weekend! Woohoo!"

She had been so engrossed in her research that she almost forgot the contact details Morales was sending over. Sure enough, her married name, address, and phone number were in her inbox. Checking the time, she guessed it was evening in France, so maybe she was home. Her hand hovered over her landline, hesitating for a moment, then proceeded to dial the number.

"*Bonsoir,*" came the feminine voice.

"*Bonsoir.* Er." None of her high school French was coming back to her. *Damn.* "Uh, hello. Speak English?"

"Yes, I speak English." The accent was pure American. "Can I help you?"

"My name is Detective Sofia Selinofoto from the New York Police Department. May I speak with Mrs. Caroline Laurent, formerly Devereaux?"

There was a long pause before the voice spoke again. "This is she."

She let go of the breath she was holding. "I'm sorry to bother you, Mrs. Laurent, but I need to speak to you."

"About what?"

"Lucas Anderson."

Another long pause. She could practically feel the hesitation through the receiver. "Mrs. Laurent?"

"Look, I know what you're going to ask me about. And I can't talk about what happened that night."

"Can't or won't?"

"I'm not supposed to."

Her firm answer made her think that she was either protecting Lucas or something stopped her from talking about that night. Like an NDA. "Will you talk about Kevin Hall?"

There was a sharp intake of breath. "Did Lucas do something? Is he under arrest?"

"He's part of my investigation." Technically, still true. "If you can't talk about Lucas Anderson, can you at least talk about Kevin Hall?"

"If you think Lucas Anderson did something bad ... you're wrong!" Her tone was vehemently defensive. "He would never—"

"Kevin was your boyfriend, right? Did Lucas try to steal you away from him?"

"What?" came the incredulous cry. "No! Of course not. Lucas was sweet and I knew he had a big crush on me for years, but he would never do such a thing."

"Then why did they fight that night?" She ignored the knot in her stomach as she continued. "I think his jealousy reached a breaking point and he snapped."

"Ha!" Caroline bit out. "Lucas isn't like that. I've known him since we were kids."

Her detective's instinct flared and she knew this was the breaking point. Years of experience interrogating all kinds of criminals and witnesses taught her when to push and when to pull back. Now was the time to drive Caroline over the edge. "Then why did he kill Kevin Hall?"

"He was protecting me!" Caroline exclaimed. "And my baby! I was pregnant, and I told Kevin it was his, and you know what he did? He *laughed*." There was righteous anger in her voice as she went on. "We'd been together a year. I ... I'd never been with anyone, and the night of homecoming we had sex. Then I found out I was pregnant ... I was so happy! I loved Kevin. And then during the graduation party, I thought it would be romantic to get him alone in the woods and tell him. He thought it was a joke, then when he realized I wasn't kidding, he became angry. Real Angry."

Sofia swallowed the lump in her throat that began to build when Caroline started talking. She was just glad she wasn't interviewing her face to face. Domestic abuse cases were one of her least favorite types of crimes to investigate. She would rather work for a dead victim than face a living one. Still, there was no going back now. "And then what happened?"

"He slapped me so hard I fell. Then he denied it was his. Accused me of being a slut. He knew about Lucas's crush on me and he said that we ... that the baby was Lucas's. His buddy Jeffrey had been there the entire time, just watching. Kevin made Jeffrey call Lucas so he could confront him. In the meantime, he was kicking me while I was still down." Her voice trembled, and Sofia could tell she was trying hard not to cry. "Lucas came right away. Kevin turned his anger at him and started screaming at Lucas. Then Lucas saw me and—" She let out a gasp. "Goddamn you! How did you—?"

"What happened, Caroline?" she pressed on.

"You sneaky bitch. I've already said too much."

"Caroline, if you don't tell me what happened next, I'm going to have to go after Lucas."

"*Fuck you.* If it wasn't for him, I might have lost my baby that night, and I would never have my sweet Amelie now." She paused. "And I swear to you on her life, Lucas Anderson is not a cold-blooded killer."

Before she could ask more, the click from the other end of the line told her that Caroline had hung up on her. She thought about calling her back, but she knew it would be fruitless. For one thing, the other woman could just ignore the phone, and short of flying to France, she didn't know how to make Caroline reveal to her what really happened that night. And another? A seed of doubt planted itself in her brain. It was small; minuscule, really, but enough to make her rethink the whole thing.

If it was truly a case of defending Caroline or himself, why didn't Lucas just let the authorities take over? If the cops had been called, they would have seen Caroline, match the evidence to Kevin Hall and arrested him. Even a cop fresh out of the academy would have arrived at the same conclusion. There might have been other witnesses too, some who would collaborate Caroline's story.

A good lawyer could plead down to manslaughter, and a great one would have been able to ensure Lucas Anderson never saw the inside of a jail cell. Why go through all this trouble to cover up the whole affair and settle the civil suit out of court? To spare Caroline the humiliation? To preserve his family name? It seemed a little extreme.

It didn't matter anyway. Her instincts were telling her to believe Caroline. Caroline was telling the truth. And if she had been in his situation and saw a man beating up a helpless, pregnant woman, she would have done what it took to protect her.

She knew all that she needed to know: Lucas was not a murderer; he was a protector. Causing someone's death was not something easy to deal with, and she understood most of all.

Always do what's right.

And sometimes what was right wasn't always the same as what was lawful.

———

Sometime that afternoon, Captain Bushnell called her in to talk. She finished her phone call and entered the captain's office, then sat on the chair opposite him.

He was at his desk, scribbling down on a notepad. "Anderson's alibi checks out," he said without looking up. "We have a written statement from his security detail from that night, plus GPS logs of their whereabouts."

So that meant he was definitely cleared of the Dixon murder. It was back to square one on his case. "Was there anything else, sir?"

"Yes." He put the pen down and looked up at her, the clear blue pools of his eyes boring into her. "The stuff about Fenrir and Anderson ... you need to drop it."

"Sir?" Her hands balled into fists.

"Aside from all these coincidences, do you have anything definitive? Any proof of criminal activity? From Fenrir or Anderson?"

Her heart sank. Of course not. All the other cases she found were only mildly related to Lucas Anderson. It was what lead her to the kidnapping case, but there was no definitive proof of wrongdoing. Her gaze lowered to her lap. "No, sir."

"Then it's best you focus your time and energy on your other active cases."

"Sir?" Her head snapped back up. "What about Dixon? He's still a victim."

"I know that, Detective, and I'm not saying to drop his case. But obviously, you're going to have to look at other angles." He sighed. "Maybe this business with Bianchi has you so tied up in knots that you're not seeing things clearly."

Her hands clenched in her lap. Did he think she was incompetent?

"It's not that I don't think you can't do your job," he said, as if reading her mind. "I can see it in your face. I've never doubted you, Selinofoto. Not even when Aarons was here. I'm just saying that maybe you need a break. Why don't you take tomorrow off? Get refreshed and have a clear head for when you start again."

"Sir, my caseload is all backed up and—"

"Should I make it an order?" When she sank back into the chair, he continued. "It's just twenty-four hours. You can do whatever you want, just don't think about work or Bianchi."

Bushnell obviously wasn't going to budge on this. "Fine. I mean, yes, sir. Is that all?"

He gave her a curt nod, and she stood up, then went straight out the door. Marching back to her desk, she sat down, staring at the blank screen of her computer.

It wasn't like she had never been wrong. When she was fresh out of the academy, she didn't yet trust her instincts.

But over the years, she had honed them, and she knew when to trust her gut. She knew something wasn't right. She'd thought the worst of Lucas, that he had a taste of violence when he was a teen and then he became a cold-blooded killer. But clearly, she had added one and one and came up with three.

She rubbed the bridge of her nose with her fingers. How could she have been so wrong? Maybe Bushnell was right. The past couple of months was wearing her down, and between what happened with Derek and now the Bianchi trial coming up.

Or maybe Lucas Anderson was making her instincts go haywire. Things hadn't been the same since the first time she walked into Blood Moon. Since she first set her eyes on him.

And then last night happened. A strange feeling came over her, and now that she knew Caroline Devereux's side of the story, she realized what it was: guilt.

Something inside her yearned for him, and she told herself it wasn't that she wanted him. Well, she had wanted him last night, but that was a moment of weakness on her part. But she needed to see him, and this time, she had to do the apologizing. She cringed, thinking of how he was the one who came to her to say sorry the other night. Not only that, he had worked so hard in the kitchen and helped out her family without expecting anything in return.

She gathered her things, determined to see him. It was the least she could do. She would explain what happened and then while they wouldn't part as friends, she could at least clear her conscience. Yes, that was it. That was the only reason she found herself driving to the Fenrir Corp. building.

She knew he would still be there, working late. She parked her car on the curb and waited.

After what seemed like forever, she saw the glass doors open and a familiar figure walk out. Lucas looked incredibly handsome in a dark formal suit. However, her heart sank when she realized he wasn't alone. A tall, blonde woman dressed in a floor-length dress was beside him, clinging to his arm. She looked up at him, smiling as he bent down to whisper something in her ear.

Her fingers gripped the wheel, her jaw tightening. Of course Lucas had a date. Why wouldn't he? She couldn't help that tiny pinprick of jealousy in her chest. Okay, not so tiny, really, but she had no right to feel it. Maybe she could just call him to apologize. Or send an email in the morning. After all, it was obvious, despite the fact that it had been less than forty-eight hours since she was in his arms, he had already moved on.

The tightness in her chest grew as she watched them step inside his town car. She shifted the gear fully intending to head home, but she was on the same side of the street as Lucas's vehicle, so she had no choice but to maneuver the car behind them. Of course, he was also heading downtown, so she trailed them for a few blocks. When it came time for her to turn east, the town car signaled west. She bit her lip and followed.

She was a damned idiot. She wasn't a police detective tailing someone now, but rather, just a woman on a fool's errand. Would she approach him with his beautiful date? Or wait until she left? Would she even leave or would they go back to his or her place? The thought made her stomach clench.

The town car headed into the trendy SoHo district, then stopped outside a restaurant. *I really must be a masochist*, she told herself as she parked across the street. Lucas stepped out followed by his date, and they headed inside. *Petite Louve* announced the elegantly-scrawled sign over the door. The restaurant sure was busy for Monday night. Several more cars arrived with people dressed to the nines. The last car that she observed was a gray Dodge Charger, and a woman wearing a red gown alighted by herself.

Sinking deep into her seat, she crossed her arms and let out a huff. She wanted to leave, but somehow, her guilt was making her stay. But then, she didn't know what she was supposed to do. Crash the party? Force him to talk to her?

She slipped out of the car into the cold night, hoping that maybe some fresh air would help her brain think clearer. She stepped onto the sidewalk and began to pace. *Go home, get to bed, and forget about Lucas Anderson.* That's what she should do, but her traitorous brain kept flashing images of Lucas and his date tangled up in the sheets.

A frustrated sound gurgled from her throat, and heat rose in her cheeks. She should—

The hairs on the back of her neck prickled. Someone was watching her.

Slowly, she pivoted. *What. The. Hell.*

A man was leaning against the hood of her car, arms folded casually over his chest, his brilliant blue eyes pinning her to the spot. A gasp escaped her mouth. At first, she thought he was an old man, with his silvery white hair, but when she looked at his smooth, wrinkle-free face, it was obvious he was only a few years older than her. Also, he was *huge*. Not just tall, but broad too. It was freezing out, but he was only wearing a white T-shirt. Tattoos snaked up his wrists and probably across his chest. How could she have missed hearing such a gigantic man approach her?

"What are you doing here?"

"I could ask you the same." His voice was low and held a quiet menace. "Are you following the Andersons?"

"No."

"Don't lie to me." There was a slight hint of an accent, one she couldn't place.

"Are you one of the security guards from Fenrir?"

"I've been tasked to protect Ms. Anderson."

"Ms. Anderson?"

"The sister of the man you follow."

"I'm not following him," she denied, but his raised brow told her he didn't believe her.

"Are you on official business, Detective?"

"How the hell did you know—" She closed her mouth. If he was Fenrir Security, of course he knew about her. They probably had her photo up in their office like a wanted poster. There was no use lying to him. Besides, his eyes, the color of which reminded her of the domed rooftops of Santorini, drilled into her with a laser-like focus. "I just need to do something. I just don't know what." God, she sounded pathetic. She probably looked pathetic too, chasing after a man across Manhattan. A man on a date with another woman.

His stony expression changed. "You need him."

"N-no!" she denied again. "I just ... I should ..." God, why was this so hard? And also, this man was a complete stranger to her, and she shouldn't be discussing her business—work or otherwise—with him. "I'll leave, okay? You can tell your bosses you got rid of me. Maybe they'll give you a raise." *And you can afford a freakin' coat.*

"Do not."

Huh?

"Detective, we have this saying where I'm from. That sometimes, you must take your heart in your teeth."

"Excuse me?"

"It means you must be brave. Dare to do something." He looked across the street, toward the restaurant.

How could this stranger read her like a book? Searching his face, she wondered if that look on his face was the same as hers—it was a look of longing. And that's what he had recognized in her.

A kind of clarity washed over her. Maybe she should confront Lucas. As soon as possible. Her heart dropped like a rock to her stomach. She needed Lucas, but would he talk to her? Well, there was only one way to find out.

"Thank you," she murmured. *I hope you can be brave too,* she added silently, then slipped back into her car. It would be humbling, but she was going to have to put on her big girl panties. And dare to do something.

CHAPTER TWELVE

"Everything all right, Lucas?"

His companion stared up at him, her delicate brows drawn together. "Yes, Barbara, I'm fine."

She smiled and ran her hand up his arm. "Then why do you seem like you're a million miles away?" Her flowery scent curled around him like talons. "You haven't even commented on how I look. This dress is the latest Armani from Milan, plus I just had my hair done." She shook her head, her golden curls shimmering.

"You look beautiful, Barbara." He forced himself to let his gaze linger longer. "As always."

"Thank you for inviting me here," she said, her eyes sparkling. "And here I thought you would never call me. I'm so happy to be meeting your parents."

"You've met them before at clan functions," he said.

"Yes, but not as your *date*." She glanced around. "Especially at such an intimate *family* gathering with important guests."

Her emphasis on the words date and family made him

wince inwardly, but he pasted a smile on his face. "You're welcome."

He turned his attention back to his father, who was seated at the head of the table as he told a funny story about one of his trips abroad. His mother, looking beautiful as ever, sat on his right, her eyes practically shining with adoration. This dinner party in the private dining room at *Petite Louve* was for their guest of honor, seated on his father's left, Count Alesso di Cavour, the Alpha of Rome. His sisters were there, except for Isabelle who canceled without telling anyone— much to his parents' dismay. As owner of the restaurant, his Aunt Holly was also in attendance.

His mother had sprung this dinner on him, and insisted he bring a date. And so he scrambled to find someone last minute. He had met Barbara Evans several times in the past, and though she was from the Los Angeles Lycan clan, she lived in New York after being transferred here for her job a few years ago. They'd met at the Fenrir Ball last spring and had been trying to get together for dinner, but their schedules didn't match. It was a stroke of luck that she happened to be free this evening.

Barbara was everything he could want in a woman—tall, beautiful, curvy, and most of all, Lycan. And she was obviously interested in him. He bet if he invited himself back to her place, she wouldn't object.

His wolf, however, did object. It scraped its claws at him, angry at him and hating Barbara's scent. He knew what it wanted, but he wasn't going to give in. Not to his wolf, not to his own desires.

Alesso must have said something really funny because everyone at the table laughed. Everyone except his sister. She seemed to have found her entree intriguing, her head bent down as she picked at her plate. No one else could tell, but he knew: she was miserable. Sure, her face was perfectly serene, and she nodded at the handsome Count next to her when he engaged her in conversation. But it was obvious she was just as happy to be here as he was.

The night seemed to go on forever, and all he wanted to do was go home. His cousin Dominic, the current head chef of *Petite Louve*, came to serve them dessert which meant that the meal was almost over. Finally, they left to let the staff clear the plates, and they all went outside to await their vehicles.

Lucas watched as Adrianna bid goodbye to the Count, her shoulders sagging in relief when he was gone.

"Lucas, darling," Barbara cooed. "Would you mind if I went back in? I need to take a quick trip to the ladies' room."

"Go ahead."

"Don't leave without me!" she jested before she stepped back inside. Her hips swayed with a practiced sensuousness that would have brought almost any man to his knees. Almost.

"She seems nice," Adrianna said, interrupting his thoughts. "Exactly your type."

His sister's words cut into him. "And what's that supposed to mean?"

The loud hum of an engine announced the arrival of another vehicle. When he saw Darius Corvinus stepping out from the driver's seat, he raised a brow at Adrianna. Not that she noticed him, because her eyes were glued to her bodyguard. Now that was interesting, because Darius was certainly *not* Adrianna's type.

He had heard about what happened to Muccino's in D.C., and more important, that Darius had been there to save her. So, it was that, and curiosity, that made him approach the other man as he exited the driver's seat.

"Darius."

"Yes?" He turned to meet his gaze.

"I heard you saved my sister's life." He offered his hand. "Thank you. If you ever need anything, just ask."

"It was my duty." Darius did take his hand, and much to his surprise, bent his head forward. "Your detective followed you here," he said in a low voice.

His shoulders tensed, not really knowing what to do with that information, and nodded a thanks to Darius before turning back to Adrianna.

"I'm glad I came, if only to see you," she said.

"I'm glad too." He glanced back at the restaurant, then turned to her. "Are you all right, Adrianna?" He'd been wanting to talk to her alone for the entire evening. Call it twin intuition, but he knew something was bothering her. Was it Darius?

She hesitated. "I'm good. You should go in and check on Barbara."

He hated that she was keeping something from him, but it wasn't like he was any better. "I suppose I should," he said with a long sigh. "Stay safe."

"You too." Lucas watched the car speed off, contemplating Darius's words. So, Sofia had been here? Did she still think he was guilty of something? Of course, she wouldn't stop digging. He would have admired her determination, but right now, it was infuriating. He wasn't worried about his own reputation at this point—there was no way Kevin's death could be definitely traced back to him. Everyone involved had been given the forgetting potion, and even official records and autopsies were doctored. But what if she were to uncover their bigger secret?

"There you go again." Barbara appeared by his side. "You look like you've tied yourself up in knots." She squeezed his bicep. "I can ... take care of those knots for you, if you like. A lot of people say I've got magic fingers."

His wolf growled and he pulled it back. "Let's go." He led her to the waiting car, where Reyes was already holding the door opened. He ushered Barbara in and then slid in beside her. Without a prompt, she rattled off her address to the driver and they were soon off to the Upper East Side.

Yes, by all accounts, Barbara was everything he could want in a woman. He *should* want her. But unfortunately, he didn't. Not when all he could think about was orange blossoms and olives and slate gray eyes. Despite everything, and the fact that she could uncover his darkest secrets, God help him, he wanted Sofia Selinofoto.

"Lucas?" Barbara's seductive voice broke into his thoughts. "Are you coming?"

He didn't even realize they'd come to a stop in front of Barbara's posh building. Reyes had already opened the door for them, and Barbara had a hand on his thigh. "Good night, Barbara." He removed her hand.

The shock on her face registered for only a moment before it was replaced by a cool mask. "Yes, I can feel my migraine coming on. You have a good night too, Lucas." She left without even looking back at him, head held high as she entered the building.

Reyes gave him a curious look. "Home, sir?"

"Yes." He leaned back in the seat and waited for the car to start moving. Maybe he should have accepted Barbara's invitation. He was sure she could make him forget his name with those magic fingers. But no, it wouldn't be fair. Besides, his wolf wouldn't have given him any peace. It seemed to hate Barbara with a passion, why, he didn't know. It didn't react this viscerally to her before, or any woman. Anyone except Sofia.

When the car slowed to a stop in front of his brownstone, he let himself out and walked up the stoop steps to his door. He was fishing his keys from his pocket when he felt his senses go on alert. Her scent called to him before she did.

"Lucas."

He closed his eyes, wondering if he was hearing things. The last time he heard his name coming from her was Saturday night. "What do you want?" he asked without turning around. Slowly, he began building his defenses. His walls going up so high that nothing would be able to tear them down.

"I wanted to apologize."

And just like that, those walls came crashing down. Slowly, he turned around. Big mistake.

Sofia looked so stunning in the moonlight, her hair tumbling down her shoulders, eyes so big and luminous as she looked up at him from the bottom of his stoop steps. "How long have you been waiting here?"

"A while." When she let out an involuntary shiver, he realized that her cheeks were red and her lips were pale. She tugged her coat tighter around her.

"Fucking hell, Sofia." He hopped down, then tugged at her hand, dragging her up the steps. Opening his door, he pushed her inside. "It's freezing out. You could have gotten sick." She looked vulnerable right now. She really could have caught a cold or pneumonia, which was a reminder of her humanness. But right now, he couldn't really care less. He took her hands into his. Just as he thought, they were like ice. Using his own palms, he rubbed them for warmth. "And what do you mean you came here to apologize?"

She hesitated. "I just ... I was wrong. You have the right to your privacy, and I'm sorry."

"You were doing your job." Her hands seemed sufficiently warm now, but he didn't release them.

"I know I can be like a rabid dog when I find something and ..."

"What made you change your mind?"

She cast her eyes downward. "Just ... I did my job. I thought I connected the dots, but it turns out there was nothing to connect." Straightening her shoulders, she faced him. "I want to offer you my apologies. From me and on the behalf of the precinct. If you want to file a harassment suit, then I wouldn't blame you."

"Harassment suit?" Shock coursed through him. Did he fall asleep and was now waking up in a bizarre alternate universe?

"Yes." She swallowed. "But I hope you won't. Because although we can't be friends—"

"No, we can't."

She faltered. "We can't be friends. But I hope we can part without any bad feelings."

"You're right." The disappointment on her face was obvious. When she tried to pull her hands away, he held them firmly. "We can't be friends. And we're *definitely* not parting."

He took a step forward, and he had to admit he enjoyed the way her expression turned to surprise before he kissed her.

She didn't respond at first, and her body went stiff. He pushed her back against the door and trapped her with his body. When she sighed against him, he deepened the kiss, sweeping his tongue into her mouth to taste her. She was so sweet, and so utterly *Sofia*.

Arms wound around his neck, and he moved his hands down to the front of her coat, his fingers deftly opening the buttons and shucking the damn thing off her and onto the floor. He bent down to cup the back of her thighs to lift her up into his arms.

She let out a surprised gasp, then a moan as he pressed his lips to her neck before wrapping her legs around his waist. He carried her into the living room, then sank down onto the sofa, letting her settle on his lap.

He needed her bad, needed to feel her bare skin, but the damned blouse she was wearing was in the way. So, he unbuttoned the front, nearly tearing them off. His patience was rewarded by the sight of her beautiful breasts encased in black lace and silk.

"Lucas," she rasped when his mouth sucked on the spot where shoulder met her neck. His lips moved down, blazing a path lower, over the top of one breast and down to the center were her nipple strained against fabric. He latched onto the nub, sucking it through the silk.

She cried out and ground her hips down. The brush of her against his hard cock nearly made him come in his pants, and so he rolled her over, pushing her down on top of the cushions. He pulled the cups of her bra down, exposing those lovely nipples. Pink and perfect, just as he'd thought. Taking one bare bud into his mouth, he teased her with his tongue, making her cry out.

Her fingers dug into his hair, pulling at the roots with just enough force to make him moan. His hand snaked down her bare, flat belly and slipped under her trousers and panties, skimming over the soft skin and traveling lower still. When his fingers slid past her neat curls and pressed against her pussy, he groaned when he realized how wet she was. He teased her slick lips before slipping a finger into her.

"Oh, God!" She threw her head back, closing her eyes. Her hips pumped up at his hand, and he slipped another finger into her tight, wet heat. Her teeth bit into her lower lip as she made a low, moaning sound.

He watched her, transfixed as her face twisted in blissful agony. He continued to thrust his fingers into her, giving her what she wanted. The scent of her arousal was filling the air, and he continued, his thumb brushing her engorged clit. That drove her over the edge, and she clamped around his fingers, her hips pushing against his hand and her expression so utterly lovely that he wanted to preserve that moment in his mind forever.

Her breathing slowed down, and her lids gradually opened. The raw passion he saw in them aroused him even more, and his cock strained painfully against his pants. He could have her now, and she would let him. It would be so easy, to strip her down fully and take her. But he didn't want just her body.

He cleared his throat and then took her hand, pulling her upright. Her eyes widened in surprise. "Lucas?"

"I ..." He didn't know what to say, so he kissed her instead. "Did you really come here to apologize?"

"Yes. Originally, I did." She blushed.

"Then I know the perfect way you can make it up to me."

"You do?"

"Yes." He grabbed her hand and kissed her knuckles. "Go out with me. On a date."

She looked at him skeptically. "Just one date?"

"Well, you're going to have to impress me on the first before I commit to a second," he teased.

She laughed. "But, come on. A date? Isn't that old-fashioned?"

"People still date these days, you know," he said.

"Yes, but not after ..." She moved closer to him, her hands landing on his chest. Her hands moved outward, pushing his jacket aside.

"Sofia." God, he wanted to let her continue but took her hands in his instead.

She raised a brow at him. "You don't want—"

"I do." Goddammit, he *wanted* so bad his damn zipper was imprinting on his dick. "But I think it would be best if we started again. Started fresh."

"Oh." She thought for a moment.

His heart pounded in his chest, waiting for her to reject him. She slipped her hands from his and his stomach dropped. However, to his surprise, she held her palm out. "Sofia Selinofoto."

It took him a moment, but he knew what this was. An olive branch. A fresh start. "Lucas Anderson." He took her hand, but instead of shaking it, pulled on it and brought her back to straddle his hips.

"Some fresh start, Anderson," she muttered.

"This is as fresh as it gets, sweetheart." He slid his fingers into her thick dark hair and brought her head down. He kissed her, devouring her mouth with his, letting the taste of her burn into his memory. He dragged his lips away from hers, trailing lower, and he brushed his nose against her pulse, getting in as much of that sweet scent as he could. "I'll pick you up tomorrow? Dinner?"

"Sure," she sighed, then slid off his lap and began to button her blouse. "I should get home, it's getting late."

He wanted her to stay. But it was probably best she go, or else he wouldn't have the strength to keep his hands off her. "I'll walk you to your car."

As they headed to the door, he picked up her fallen coat from the foyer floor and then helped her put it on. "Aren't you cold?" she asked.

He opened the door and gestured for her to go first. "We're only going to be outside for a minute." They walked out to her parked car across the street.

"What time should I be ready?" she asked.

"Six," he said. "Should I pick you up at work?"

"No!" she said vehemently. "I mean, I'm not working tomorrow."

"You're off?"

She nodded.

He was tempted to take the day off and just spend it with her. But he knew that he had a million things to do. "All right. I'll pick you up at home." Then, he wrapped an arm around her waist and pulled her to him, planting a long, lingering kiss on her mouth. "Drive safe."

"I will." She gave him one last look before she got into her car and drove off.

He stood there, watching her car disappear down the street. Tonight's events had certainly turned out differently than he'd thought. But it was like a runaway train going full speed ahead: He couldn't stop it. And he wasn't sure if he wanted to.

CHAPTER THIRTEEN

Sofia sighed for what seemed like the hundredth time that hour, staring at the piles of notepads in front of her spread out on her coffee table. Despite the captain's advice of taking a break from her work, she could hardly do that. First of all, the date of her testimony was coming up, and she had to make sure she could remember all the facts. And second, if she didn't find something to occupy her time, she would surely go insane waiting for six o'clock to arrive.

Could they really start afresh? As she told him and herself, she was done with looking into his past. Sometimes, it was better to let things be. It wasn't easy killing someone in order to protect yourself or those around you, but sometimes it had to be done.

But now, things were different. She never liked feeling vulnerable, and Lucas seemed to be breaking every one of her walls. Sex, she could do. God knows, she and Derek never even went on a real date; they just kind of fell into bed after a particularly long, hard day at work and she was feeling weak.

She told herself that she would never be vulnerable like that again, but now ...

This was different, right? Lucas wasn't a corrupt cop on some crime boss's payroll. She hardly thought anyone was paying him to get close to her. He was just a man. A man who kissed her so hard she forgot her own name. And those fingers of his. She hadn't come that hard in a while, not even with her vibrator. And that wasn't even the main event.

A shiver of anticipation ran through her. What should she wear tonight? Would Lucas expect her to jump into bed right away? It sounded like he wanted more. But what was more? Could she even give more of herself? What would it be like to date someone like him?

It was a good thing her phone ringing interrupted her thoughts or she would have spiraled down into her own thoughts. The number flashing on the screen was unfamiliar.

"Selinofoto," she answered briskly.

"It's me."

"Oh. Hey, Lucas."

"Sofia." There was a long pause, but the tension in the silence that spanned across them was obvious. "I'm sorry, I can't make it tonight."

She tried to hide her disappointment. "Right. I mean, that's all right."

"Sofia, I ..." He let out a frustrated sound. "It's not what you think. I've got a crisis on my hands. A family crisis."

The panic in his voice erased her doubts. "Crisis? What's wrong?"

"It's my sister. She's in a lot of trouble." The anger in his tone was barely contained. "My parents are doing what they can, but I have to stay home and hold the fort, so to speak. I hate to cancel our date."

"It's okay," she soothed. She wished she was there beside him right now. "We can re-schedule. Is there anything I can do?"

"No, we can handle it. But, are you sure this is okay?"

"It's fine," she assured him. "Take care of your family." God knows, if it was Dad or *Pappoús*, she would have dropped their date too. "But promise you'll tell me right away when things settle down." She'd never heard him sound so alarmed before.

"I will, Sofia. Thank you."

"No problem."

The click from the other end told her he had hung up. What could possibly have gotten him shaken? It sounded like a life or death situation, but if that were true, surely the Andersons would get the authorities involved?

With a deep sigh, she turned her attention back to her notes. Looks like she was having a date tonight with General Tso and his friends, egg rolls, and fried rice.

———

Sofia woke up with a start as she straightened up from her sleeping position. Glancing around her, she realized she had fallen asleep on the couch, surrounded by her notes and left-over Chinese food. A crick had developed in her neck because of her lumpy cushions, but that wasn't what woke her up. It was the sound of knocking on the door.

"Hold your horses!" She scrambled to her feet, trying to put some semblance of order to her hair. The knocking was so insistent and she was still half-asleep that she didn't check the peephole, though she at least had the sense to keep the door chain in place. "What the hell—Lucas?"

She quickly slammed the door closed and removed the chain before flinging it open. "Lucas? What are you—" She checked her watch. "It's five o'clock in the morning."

"I know. But you said you wanted to know right away when things settled down." His voice was raspy, and from the rumpled suit he wore and the dark circles under his eyes, it was obvious he'd hadn't been home or had any sleep. "Can I come in?"

She moved aside. "Of course. Have a seat." Then, she cursed silently when she realized what a mess her living room was. "Oops," she swooped in and grabbed the half-empty boxes of takeout. "I'll be right back." Running to the kitchen, she deposited the boxes in the garbage. When she came back to the living room, he was seated on the couch, one of her notepads in his hand.

She snatched the pad from him. "Confidential police business," she bristled.

"I'm sorry," he said, looking up at her with those incredible eyes of his. He looked exhausted. "I sat down and it was under me."

"No worries." She put the pad aside, discreetly closing the pages and shoving it under a bunch of magazines. "Now, is everything okay? With your sister?" Moving closer, she placed a hand over his. "What happened?"

His shoulders sank and he let out a long breath. "Adrianna was attacked."

She tensed and he lifted her hand to his cheek, the day-old growth of rough bristles rubbing on her skin. "I'm sorry. Is she all right? Did you call the police?"

"She's fine. She wasn't hurt or anything, but she was threatened in her own home in Jersey. My mother and my other sister were there with her, but these men ... let's just say they've been causing trouble in the area and when my mom tried to put a stop to it, they retaliated."

"Was it some kind of gang?"

"Sort of." He pressed a kiss to the inside of her palm, making her shiver. "But it doesn't matter now. She's safe. They all are."

"I'm glad."

"Me too, but," his brows drew together, "I'm sorry I missed our first date."

"You had more important things to attend to," she reminded him.

His gaze fixed on her. "Other important things. Not more important."

"Well, I'm free now." She smiled at him. "Why don't you give me fifteen minutes and then you can take me to breakfast? There's an all-night diner on Third Avenue."

The corner of his mouth quirked up. "I'm still wearing the same clothes from yesterday."

"Well, you'll have to hold your head up high when you do the walk of shame past my neighbors." She winked at him before disappearing into her bedroom.

CHAPTER FOURTEEN

DATING SOFIA WAS A LESSON IN PATIENCE.

They'd had two dates now, but he always went home afterwards, alone. He knew he had to take it slow with her, but it was hard when all he wanted to do was to bring her to his bed and fuck her senseless. Every minute he wasn't with her, all he could think about was that night on his couch. How sweet she tasted. And what she looked like when she came. His wolf, too, was urging him on to make her theirs. It didn't want to be patient. It wanted to own her. Dominate her.

Having dated Lycan women exclusively, most of his bed partners had been eager to please him—no, scratch that, they were eager to please the future Alpha of New York. They all acted submissive in bed, letting him take over and dominate them. But Sofia didn't have a submissive bone in her body, and he was looking forward to find out what she was like in bed.

And the other problem was that the damned woman refused to let him sweep her off her feet.

Not counting their breakfast date, he had taken her out two nights in a row, one to a Japanese restaurant with a famous celebrity chef, and the other was a Michelin-starred restaurant that usually needed a year's reservation in advance. Though she seemed happy enough with the food and even gracious when they met the chefs at both places, she just didn't seem impressed.

He was used to women being dazzled by the glitz and glamour of what he could offer, but Sofia didn't have the usual wide-eyed surprise most of his previous dates did. Instead, she seemed eager to get on with the meal. He was pulling out all the stops and she didn't even seem fazed, like she dined at exclusive restaurants all the time. She was also annoyed that each time she tried to pay, the waiter told her that the bill had been taken care of and refused to let her see the check.

So now, on their third date at the private-dining room of a famous TV chef, she shot him a dirty look when the waiter shook his head when she handed him her card.

"Will you stop doing that?" she huffed, training her annoyed gaze on him. "You can't expect me to just keep letting you pay. I do hold a job, you know."

He did know that, but also knew that detectives probably didn't make a lot, at least not enough to be able to afford all these places. "What's wrong with the restaurants I've been taking you to? Aren't they good enough?"

"Good enough?" she asked, puzzled.

His irritation was rising. "I've taken you out three times now and you don't seem impressed."

"I don't?" Her expression changed. "Oh, no. I'm sorry, Lucas." She shook her head. "It's not that I'm not impressed—

I don't even know how you managed a reservation at the last place. It's just that ..." She let out a breath. "I don't know. These restaurants, they all seem stuffy and boring. You don't have to take me to these fancy places to impress me, you know."

Her explanation rendered him speechless.

She gave him a smirk. "And I know I can't afford these places, but you really have to let me pay sometime. At least half."

"I'm the one who invited you out, so I should pay," he insisted.

"Fine." She put her napkin down. "Lucas, will you go out with me?"

That took him aback. "Go out with you?"

"What? I haven't made a good enough impression to warrant a fourth date?" She sounded hurt but was grinning when she said those words.

"All right," he said. "I'll go out with you. When?"

"Tomorrow's Sunday, and I have to go home to Queens, so it'll have to be Monday."

He didn't want to wait more than twenty-four hours to see her, but he knew how important her family was. "All right, I'll be ready."

"I'll choose the restaurant, I'll pick you up, and *I'll* pay."

The smile on her face was worth swallowing his pride.

———

On their last three dates, he had picked her up at home, but this time, Sofia insisted on doing the same for him. She showed up at exactly six o'clock on the dot.

"You look beautiful," he said, his eyes roaming over her face. Her hair was done up, and she wore only the most minimal makeup to enhance her features. As always, he found himself staring at her lips, thinking about kissing them again.

"Thank you, but I'm taking you out, so I should be the one giving the compliments."

"All right then," he challenged, spreading his arms. "What do you think?"

"Meh, you clean up nice." A smile tugged up at the corner of her mouth as he gave her a mock hurt expression. "Just kidding. You're beautiful too. C'mon."

"Where are we going?" he asked.

"I have the whole night planned, but it's a surprise." She led him down the steps, where there was a waiting yellow cab. "Come, my finest chariot awaits."

"You're not driving?" he asked.

"This place has great, if overpriced, wine, so I'm planning to splurge," she said. "And besides, parking downtown is hell if I'm not on official duty."

"And where is this place?"

"I'm not telling." Her eyes sparkled with mischief. "Don't worry, it'll be up to your standards, but I promise you, it isn't stuffy or snooty."

When she attempted to open the door, that was where he drew the line. Instead, he pushed her aside gently and pulled on the handle, then let her go in. He sent a quick text message to Reyes, who was in the town car parked behind the cab, then slid inside to join Sofia.

"You've been to this place before?" he asked as the vehicle began to move. She didn't even have to tell the cabbie the address, which meant he had no idea where they were going.

"No, but my parents went twice," she said. "The first was on their first date and the second when my dad proposed to my mom."

He felt her tense beside him, and her cheeks went pink. The implication, of course, wasn't lost on him either. "So, the food's good, huh?" He wanted to spare her the embarrassment. "Even better than your grandfather's place?"

She laughed. "Supposedly, though I'm not really fond of Italian food. My mom said the chef was even nice enough to come out of the kitchen and give them his congratulations. Even comped the meal."

"Hmmm." So, they were going to an Italian place downtown. He hoped it wasn't to one of those touristy restaurants in Little Italy. Not that he would look his nose down at her choice of restaurants, but he had eaten real Italian food all his life. He would be as gracious as he could of course.

"We're almost there," she said cheerfully.

He looked outside the window and realized they were on a familiar street on SoHo. A bad feeling suddenly came over him. *Oh, no. Please don't let it be—*

"We're here," she announced before stepping out of the cab. "Lucas? Are you all right?"

Shit. Just as he'd thought. They were standing right outside Muccino's. "I'm fine."

"Are you going to come out of the cab at all?" she asked wryly.

"Yeah, yeah," he muttered. The red neon sign that was his impending doom seemed to mock him as he stepped out. *Fuck.*

It wasn't that he was ashamed of being with Sofia. It's just that he hadn't had time yet to prepare her to meet the Muccino–Anderson clan. Hell, he hadn't prepared *himself*. And now she was walking into the wolf's den. Oh, fuck. *Gio*. If his cousin was working the kitchen tonight, the gossip would spread like wildfire. And everyone would want to know about Sofia.

"Say, Sofia," he began. "Wouldn't you rather have French food?" He jerked a thumb across the street. "I heard that restaurant is much better." And his other cousin, Dom, would be much more discreet; hell, he probably wouldn't even notice if Lucas brought an entire harem.

"You mean, the restaurant where you took your blonde date to?" Her voice was cold enough to freeze the blood in his veins.

"Right." Ouch. Darius had warned him that Sofia had been at the dinner for Alesso the other night. He was going to pay for that one. "Muccino's is fine."

"I hope it's more than fine." She led him toward the entrance, though he stepped ahead to open the door for her. "I couldn't get a reservation for another two weeks, so I had to come during my lunch hour to see if they could fit us in. That snooty hostess wouldn't even look at me, and when I finally got her attention, she said the only table she had wasn't in the best location."

She went inside and headed straight for the hostess' station. He followed a step behind, praying that no one would recognize him.

"Reservations?" The female hostess asked.

"I was just here during the lunch hour," Sofia said. "You can't have forgotten me already."

"Sorry, ma'am," the girl smirked at her. "We do get an awful lot of people in here. What was the name again?"

"Selinofoto."

"Just a moment." The hostess looked down at her notebook. "Hmmm, I don't see it."

"What?" Sofia exclaimed. "I was right here when you wrote it down."

"Was I?" She crossed her arms over her chest.

Lucas placed a hand on Sofia's arm. "It's okay, we can go somewhere else."

"No, it's not okay, Lucas." She looked like steam should be coming out of her ears.

Suddenly, he felt the hostess's eyes dart over to him. It took a second, but a flash of recognition crossed her face, and she went red. "Mr. Anderson! Sir, I ... I didn't know you were ... I mean ..." She swallowed. "I'll find you a table right away, sir. Sorry!" She pivoted on her heel, and Lucas could hear her muttering under her breath.

Sofia turned to him, a delicate dark brow raised. "Does every restaurant in New York train their staff to recognize you or something?"

"Something like that." At least the girl didn't reveal to Sofia who he really was. Maybe this would work. And he could keep Sofia to himself, just for a little while longer.

"I wonder what the hell is taking so long." She tapped her foot impatiently. "Ah, here she is."

The hostess was walking back toward them, but she wasn't alone. *Oh, no.* Lucas wanted to bang his head on the wall.

"What's going on here?" Gio Muccino's dark brows were

furrowed together. "Gretchen, stop begging me not to fire you. Who the hell—Lucas?"

It was probably too much to hope that Sofia didn't realize what was going on, but her keen detective's eyes couldn't have missed it. She did a double take, first at Lucas, then at Gio and then back at Lucas again. There was no way she would have missed the similarities in their features, and even if she did, the color of their eyes gave everything away. "Lucas, what's going on?"

"Sofia, I'd like you to meet my cousin, Gio Muccino. Gio, this is Sofia Selinofoto."

Gio's face turned from confused to surprise and then finally, his handsome face broke into a big grin. "Sofia! Nice to meet you! Are you Italian, *bella*?"

"No, I'm afraid not. Greek, actually."

"Even better." Gio winked at her. "Because you are as beautiful as a goddess."

To his surprise, Sofia actually laughed. "You're too kind, Mr. Muccino."

"Ugh! Mr. Muccino is my father, please, call me Gio."

"Nice to meet you, Gio." She held her hand out, which Gio took and kissed.

"Can we get a table, please?" Lucas muttered, not liking how his cousin was touching Sofia.

"Of course! And you'll get the best table—my table, in the kitchen. Come on," he gestured for them to follow him. Soon, they were crossing through the kitchen and then Gio led them to the chef's private dining table. Lucas had dined there many times before of course, but he always loved it. Watching the people working in the kitchen reminded him of those summers spent here.

"So," Sofia gave him the stink eye as he pulled a chair out for her. "Cousin, huh?"

"Guilty," he said sheepishly.

She sat down and allowed Gio to put the napkin on her lap. "You could have told me your cousin owns the restaurant, it's not that big of a deal."

"Actually," Gio began, "I'm only co-head chef here. And Lucas's family owns most of this restaurant."

"What?" she exclaimed. "Why didn't you tell me you owned this place as soon as we got here?"

"My mom and Gio's father are siblings," he explained. "Their grandparents immigrated here from Italy and then opened a restaurant in New Jersey, the original Muccino's. And when my parents married, my dad personally invested in this branch of the restaurant and put in my Uncle Dante— that's Gio's dad—as head chef. They opened more restaurants, plus expanded into food manufacturing, kitchen tools and appliances, and other related businesses. It's totally separate from Fenrir, and I don't personally own any stake in here."

"But he did work in the kitchens for a while," Gio added. "I remember him in the kitchens when Pops used to bring me to work. He would watch over me sometimes when he was taking a break." His cousin was a few years younger than him, though he'd already spent half his life in the Muccino's, since Uncle Dante brought him and Dominic around all the time.

Her face lit up, then lifted a brow at him knowingly. "No wonder you know your way around the kitchen. Why keep it a secret?"

Gio cleared his throat. "If you guys don't mind, why don't

you let me take care of dinner—off the menu, stuff prepared just for you, okay?"

"That's too much," Sofia said. "I don't want to be a bother."

"You're not a bother, *bella*." When Lucas sent him a sharp look, he added, "I mean, Sofia." He gave her a dramatic bow and excused himself.

"It's not a secret or anything," Lucas began, hoping she wouldn't think he deliberately kept this from him. "It's just that ... it's not my thing, you know?"

"You seemed perfectly comfortable in the kitchen. You really worked here?"

He nodded. "Yeah. It was my parents' idea. They wanted to teach me and my sister the value of hard work." And they really did, and Lucas had been grateful for the lesson. He'd learned to be thankful for what he had.

"I just ..."

"You can ask me anything," he said in a quiet voice. "Just don't be mad at me."

"I'm not mad at you, Lucas," she said quickly. "I'm just ... amazed."

"Amazed?"

"Yeah. You and I, we have so much in common. My grandfather and his restaurant. I mean, it's nothing like Muccino's, of course."

"It could be," he said. "The food there was amazing. They could expand and open up other branches if they want to."

"I know." Her eyes sparkled. "But both my grandfather and dad are too set in their ways. Anyway, they're happy with the way things are. So," she glanced around, "This isn't going to cost a fortune, is it?"

He chuckled. "Don't worry—"

"Oh, no, you're not going to pay, mister! I invited you out, and I'm going to pay." She fiddled with her napkin.

He made a mental note to pass a message to Gio about a large family discount. "You did. And I expected to be wined and dined, if you want me to put out."

Though he meant it as a joke, the sudden flush of her cheeks made heat creep up his collar, and a surge of desire went straight to his cock. Good thing they were interrupted by Gio's arrival along with their wine, but he couldn't get the image of Sofia, naked in his bed, out of his mind.

"You okay, Lucas?" Gio asked as he poured him a glass.

"I'm great." He took a sip and looked over at Sofia over the rim of his wine glass. Her face was still pink. "Just great."

The rest of the evening went well, though he was annoyed by Gio's multiple appearances. While he loved his cousin, he just wanted to be alone with Sofia, plus Gio kept telling embarrassing stories about him whenever he got the chance.

"I do remember you had that crush on that waitress," Gio said. He announced he was on a break and sat in one of the empty chairs, wiping his face with a towel. "What was her name? Nina?"

"Nia," Lucas corrected. "And I didn't have a big crush on her."

"Yes, you did," Gio teased. "I don't blame you." He lifted his hands to his chest, making big circles. "She had these huge—"

"Gio!"

"Heart." Gio looked wounded. "I was going to say heart."

Sofia guffawed, which made Lucas groan. "You were nine years old, how could you know that?"

"I know everything." He stood up and winked at Sofia. "I'll be bringing your dessert soon. Unless you already had other plans for dessert?"

"Your diners are waiting, Gio," he told his cousin. As soon as he left, he turned to Sofia. "Sorry about Gio," he said.

"He's interesting."

A surge of jealousy ran through him. "Oh?"

"Yeah, he kinda looks like you, but he isn't," she said.

"What do you mean?"

"He's so cheerful and open." She took a sip of her wine. "I can read him like a book."

"Oh?" His attempt to sound casual wasn't working. At all. Not when all he wanted was to punch Gio in the face. "Is that what you like then?"

"Not at all." Her eyes met his. "I prefer brooding, mysterious men."

The look she gave him was pure passion and desire, and he could barely stop himself from getting up from his chair and dragging her home now. But, as Gio said, there was dessert, and he didn't want her to miss it.

At some point during the meal, Sofia told Gio about her parents and how Uncle Dante prepared a special dessert for them—Nonna Gianna's zeppoles. It wasn't on the menu tonight, but he promised to make it for her. Sure enough, his cousin came back minutes letter, a plate of the said desserts on hand.

Finally, the end of the meal arrived. "Thank you," Sofia said to the waitress who had taken the small black folder from her. "These prices are so reasonable, it's a wonder you stay in business." She shot Lucas a meaningful look. The waitress didn't say anything, but nodded a thanks to her before leaving. "Well," she put her napkin down and stood up. "I'm going to head to the ladies. Be back in a few."

On her way out the door, she nearly bumped into Gio, who stepped aside gallantly and then pointed her to the direction of the facilities. Obviously glad to be alone with him, his cousin leapt to his side.

"She's not your usual type," Gio said as he sat down. "But then again, she's gorgeous. I don't know what she sees in your ugly ass mug."

"I don't know either," he replied. "Gio, I need a favor. Don't—"

"Say no more!" He put a hand on his heart. "I won't breathe her name to anybody. Your secret is safe with me."

"Thanks." Relief poured through him. "You know what my mom and my sisters are like. I just ... want to keep her to myself for a bit, you know?"

"I do." He stood up. "She's special, you know."

And mine. The declaration came out of nowhere.

"Hey calm down, Lucas. No need to rip up my table."

He looked down and saw that his knuckles were white from gripping the edge of the table. "Sorry."

"I wouldn't dream of stealing her from you. Besides, she's the only woman I've ever seen you with that makes you smile."

"I do smile, you know."

"I know," Gio grinned. "But it never reaches your eyes. But that one," he gestured to Sofia, who was walking back toward them, "that one makes you smile all over." When

Sofia reached the table, he turned to her. "I hope you enjoyed your meal."

"I did, thank you very much."

"Please come back anytime. I'll put your name on a list to make sure you get a table anytime you want."

"That's very kind of you," she said. Gio waved goodbye to them and then headed back into the kitchen.

Lucas stood up and helped Sofia with her coat, and they walked out of restaurant. "Thank you for dinner," he said.

"You're welcome." She fiddled with the buttons on her coat.

Usually at the end of a date, he would offer to bring her home. He'd walk her up to her apartment, kiss her by the door, but never pressed her to invite him up. "Sofia," he took her hands in his. "Why are you nervous?"

Her eyes seemed even larger as they looked up at him. "Nervous?" she laughed.

"Yeah." He could feel it. "There's no pressure at all." And really, he didn't want to. He'd wait for her for as long as needed.

"This is the fourth date," she finished. "And ... and I do want to be with you, Lucas."

The confession made him release the breath he'd been holding since they finished dinner. "There are no rules here, sweetheart. Just you and me, okay?"

She nodded.

He wanted to put her at ease. "Look, it's not even nine o'clock. How about we go somewhere for a drink? Do you know any good places here? Not one of those trendy bars, but somewhere we can have a beer and just talk?"

"As a matter of fact, I do know a place," she said. "It's kind of a cop bar, if you don't mind."

"Not at all," he replied. "I've never been to a real cop bar."

"Well, it doesn't get more real than this."

CHAPTER FIFTEEN

EVEN THOUGH IT WAS TECHNICALLY HER INVITATION TO go out, Sofia let Lucas call his car to bring them to McKilleney's on Third Avenue. It was a quintessential cop and fireman bar downtown, with no hip decor or fancy drinks. Just cold beer, greasy food, and great company. She had always felt at home here, probably because the staff and owner were all former policemen and firemen. In fact, Mac, the owner, was behind the bar when she and Lucas walked in.

"Well, now," Mac said as he wiped the bar with a rag. Broad-chested, white-haired, and hard-eyed, John "Mac" McKilleney looked every bit the typical retired cop. "Haven't seen you around here in a while, Detective. I was beginning to think you'd forgotten about us."

She winced inwardly. "I haven't, Mac. It's just been really busy."

Mac laughed, then walked around the bar to give her a hug. "You're here now. Glad to see you doing well. And who's your friend?" He raised a bushy white brow at Lucas.

"This is my date, Lucas," she introduced. "Lucas, this is Mac McKilleney."

"Nice to meet you, sir," he said as he took the hand the other man offered.

His eyes narrowed at Lucas. "You're not P.D. or F.D., are you son?"

"He's not." Sofia rolled her eyes.

"I promised your Ma I'd take good care of you and that I'll help you find a nice boy," Mac declared, then made a sign of the cross. "God rest her soul."

"Oh, and cops and firemen are the only 'nice' boys?" she retorted.

"The only ones I trust," he declared. "So? You do work, don't you, Lucas?"

"I worked in Giorgios's kitchen, if that counts," he said matter-of-factly.

"Ha!" Mac slapped him on the back. "A working guy. I like you already. From your fancy suit, I thought you were some big shot billionaire or something."

Sofia couldn't stop the smile from tugging up at her mouth. "Or something."

"So," Mac went back to the other side of the bar. "What can I get you?"

"A beer," Lucas said.

"Make that two," Sofia added.

"Coming right up." He turned around and then produced two mugs of ice-cold beer.

She took out her wallet, but Lucas had already beat her. "Hey! I invited you."

"And you paid for dinner."

"But this is my night—"

"Well I—"

"Stop!" Mac pushed Lucas's money back at him. "First one's on the house. You can fight about the check later." He shook his head and tsked at Sofia. "You're such a ballbuster like your ma. You really can't let a guy buy you a beer?"

She harrumphed but didn't say anything, instead took a sip of the beer.

"So," Lucas began. "Sofia tells me this is a cop bar."

"Cop *and* firemen." He nodded to one wall where over a dozen portraits hung of various men and women in formal police and firefighter attire. "Almost everyone in my family's P.D. or F.D. My dad was a cop, and mom was a dispatcher."

"And you knew Sofia's mom?"

"Of course, she was a regular and this was her beat." Mac smiled fondly. "She was one of the best, you know?"

She felt that familiar pang in her heart. "I know."

"She was too young when ..." Mac paused. "Well, she used to come around here when she was single, then less so after she married Sofia's dad. But, when she did come, all she talked about was her daughter. She was so proud of you." His eyes shone with pride. "She came here to tell me about that day you said you wanted to be a cop like her."

"She did?" That she didn't know.

"Yeah, she was so happy."

She swallowed the lump in her throat. "I didn't know. Thank you."

"She's a great detective," Lucas answered. "And devoted to her job." He winked at her, then raised his glass. "To your mom."

"To mom." She clinked her mug against him then took a sip, allowing the cold liquid to wash away the emotion building in her throat.

Lucas flashed her a sympathetic smile, then turned to Mac. "Say, Mac, I bet you have some great stories about when you were a rookie."

"Do I?" Mac wiped his hands on the towel wrapped around his waist. "There was this one time ..."

Sofia sighed inwardly with relief, glad to have the attention off her. She loved talking about her mom, but it was these moments that she wished Nadia was still alive. She never had a lot of girlfriends; she didn't have any friends, period, but it would be nice to talk to a female about certain things. Like how she was feeling about Lucas and the fact that she was nervous about what she knew was inevitable. Because she knew if she had sex with Lucas tonight, well, it wouldn't just be about sex. There was a dam inside her, waiting to burst. With passion. With emotion. And possibly something deeper.

Plus, there was the fact that her last sexual encounter wasn't exactly ideal. Sure, Derek was good in bed, but then all the mess that came after ... It was silly because he and Lucas were nothing alike, but still, there was a part of her that was afraid of what would happen after.

As Mac continued to regale them with tales of his youth, Sofia felt her cellphone buzz in her purse. It was a message from an informant on another case. Though she hated to be rude, this was important and she excused herself so she could call the number back, crossing the main bar room to make her way outside. Stepping a few feet away from the front door, she dialed the number back and spoke to the person who picked up the phone, and scheduling another time they could speak longer.

Being a weekday, the bar wasn't full, and there were only two tables occupied in the entire place. However, when she finished her call and walked in, she noticed a big group that must have just arrived. They were all dressed in street clothes, but her instinct told her they were all cops. It looked like they had been celebrating, as they were all loud and raucous. Ignoring them, she focused her sights back on the bar where Lucas and Mac were waiting.

"Well, look what the cat dragged out."

She froze at the familiar voice. *Fuck me.*

"Yeah, didn't think she'd show her face at a place like this."

Fleetwood and Benito. *What the hell were they doing here?* She specifically chose this place because it was far from her precinct.

Sofia knew she had two choices. Ignore them as she had always done or ... not. She chose the latter. "Detective," she nodded at Fleetwood, then turned to Benito. "Sergeant."

"When we chose this place for Barret's retirement party, I was told this was a cop bar," Fleetwood sneered.

"Yeah, seems like they just let anyone in here," Benito spat. Behind the two, the rest of their party had gone quiet.

She felt her temper rise. "Why not say what you really mean *to my face* instead of doing this pathetic mean-girls act." Her words stunned them and both men went quiet. "What? Don't have the balls, cowards?"

Fleetwood went red. "You're a rat, Selinofoto, is that

what you wanted to hear? That you sold out one of our own—"

"Who was dirty! Derek was doing Bianchi's bidding and you all know it." She didn't even realize she was shaking with anger. This was it. After months of keeping quiet, it was all going to come back now. "You don't even know half of what he did. What Bianchi told him to do and how he enjoyed doing it. That—"

"What's going on here? Sofia?"

The voice was soft, but she could hear the deadliness just underneath the surface. Turning her head, she saw Lucas standing behind her, his blue-green mismatched eyes looking straight at Fleetwood. The cold, hard expression in them made her shiver.

"What's the matter?" Mac said, his voice booming as he approached them. "Are you guys making trouble?" He folded his arms over his wide chest.

"Not at all," Benito swallowed. "Just ... saying hi to a friend." He pulled on Fleetwood's arm. "C'mon, let's go back to our table."

Fleetwood huffed. "Fine. Let's finish our drinks and go." His eyes flickered at Sofia, before allowing Benito to drag him back.

Sofia counted to ten, then turned on her heel. She thought she heard Lucas and Mac call after her, but she didn't want to stop. She would not cry in there, not show them how affected she was by their words. Pushing the door open, she stepped out into the cold night.

I wanted to do the right thing, Mom. Her throat burned as she choked on the tears she refused to spill. *I did it for you.*

But what was the right thing? Was handing over a dirty cop the right thing? Or keeping with the blue wall of silence? Frankly, she didn't know anymore.

"Sofia!"

Lucas.

"What's going on, Sofia?" He stepped in front of her and placed his hands on her upper arms. "Please. Look at me. Tell me what's wrong."

"Nothing," she said through gritted teeth.

"That's *not* nothing." His hands gripped her tighter. "Tell me."

"I ... I ..." She looked up into his eyes, wanting to get lost. To forget. "I want to go, Lucas."

He let out a sigh. "All right. I'll take you back to your apartment."

"No." She took a step forward and placed her hands on his chest. His muscles jumped under her touch, and she moved her hands up to his shoulders. "I don't want to go home. Take me back to your place." His eyes darkened and he nodded, then took his phone out from his pocket to call, she assumed, Reyes. She gripped the soft wool of his jacket, flexing her fingers. She just wanted to forget about what happened. Forget about Derek. Forget about Bianchi. Just for one night.

———

She wasn't sure what to expect when they arrived at his place. The ride uptown was silent, the tension growing between them. She hoped it was just the sexual tension and not anything else. Lucas never said a word the entire time, and he sat away from her, his face turned to the window. What was he thinking right now? She was desperate to know because she knew there was something going on. Isn't this what he wanted?

The car slowed to a stop, and her heart began to pound in her chest. He slipped out of the vehicle and held the door open for her. This was it. When she stepped out and followed him inside, there was no going back. She slid across the luxurious leather seat, then stepped out of the car. Lucas placed his hand on the small of her back, guiding her up the steps. When he opened the door, she stepped inside, holding her breath as she heard the door lock behind them.

"Lucas." She spun around, then pressed herself up to him. Getting on her tiptoes, she pressed her mouth to his. His lips were warm and she let out a soft sigh when his hands encircled her waist. "Lucas, please."

He moved his lips lower, down her neck, tickling her with his lips. "Sofia."

"Take me to bed." *Or the couch. Or the floor. Or against the wall.* She didn't care. She just wanted to lose herself in him.

"I will." He lifted her up into his arms and carried her away. To her surprise, they went past the stairs and into another room down the hallway.

It was dark inside, but when her vision adjusted, she could tell it was some kind of office. Leather-bound books lined one wall and there was a fireplace on the opposite side. Lucas sat her down on a comfortable settee, then promptly stood up.

As she took off her coat, she watched him walk away from

her, toward the fireplace. He flicked a switch, and it turned on, the flames leapt up, bathing the room in a soft light. Unbuttoning his coat, he folded it neatly and placed it to the side, then loosened and removed his tie. She waited for him to come back, but he remained in the same spot, his back to her. "Lucas? Why are you all the way over there?"

He turned, slowly. "Because I can't keep my hands away from you."

"All the more reason to come back here." She tried to sound light-hearted, but the expression on his face remained stony. "Lucas?"

"Who's Bianchi?" he asked, his voice flat. "And who's Derek?"

The last name he said made her stomach twist into knots, and she shot up like a rocket. "It's getting late, I should get going."

Before she could even take a step toward the door, he was right in front of her. *How did he move so fast?* Maybe it was the wine and beer making her see things. "Get out of my way, Lucas." He wrapped his fingers around her wrists. "Let go."

"No, not until you tell me who they are. I've seen their names before. In your notes."

"That was confidential!" Anger bubbled inside her. "You want to know? You want to know how I ruined my career? How I slept with a man who broke my trust and turned out to be a monster? And when I tried to do the right thing, everyone hated me for it?"

She gritted her teeth and tried to turn away, but he tipped her chin up. She expected disdain or even disgust from him. Not the quiet and gentle look of understanding.

"I'm sorry for bringing this up." His voice was steady, but

strong. "But we're not going to jump into bed so you can forget your problems."

That cut into her deep, because it was the truth. She would have used him tonight, because she just wanted to feel something else aside from the hurt gutting her deep. It wasn't fair, and he didn't deserve that. "I'm sorry." God, she was a terrible person.

"Tell me." He brought her hands up to his lips and kissed them.

She took a deep breath and looked up to him. The light from the fireplace turned his eyes all molten. There was something in them she couldn't quite name. Or didn't want to. So she turned away and sank back into the settee. He joined her, never letting go of her hands. "Derek Hastings was my partner. We'd been paired up for a couple of months after my old partner retired. This job, it can get lonely you know, and we just ... turned to each other."

She felt him tense, but continued. "It was just scratching an itch, trying to feel something after you've numbed yourself because all you can see is the worst in the world. But it turns out ..." She took a deep breath. "I heard him talking on the phone one night. He thought I was in the bathroom. He was talking in a low voice, but I heard some words that sounded familiar. From a case we were working on. I followed my instincts and dug deeper. Followed him one night." Her throat went dry, thinking about what she had discovered.

He squeezed her hand. "What did you find out?"

"He was meeting with the head of an organized crime family. Anthony Bianchi. Derek wasn't just dirty, but he was involved in a lot of illegal activities. He not only passed information along to Bianchi but would sometimes do jobs for him. His favorite ones involved Bianchi's human trafficking ring because he could sample the goods." Bile rose in her throat. Those poor women.

"Take deep breaths." A hand soothed her back, rubbing slow circles. "It's okay, you don't have to tell me more."

But she had to. So he could understand. "I reported him, of course. And IAB was all over me to bring him in and testify. So, I collected all the evidence and made the arrest myself at a warehouse where they kept the new girls. It was a big bust because we got Bianchi too." It had been the greatest moment of her career. At least, it should have been. "My testimony in a few weeks will put him away for good."

"You did the right thing," he said.

The irony of his words weren't lost on her. "I thought so too. But the other cops and detectives didn't see it that way." She pulled her hands away from him and wrapped them around herself, feeling a sudden chill. "I've been ostracized ever since then. I can hear them whispering behind my back. Been called all kinds of names. No one wants to work with a rat. Because that's what I am."

"No." He moved closer to her, so close that she could feel the heat radiating from his body. "Sofia, you did the right thing. Derek was hurting people, and he deserved to be put away."

"You know what they do to cops in prison?" she asked. "The first day he was there, he was beaten up so bad, he had to be fed through a tube for weeks."

"That's the prison warden's fault, not yours. Sofia, look at me." He slid his palm up to her jaw in a soft caress.

"It doesn't change the fact that I turned on my own. My mother would—"

"Your mother would have been proud," he insisted. "You upheld the law. Made sure justice was served."

"You don't understand, you're not a cop." The brief flash of hurt in his eyes made her chest ache. "No! Lucas, I didn't mean—"

"I know." He cupped her jaw so she couldn't turn away. "You put away some very bad people and you should be proud of that. You saved a lot of people and probably stopped more from getting hurt."

It was the one comfort she took in, knowing those girls with the haunted looks on their faces were all free now. "Thank you for saying that."

His arms wound around her, and he drew her close. She lay her head on his chest, listening to the soothing beats of his heart. A hand came up to stroke her hair.

"I'm sorry for what you went through and what I said about you wanting to forget your problems."

"No, don't be sorry." She rubbed her cheek against his chest, breathing in that ocean-breeze scent. "You were right about one thing. I was trying to use you, and you deserved better than that." *Better than me.*

"Sofia, you have no idea how much I want you. You're so beautiful, but also so fierce. You're passionate about your job, and I admire that." He rested his chin on top of her head. "I didn't want to sleep with you if you weren't doing it for the right reasons, because you have to know, this won't just be about scratching an itch for me."

She shut her eyes, wondering if she heard him correctly. What he said shook her to the very core because if she were honest with herself, it was the same for her. Pulling away from him, she slid her hands up his lapel and pulled him down to touch her lips to his. Pouring every ounce of desire and passion in the kiss, she hoped he could feel how much she wanted him. *Him*, not just because he could make her forget.

His mouth moved against hers, slowly, almost reverently. His hands went to the back of her dress, and his nimble fingers eased the zipper down, exposing her back. He pushed her on her back, sliding the front of her dress down to her waist.

"Beautiful," he murmured as his warm palms cupped her breasts through her black lace bra.

She moaned when he pulled down the cups, her nipples instantly pebbling under his gaze. He brushed the hardened tips with his thumb and forefinger. It sent zings of pleasures straight down to her pussy, making her wet.

His nostrils flared and his eyes blazed. Leaning down, he drew a nipple into his mouth, sucking back hard. His tongue was wet and warm, licking and torturing her until she was squirming under him.

He shifted his weight, sliding her across the settee until she was sitting on the edge and her legs spread. He was kneeling in front of her, his gaze never leaving hers even as he pulled the rest of her dress off.

"I need to taste you," he growled. Fingers skimmed over her stomach, moving lower to hook into her panties and peel them off. Lowering his head, he pressed his tongue to her.

"Nnggghhh!" The sensation of his mouth on her was too much and she began thrashing her hands. His hands caught hers and pinned them down. He was looking at her even as he licked and sucked at her, as if daring her not to look away.

God, it was so hot watching him like that, enjoying himself as he gave her pleasure.

When his mouth encircled her clit, he let go of her. Her fingers dug through his thick hair, raking her fingers down his scalp. He ate at her enthusiastically, licking and sucking at her until she felt the pleasure building in her. One, then two, and finally three fingers thrust into her, and she felt her entire body explode with pleasure.

As she was coming down, she felt herself lifted up. She thought they would be making their way to the bedroom, but he only took a few steps, laying her down on the soft, plush rug in front of the fireplace. He pushed her thighs apart and crawled between them and began to unbutton his shirt.

Good God, he was magnificent. That brief glance she saw that first time in the darkened club didn't do him justice. His tanned, muscled skin slowly exposed to her as the shirt parted. A soft mat of dark hair covered his broad chest, trickling down to a line over his perfectly-formed six-pack abs. After he tossed the shirt aside, he began to unbuckle his belt.

She wanted him so bad, but at the same time, she couldn't be irresponsible. Which was why she sat up and placed her hand on his to stop him. "Lucas ... my purse." She nodded her head to her bag, which was on the couch.

It took him a second before he understood, then shot to his feet. He was back in no time, foil packet in hand. Thank God she was prepared and it didn't ruin the moment. She took it from him and he removed the rest of his clothing.

She couldn't help but gasp when his cock was free of his underwear. He was already hard and so thick and long that her pussy clenched at the sight. Unwrapping the packet, she unrolled the condom over him.

He pushed her down. "I need you so bad, Sofia."

"Then take me," she urged, spreading her legs.

He didn't need any further invitation as he covered her with his body. She bit her lip as she felt the blunt tip of his cock at her entrance, pushing slowly. Her hands went to his shoulders and she could feel how tense he was and how much he was holding back as he waited for her to accommodate him. She wanted him bad too, the sensation of being stretched was thrilling, and soon he was all the way in her.

He paused, as if waiting for her. She lifted her hips up, pushing against him to let him know she was ready. She braced herself, waiting for him to start moving and thrusting. But instead, he slid his hands under her, cradling her body to his as he captured her mouth in a slow, sensuous kiss.

She sighed and opened up to him. His hips moved at the same time as his mouth and tongue. Slow. Teasing. His cock slid in and out in a slow rhythm, building up the sensations in her.

"Lucas," she moaned as his mouth lowered down to her neck and the tops of her breasts, licking and kissing and sucking at her most sensitive areas, then moving up again to taste her mouth. His cock teased her tight passage, sliding along and causing pleasure to ripple through her. It was exciting. It was maddening. The pleasure didn't crescendo as much as build up.

"Stop teasing," she begged, tugging at his hair. She felt him smile against her neck.

"All right," he rasped. "But you take what you want, sweetheart."

One moment she was under him, and the next, she was on top. He had rolled them over so she straddled him, his blue-green eyes blazing with lust. "Go ahead. Ride me, Sofia."

She gasped when he pushed up at her. God she'd never been so filled before. She braced herself on her knees, sliding him out of her before sinking down on him again.

She set the pace, slow and steady at first. But soon, she was moving faster, the pleasure erasing the burning of her thighs as she rode him. He let out a strangled growl when she squeezed around him, his fingers digging so hard into her hips she knew it would bruise. She was so close ... closer ...

"Lucas!" She sobbed his name when the orgasm took over her body, washing over her, making her want more. His hands found hers, their fingers entwined as her pleasure ripped through her. He let out a grunt as she felt his cock pulse inside her, his hips thrusting up erratically as his pleasure peaked. He reached down to pinch her clit which made her body shudder in surprise as another wave of pleasure coursed through her.

She let out a whimper and collapsed on top of him. Her breathing was heavy and ragged, but as she pulled more air into her lungs, it slowed down to a more normal pace.

She lay there for a few minutes on top of him, awareness slowly coming back to her as the feeling in her legs and thighs did as well. His cock slipped out of her as he shifted his hips. She moved her head up to look at him, only to find him staring back at her with those strange eyes. A hand cupped her chin and she turned to press a kiss to his palm.

"Are you okay?" he asked in a soft voice.

She couldn't stop the smile spreading across her face. "Yes. More than okay, although," she looked around them, "you couldn't have brought me to a bed?"

"I had to have you," he said.

"I—" She let out a yelp as all of a sudden, she was swept up into his arms. Maybe it was the post-orgasm buzz, but how could she miss how fast he moved or how strong he was?

"But don't worry," he nuzzled at her ear, "we'll be making use of my bed a lot more."

CHAPTER SIXTEEN

EVEN IN THE DARKNESS OF HIS BEDROOM, SOFIA LOOKED so incredibly beautiful. He was glad for his Lycan eyesight, so he could watch her like this—curled up against his side, long, dark curls spread over her shoulders, her skin smooth like marble, and those lush lips parted slightly as she breathed evenly. He wanted her again, even more this morning, even though they'd already had sex twice after that first time.

As he continued to watch her, his wolf lay inside him, quiet. For the first time, it wasn't restless or fighting him or wanting to take over. It was simply content to watch her too. *You and me both.* He wished he didn't have to leave this room, or this bed, ever. That he and Sofia could just stay here and not have to deal with the outside world.

Whatever had possessed him to say those words to her, that this was more than sex for him? Well, it was the truth. This wasn't about fucking or fulfilling a biological need. And he'd always been honest with the women he'd slept with in the past. If it was a one-night thing, he would tell them. If he was dating them and he lost interest, he told them too. He didn't lie to women, and he certainly couldn't lie to Sofia.

She was beautiful and he admired her and the sex was mind-blowing, but there was still the irrevocable fact that she was *human*. Yes, this wasn't just fucking and it was certainly not a one-night stand. But he didn't trust humans and there would always be a part of him that would never fully trust her, so what would become of them?

"You're thinking awfully hard so early in the morning." She still looked half asleep, with eyes cloudy and just the barest hint of a smile curving her lips.

"I think you're awfully beautiful."

She blinked. "It's too early, and I haven't had coffee, so I don't know if that's a compliment."

"It is." He rolled her over, her body so pliant and soft under his. She spread her thighs easily, cradling his already hard cock between them. He growled, feeling her cunt rubbing along his length, smelling how quickly she became aroused. He knew he could slip into her right now and she wouldn't protest. He desperately wanted to know how she felt without any barriers between them. Protection was one thing he was careful about, even with Lycan women. Sofia made him want to forget about that.

But he used every last ounce of control he had to stop. Just for a second. Enough time for him to reach over to his nightstand and grab the last condom he had. He quickly ripped the packet open and put it on.

She was wet and ready for him, and he braced himself as he plunged into her. Their joining was fast and urgent this morning, and she cried out as he pummeled into her with long, hard strokes. He made her orgasm twice before he did and then fell on top of her, his heart beating a mile a minute, and his lungs burning with exertion.

He kissed her soft, damp skin and then rolled over, discreetly disposing of the condom into the bin before slipping back into bed. He gathered her against him, pressing her body against his.

She sighed and turned her head. "What's wrong?" he asked.

"I should go."

He only tightened his hold on her, and his wolf growled in protest when she wiggled.

"I have work, you know," she said, but the doleful tone in her voice mollified him.

"Then I'll see you tonight." He took in a long, deep breath as he nuzzled her neck, trying to make her scent imprint in his brain.

"Yes, I—crap." Her shoulders tensed.

"What's wrong?"

"It's just ... yesterday the captain asked me to relieve someone on stakeout duty tonight. It's not hard, but I'll be babysitting some techs in a van the whole night." She twisted around to face him. "Tomorrow night?"

"I—" He shook his head. "I have a family thing tomorrow."

"A family thing?"

"Yeah. I can't miss it." He almost forgot what tomorrow was. Adrianna's ascension ceremony. "My sister, Adrianna, is getting a ... promotion and we're celebrating. My grandparents and uncles are flying in."

"Oh, congratulations. Not that I've met her or anything."

He chuckled. "You've almost met her. She was with me at the diner in Jersey"

"Ah."

He rolled her over so she lay on him, her chin propped up on his chest. "I wish we didn't have to wait two days to be together again."

"But the world keeps turning. You have to go make your billions, and I have to catch more criminals."

He knew she was joking, but the reality of her job suddenly hit him. Brushing away a lock of hair from her face, he sighed. "You're always careful when you're doing your job, right?"

"Of course." She narrowed her eyes at him. "You're not doing this macho thing are you? You do know I've been a cop for years."

He could see the disappointment in her eyes, but he couldn't help it. When he thought about how dangerous her job was, a surge of protectiveness rose in him and his wolf. It didn't want her in the danger, and neither did he. "I know." He tried to soothe her hurt feelings. "And I know you're good at it."

"I am." When she tried to move away from him, he held her tighter.

"Sofia, I'm just concerned." He didn't want her like this, with her walls up. "You're a great detective. I'm just worried about those criminals you have to deal with. I don't want to say goodbye like this."

"Like what?" Her voice was edgy.

"With you, being mad at me for saying something wrong that I didn't know was wrong."

Her expression softened. "And how do you want to say goodbye?"

He took the opening and kissed her on the mouth, rolling her over onto her back. There were no more condoms left, so he pleasured her with his mouth, licking her to another orgasm. By then it was really late and she had to rush so she had time to go home and get dressed. He offered to have his driver bring her home, but she said she would rather take a taxi. He brought her outside, hailing a passing cab for her, then kissing her goodbye before she got in. When he turned back to the townhouse, he saw Reyes waiting for him by the door, his face expressionless, though the bodyguard did crack a small smile when he passed by.

He got ready for work and was soon on his way to the office. As he walked by David's desk, he greeted his assistant good morning. As usual, his wolf went on full alert, clawing at him, trying to get to the human. It seems the good mood it had been in was now gone. *Damn animal.* He took a deep breath, trying to find good memories to ground him. Of course, the first thing that popped into his mind was this morning, of Sofia on his bed. Instantly, the wolf calmed down.

"Good morning, Mr. Anderson," David greeted. "Your calendar has been updated. Your first appointment is with Mrs. Vrost."

"Thank you, David." His wolf growled, but he pulled it back, then headed into his office. What was wrong with his wolf today? He honestly thought that now that Adrianna was safe, it would at least mellow down. She had Darius to protect her, and Lucas knew he would do anything for her.

He settled down into his chair, going through his emails

and messages. But he could only half concentrate on them because his mind was still on Sofia and their incredible night, wishing he didn't have to wait so long to see her. He was glad they were able to make up this morning, but it didn't change the fact that she would always be in danger.

His wolf's hackles raised, thinking about her old partner and that mob boss. *Bianchi.* He didn't know the man personally, but if he was the head of a successful organized crime family, he didn't grow his empire by letting police detectives testify against them. A dread came over him. Surely Sofia or her boss had thought about Bianchi retaliating or possibly doing what he could to stop her from testifying. Lucas wanted to make sure she was safe, but short of locking her up and putting armed guards on her, he didn't know how. If only there was a way he could get close to Bianchi and find out if he had plans for her.

"Lucas?"

Astrid's voice cut through his thoughts and he immediately straightened his posture. "Hello, Astrid."

"Are you ... all right?"

As a Lycan, she could probably feel his wolf getting worked up. "Yes, I'm fine. Shall we begin?" They had briefings at least once a week, since his own ascension ceremony would be coming up as well. He wanted Adrianna to have hers first though, and he was going to decide on a date after tomorrow night.

She sat on the chair opposite him. "We have a couple of things to discuss. First...."

The meeting with Astrid distracted him from most of his thoughts. Being Alpha was still important to him after all, and there was so much they needed to do.

"Anything else?" They had spoken for the good part of an hour at this point.

"That's about it." She closed her tablet PC. "I should get going, Nick wants me at the security office. Oh, wait!" She snapped her fingers. "Yes, one more thing. Reyes needs some time off."

"Of course." His bodyguard had been working long hours and extra shifts for the past weeks.

"We're still looking for someone to cover him tonight. If we can't find anyone, do you think you can stay at The Enclave? Just until he comes back."

"Sure." Maybe it was a good thing Sofia was working. There was no way she'd be allowed to visit him at the clan's super secure private compound. In fact, it had magical protections just to make sure humans ignored the mini-city hiding under their very noses.

"Great! That'll save me a lot of work. I'll leave word with David either way." Astrid got to her feet. "I'll see you around. When you see her tomorrow, tell Adrianna I said congratulations." With a final wave, she headed toward the door.

"Wait, Astrid." An idea popped in his head. Of one way he could find out about Bianchi.

Astrid spun around. "Yes?"

"Your uncle Quinn, he still works for Lone Wolf, right?"

She quirked an eyebrow. "Yeah?"

"Do you think I could have his contact?"

"Sure, but you can call the office." She frowned. "What do you need him for?"

Hesitation made him pause. However, he chose Astrid as his Beta, which meant he had to learn to trust her. "He's a hacker, right?"

"Yeah."

"I have something I need to ask him. Not related to Fenrir or the clan. But it has to be discreet, and I need the best." As future Alpha, he knew about Quinn Martin, of course. He was the Lone Wolves' resident hacker and information specialist. He hoped he wouldn't ask too many questions.

"Yeah, Uncle Quinn's good. But if you want *the* best, then you gotta talk to his kid. My cousin. Let me find that number ..." She took her phone from her pocket and tapped on the screen. A beep from his own phone told him she had sent him a message. "There, I sent it to you."

"Thank you."

"You're welcome. And Lucas?"

"Yes?"

She put her hand on her hip. "You will tell me if I need to know anything with the clan, right? So I can do my job properly?"

Technically, Sofia and Bianchi weren't clan-related. "I promise."

She nodded her head and then left without another word.

Lucas grabbed his phone from his desk and opened the contact Astrid had sent him. "*Huh.*" He didn't expect *that.* Was this person really the best? Astrid wouldn't lie to him about this. His finger hovered over the screen. He thought back to their conversation this morning, about him being macho. This might be an invasion of Sofia's privacy. His wolf growled at him, and for once he understood. This was about her safety. He tapped on the contact.

After two rings, the caller on the end other picked up.

"Good morning, this is Acme Crematory Services. You bring 'em, we bake 'em."

Raucous music played in the background so Lucas raised his voice a decibel. "Uh ... I must have the wrong number. I'm looking for Lizzie Martin?"

A feminine chuckle burst through the line. "Yep, that's me. What's up?"

"Uh, hey, Lizzie." Only a year or so younger than him, he tried to recall the last time he'd seen Lizzie. He remembered playing with her when they were kids at various parties and picnics. "This is Lucas."

"Who? Wait, hold on." There was shuffling and then a shout of, "No, Dad, I will not turn off that racket ... yes it's music, and I need it to work ... you know what, I'm going to turn it up *louder*." The music he heard in the background became a full-out cacophony of wailing guitars and cymbals. A second later, he heard a thunder of footsteps, a muffled male voice, then a loud crash before the music completely stopped.

"Seriously, Dad? That was my favorite speaker." Lizzie let out an incredulous gasp. "You have no chill! Ugh!" There was a deep breath. "Sorry, who is this again?"

"Lucas," he repeated. "Lucas Anderson."

"Lucas—" Another gasp, then a nervous giggle. "Oh. Hey. Mr. Anderson."

"Lizzie, please. I watched you streak down the backyard of our Long Island house during our annual Fourth of July barbecue. You can call me Lucas."

"I was like, a toddler, right?" she asked.

He laughed. "Yeah. You were probably six."

"Oh, good." There was a pause. "So, what's up, Lucas?"

"Astrid gave me your number. She said you were the best hacker around."

"Weeeeelllll, I don't know if I'm *the* best, but I'm flattered you called me anyway," she said with a chuckle. "So, what can I do for you? Do you need me to hack into some secret government files? Or change your competitors' stock prices? Or maybe I can help you overthrow a South American dictator?"

"You can wha—you know what? Never mind, I don't want to know." He rubbed the bridge of his nose with his fingers. "I just need you to find some information for me about someone. Anthony Bianchi."

She cleared her throat. "Um, you mean the Don of the Bianchi Crime Family and current guest of the New York State Penitentiary System?"

"Yes, that one."

"I need you to be more specific. What kind of information do you want on him? About his childhood? Business dealings? What he had for lunch?" she asked.

"You need specifics?"

"If you don't give me specifics, it'll be like walking around in the dark. Unless you want to know everything about him, but that might take a while to compile."

"Oh, I see." That made sense. But where to begin? He supposed he only needed to know one thing about him. "Well, if you could cross-reference anything important about him that happened in the last year before he was arrested and the name Sofia Selinofoto. I mean, Detective Sofia Selinofoto of the NYPD."

"Uh-huh." There were audible clicks on a keyboard in the background. "Gotcha. I'll see what I can do."

"Thank you. Let me know your fee, and I'll take care of it."

She chuckled. "Fee? Nah, I won't even break a sweat with this one."

"I insist—"

"Pshaw, don't worry about it."

He didn't want to have her work for free. "Well, how about we say I owe you one?"

"A favor?"

"Sure. You can ask me a favor anytime."

There was silence on the other line, as if she was contemplating it. "Okay, that sounds fair."

"And, Lizzie," he lowered his voice. "This is just between you and me, okay?"

"My lips are sealed," she promised. "I'll work on this right away. And if you ever need to destabilize a government—"

"I'll know who to call," he said wryly. He gave her his personal cell phone to call once she found anything interesting, then hung up after saying goodbye.

Maybe he was being overly cautious or even paranoid, but if anything happened to Sofia, he wasn't sure what he'd do. His wolf seemed restless, pacing inside him, like it was nervous, angry, and excited at the same time. It wanted him to do ... something. But what? He had done what he could to protect Sofia without pushing her away.

He turned to his computer, hoping to get some work done. It was going to be a long two days without Sofia. Maybe he should call her—

A soft beep interrupted his thoughts and he grabbed his phone. It was a message from Sofia.

I barely made it to work on time.

He grinned and replied, *You're welcome.*

She sent back a rolling eye emoji.

He thought for a moment, then replied, *That was the expression on your face this morning before you got up to leave.*

You're evil, Mr. Anderson, she replied.

I aim to please, Detective Selinofoto.

The rest of the day seemed agonizingly slow, but the flirty messages they sent back and forth made him less antsy about their separation. Later in the evening, she sent a message saying she was about to go on the stakeout and she was about to turn her phone off. He replied and asked her to message him as soon as she was off-duty.

He glanced at the clock and realized that it was eight-thirty. Pressing the button on the intercom on his desk, he called his assistant. "David, are you still there?"

"Yes, Mr. Anderson."

Huh, he usually didn't stay as late as he did. "You didn't have to wait for me, you know."

"I, er, have work to do, sir. And Mrs. Vrost left you a message."

Right. "And?"

"She said you can go home to the townhouse. She has someone covering you there and you should just have your driver drop you off."

"Excellent. Have the car ready for me. I'm headed home."

———

"Congratulations, Alpha," declared the leader of the Lycan High Council.

The reverent silence in the room was broken by loud cheers. Even Lucas found himself clapping and whistling in happiness as Adrianna was finally proclaimed Alpha of New Jersey. Everyone surrounded the new Alpha. When Gio declared that it was time to eat, everyone filed out of the living room and into the dining room.

Not really feeling hungry, he let everyone crowd the buffet table and sought out a quiet corner. Last night, he went home and spent the whole night alone, unable to sleep, wondering if she was okay. It was just a stakeout, nothing to worry about according to her. But so many things could go wrong. He slipped his phone out of his pocket, checking to see if he had any new messages from Sofia. She did message him when she was done, at around six o'clock this morning. She probably crashed the rest of the day and didn't send him any more messages. However, he was glad to see a new message from her, saying she was okay and just got up.

He was glad to know she was safe, but wished she was here. If she was a Lycan, she could have been here to witness this.

But she wasn't.

She was human. A fact that he kept forgetting.

"You're texting her, aren't you?" Adrianna said. She had crept up behind him and he'd been so distracted he didn't realize she was there.

"Fucking Gio." Despite his promise, Gio had let it slip to his sisters that Lucas had been at Muccino's with a 'gorgeous brunette'. "Yes."

"I'm so happy for you!"

"She's human, you know," he said glumly.

"So?" she asked. "Only *you* cared about that part."

That made him wince, the reminder of how much he hated humans. Well, he hated humans with the exception of one beautiful and stubborn detective.

"And everything is going well between you two?"

"So far," he said. "I'm just ... I'm not sure what to do. Especially, you know, telling her about the clan." The words came out of his mouth, but he wasn't surprised. Adrianna was his twin sister after all, and he could tell her everything.

"Just take things one day at a time, Lucas. You don't have to commit. I mean, you might not even get to that point, right?"

His wolf growled in protest, not liking those words that implied Sofia wouldn't be around for too long. Damn, if he wasn't gone already, his wolf was certainly head over heels. For a human, of all things.

"Looks like Darius needs me."

He followed Adrianna's gaze. Darius was by the buffet table, trapped between Isabelle and his cousin, Maxine Muccino. The look on his face made Lucas feel sorry for him. "Go rescue your mate," he said with a chuckle.

"I'll talk to you before you leave."

He watched his sister as she walked over to Darius and the two girls, grinning to himself. If there was something he was glad for, it was that tonight they were all here. Even Grampa Noah and Grandma Callista. His grandfather was a quiet man and they hadn't had a chance to talk yet. Lucas was trying to avoid him, because the old man was sometimes too perceptive.

He lingered another hour, chatting with various members

of his family, especially those who lived far way like Uncle Rafe and Uncle Matt and their families. Finally, he was ready to leave and sent a text to his driver to bring the car around.

"Lucas."

He turned to face Darius, who had caught up to him as he was leaving. "Hey. Sorry, could you tell Adrianna I had to go?" He knew he was being a coward, but he didn't want to talk to Adrianna about Sofia. He couldn't lie to his sister, but he just wanted Sofia to himself for a bit longer.

"Of course. But I actually wanted to talk to you. About Adrianna."

"Is she okay?"

"Yes, she is all right, but ..." He took out something from his pocket. A velvet box. "I was hoping to speak to you and your father."

Lucas didn't need to know what was inside. "You don't have to ask me or Papa for permission. But you do have my congratulations." Adrianna was going to be thrilled and he felt genuine happiness for his sister.

"Thank you. I mean, she needs to say yes first."

"She'll say yes," he said, but Darius almost seemed ... nervous? "And my father will definitely give you his blessing."

"Thank you for saying that."

"I look forward to calling you brother." And he meant it. He owed Darius for saving Adrianna's life, more than once. They shook hands and Lucas bid him goodbye before slipping out of the house and into his waiting town car.

The drive back to Manhattan was uneventful and quick. He was looking forward to getting home and getting some sleep—because that would mean it would be tomorrow and then he would be seeing Sofia again.

They had already crossed the Lincoln tunnel when his phone vibrated in his pocket. *Sofia.*

"Hello," he greeted as he answered the phone.

"Hey, you. How was the party?"

"It was fun. But I'm on my way home now, since it was getting late. What time should I pick you up tomorrow?"

"Oh." She sounded disappointed. "I was hoping you'd want to stop over tonight. Here. At my place."

The invitation surprised him. Of course, he was as eager as she was. "I'll be there in ten." He gave the directions to his driver and in no time, he was at the entrance of her building. She buzzed him in and he took the steps two at a time, all the way to her fourth-floor walk-up, not even breaking a sweat as he made it to her front door. He didn't need to knock as she opened it.

"Hi." She stood in the doorway, her fingers playing with the tie on her robe.

"Hi." God, he didn't realize just how much he missed her until this moment, when her scent enveloped him. She looked absolutely beautiful, her face free of makeup and her long hair tumbling down her shoulders.

He stepped inside and closed the door behind him. "I missed—" His mouth went dry when she dropped the robe. She was wearing a pair of white lace panties and a bra, as well as matching stockings that went up to mid-thigh.

They didn't even make it to her bed.

CHAPTER SEVENTEEN

"My, don't you look like the cat that got the cream," Sergeant Winters said as she stopped by Sofia's desk.

"Hmmm?" She looked up from her computer screen. "What do you mean?"

"You don't have your patented resting bitch face this morning." Winters narrowed her eyes. "Either you got a lot of sleep last night or ..." She gasped. "You didn't get any sleep at all!"

Sofia felt her cheeks go hot.

"Oh. My. God." Winters squealed. "You got some."

"Shhhh!" She didn't need it announced to the entire precinct. "Pipe down."

The other woman's smile was as wide as the Queensboro bridge. "I'm just glad you're finally having fun, Detective."

The corners of her mouth curved up involuntarily. Sex with Lucas was definitely fun. And thrilling. And quite possibly, addicting. God, the man was like a caged animal who hadn't been fed in days, and she was his first meal. She honestly thought it was just that first time, but then last night

... she was glad she invited him over. They were at it the entire night, and she was almost late again this morning.

"Wooo!" Winters fanned herself with her hands. "I need a cigar just by looking at your face, Detective."

"Shut up, Winters." But she was grinning when she said it.

"So, who—"

"Officer," Bushnell's stern voice made Winters jump. "Don't you have somewhere to be?"

"Uh, yes, sir!" Winters croaked before scampering away.

When the sergeant was well beyond hearing range, Bushnell trained his blue gaze on Sofia. "Selinofoto, we're a bit shorthanded today. I need you to assist on a case. The lead detective is a new transfer here, but he's a veteran. He'll need a hand since it's his first day with us."

"Of course, sir." She got up and grabbed her things.

"Detective Sharpe's already on the scene, I had dispatch send him straight there."

He rattled off the address to her, and she wrote it down on her pad. "I'll head there now."

The scene of the crime was just a ten-minute drive away in an alleyway behind a church. The yellow tape was already strung across the entrance of the alley. She flashed her badge to the uniformed officer guarding it, who immediately lifted the tape to let her through. She walked toward the man standing by a dumpster in the corner, whom she assumed was Sharpe.

"Detective Sharpe," she called out.

The man turned to look at her. He was a few inches taller than her and had smooth skin the color of dark chocolate. He didn't look much older, but the wrinkles in the corner of his keen eyes told her differently. "You must be Detective Selinofoto." He held out his hand. "Henry Sharpe."

She shook it. "Some first day, huh?"

Sharpe grimaced. "It's one for the books for sure. Want me to brief you?"

"Sure."

He took a deep breath and jerked a thumb at the dumpster. "D.B.'s in there. Garbage men found him this morning. They only pick up every other day, which means the vic's been in there for less than forty-eight hours."

Sofia peeked into the dumpster and instantly regretted it. The smell alone made her want to retch, but the sight of the body turned her insides. The victim was probably male based on the clothes, but that's all she could tell. The body was beaten and bloody beyond recognition.

A chill went down her spine. Why did this feel like déjà vu?

"Detective?" Sharpe asked. "Are you okay? It's pretty ripe, you might want to step back."

"I'm fine," she snapped, then shrugged her shoulders. "From the smell in there, he's probably been dead for more than a day."

"Rigor's passed for sure," Sharpe observed. "I spoke with the parish priest. The church"—he pointed with this chin at the building behind them—"is also a homeless shelter. He think's our vic is Alfie Fraser, one of their more recent residents."

"How recent?"

"Five days, according to Father Joseph." Sharpe took out his notepad. "Apparently Fraser just got out of prison."

Just like Thomas Dixon. She supposed it was a valid

observation, but also a coincidence at this point. "Tech lab guys should be here any moment," she said. "We'll know more when they do their examination."

"Yeah, if he's in the system, then fingerprints would confirm it."

"Detective Sharpe!"

They turned toward the young police officer jogging toward them, his face red from exertion.

"Take a deep breath, son," Sharpe said. "What is it?"

"Come with me. There's something you should see."

They followed the officer out of the alleyway and to the street. One of the trashcans on the sidewalk had its top removed. Sharpe peered inside and frowned, then took out gloves from his pocket. Sofia did the same and watched as the other detective picked out something white from the bottom of the can. It was a shirt covered in blood.

Sharpe gestured to Sofia, and she took the other end of the shirt to spread it out. Another chill ran through her.

"Looks expensive," he said. "Tailored maybe. I think that label is from a shop in London."

Sofia swallowed hard as she recognized the label. She'd seen it twice before. *No.* Her stomach twisted into tight knots.

"If the blood is the vic's then this has to be the murderer's shirt," the officer said.

"Good observation, Officer," Sharpe began. "But, let's wait until we have all the evidence to make that assumption."

The tension in her body eased somewhat, but her heart now pounded in her chest like a jackhammer. Her mind was spinning with all the possibilities and explanations.

"Are you okay, Detective Selinofoto?" Sharpe's gaze narrowed at her. "You're looking pale."

She wanted to throw up. She wanted to let go of this shirt and never see it again. "I'm fine. Let's get this bagged and sent to the lab." She wanted to know right away. Because if she was right, then Lucas might be in big trouble.

———

Sofia and Sharpe waited for the coroner to come and take the body away before they went back to the precinct. He headed straight to the captain's office, and she went to her desk, and quickly booted up her computer. She had to know now.

Clicking on her old case files, she opened the one from Lucas's kidnapping. As she went down the list of the kidnappers, her heart sank. Alfie Fraser was one of the people convicted of kidnapping Lucas and his sister. He also just got out of prison a week ago.

She clenched her jaw and balled up her fists, and her vision blurred at the edges from the anger she was trying to contain. Because she was 100 percent sure that this was bullshit.

Someone was trying very hard to make it look like Lucas was a murderer. He didn't kill Thomas Dixon and he didn't kill Alfie Fraser, and she knew it not because she was sleeping with him. Her detective's instincts were telling her something was very wrong with this whole scenario.

Besides, she knew Lucas already had a solid alibi. He was at that party for his sister and then he came to her place. But she just knew Lucas could never do such a thing.

It was early yet, and they weren't even sure if the body

was Fraser or whose blood was on the shirt. It might take a couple of hours still for the ID on the body. She glanced over at Bushnell's office. Sharpe was still in there talking to the captain.

Wait and see. This whole thing might be a big coincidence anyway. And she was worried for nothing.

When Bushnell and Sharpe finally finished talking, the captain led the detective out of his office and began to walk him around, giving him a tour. Sofia turned to her computer, trying to ignore that dreaded feeling in her stomach.

"Detective Selinofoto."

She nearly jumped out of her chair at the captain's voice. "Sir?"

"Detective Sharpe will be taking this desk." He gestured to the empty one beside her. Derek's old desk. "I know you're not leading the investigation on the D.B. from the church, but I hope you'll help him out any way that you can."

"Of course, sir," she said. "I'd be glad to help in any way I can, Detective Sharpe."

"I appreciate it," Sharpe replied. "Thank you."

As Sharpe settled into his new desk, Sofia turned back to her computer, trying to concentrate on her other cases. Of course, she kept on eye on the other detective, waiting to hear for news on their D.B. It wasn't until it was late in the day that he got the call.

"And you're positive?" Sharpe's brows were furrowed together as he scribbled on this notepad. "Okay, thanks." He put down the phone.

She waited with bated breath as Sharpe turned to her.

"It's definitely Fraser. Fingerprints confirm it."

Her blood pounded in her ears, and a pit in her stomach

grew. There was a definite link now between Dixon and Fraser.

What she *should* do was give all her previous evidence to Sharpe and tell him about the connection. But what she wanted to do was get to Lucas. *Now.* Someone was trying to frame him. She knew it, and she almost fell for it the first time. If she could warn Lucas first, then he'd at least know he had an enemy.

Her fingers drummed on the table, thinking of what to do. She had to protect Lucas. But at the same time, her own involvement could put him in further jeopardy.

The best thing she could do right now was tell Bushnell her suspicions, then remove herself from the case. Though he was always by-the-book, the captain was a smart man and always considered all sides and possibilities before making a decision.

"Detective?" Sharpe cocked his head at her.

"Sorry, I have to talk to the captain." She stood up and walked over to the captain's office, not even bothering to knock when she strode in.

"Detective?" Bushnell put his pen down. "What's wrong?"

"Sir, I need to tell you something." And she told him everything. About the connection between Dixon and Fraser and about Lucas, including sleeping with him. She tried to be as objective as possible, but she knew this wasn't going to turn out well.

Bushnell's jaw tightened and his blue gaze bore into her. "Detective, I don't even know where to begin. We're talking about a massive conflict of interest here, not to mention possible misconduct on your part just by being at the crime scene."

She flinched. "I know, sir. But I didn't know the connection of the two cases until we got positive I.D., and I assure you my ... personal involvement with Lucas Anderson isn't affecting my work. But still, I'm going to remove myself from the Fraser case."

"This is extremely disappointing. I like Sharpe, and I was hoping you would get along and you could be partners." He sighed. "You'll be removed from the Fraser case, as well as Dixon's."

"But we've already proven Lucas didn't do it! He's being framed." She bit her tongue when the captain scowled at her.

"He was your prime suspect, and now you're sleeping with him!" His face was red and blustery. "Selinofoto, you're the last person I'd expect this from."

His disappointment in her stung. "I'm sorry, sir."

"You really don't think it's him? What if the shirt is his?"

If it was, then that made her even more suspicious. Someone as careful and smart as Lucas wouldn't leave around evidence like that. "I can alibi him for last night, sir." She winced when he let out a curse. "And before that, he was at a party surrounded with family. Lucas—Anderson's got round the clock bodyguards. You know that yourself. I'm sure if you call Fenrir's security team, they can confirm his whereabouts and have GPS logs."

The captain leaned back in his chair and massaged his temples. "All right. But as of right now, I'm putting you on a couple days' leave."

"Sir!" she protested. "You can't—"

"It's a paid leave," he said. "You can't be here. At least,

not until we've totally cleared Anderson. This is the best thing you can do for him."

Fuck. He was right, and she knew it. Any hint of impropriety could jeopardize the precinct, the captain, even the entire case. "Fine." She stood up. "Is that all?"

"Yes, Detective."

It took all her self-control not to storm out of his office and slam the door behind her. But she had to act professional. After a deep, calming breath, she walked to her desk, then grabbed her things. Thankfully, Sharpe wasn't there so she could make a clean escape. Picking up her pace, she quickly headed outside, then took her phone out of her purse to call Lucas.

"Hey, you," he answered. "Miss me already?"

"Lucas." Her voice was shaking as she spoke. "I need to talk to you."

"Sure, what is it?"

"I—not over the phone." She lowered her voice. "Can you come to my place?"

"Of course." There was a pause. "What's wrong? Are you in trouble? Tell me."

"I can't tell you over the phone, but I promise I'll explain everything when we're alone." Her heart was beating a mile a minute. "Will you trust me?"

"Of course. I'm headed to your place now."

"Thank you." She put her phone away and headed for the parking lot. Driving home allowed her to keep her mind off things, and helped her calm down and think. Everything would be all right. Lucas had a solid alibi. There was no need to panic. Maybe she had overreacted. But all her alarm bells were ringing. Someone was trying to harm

Lucas, and there was no way she was going to let them succeed.

She parked in her garage and walked back to her building. Her keys were already in her hand as she approached the building, but she slowed down when she saw two men waiting just outside. They shuffled aside when she approached them. But before she could slip her key into the door, she felt their presence behind her.

Ugh. This was one thing she hated about living in an apartment building. These guys were attempting to slip inside with her. Maybe they had a friend who lived inside or they could be neighbors who forgot their keys. Being a New Yorker, she didn't know all her neighbors of course, so she wasn't sure what their business was. She straightened her shoulders and turned around.

"Excuse me, but are you—" Her heart leapt to her throat. Both men crowded into her, and one of them held something shiny. A gun. "Hold on, gentlemen," she said in her calmest voice. "I have a hundred in my purse. You can have it now and I won't—"

"Ha! Stupid bitch!" The man holding the gun spun her around and pressed the gun to her back. "Open that door and let's go up to your place."

Sofia hesitated, but the muzzle dug into her. What did they want? Did they mean to rob her place? Or worse?

"Go, bitch!"

"All right!" Her hands shook as she turned the key and let them in. She considered calling for help, but that would put her neighbors in danger. These men obviously meant business, and the only two choices in this situation were to follow their instructions or get shot.

She took her time getting to her fourth-floor walkup, trying to figure out what she could do. Given that she was on leave, she had to leave her gun at work. She had a weapon in her dresser, but that would mean having to go into her bedroom.

"Stop stalling!"

Gritting her teeth, she picked up her pace, and soon they were entering her apartment. The sound of her door closing behind them seemed to underscore her impending doom.

"Move," the man said, pushing her into the middle of the living room, his gun trained at her.

Slowly, she turned around. As a detective, she couldn't help but observe him. He was massive, probably half a foot over six feet and completely bald.

His companion, on the other hand, was tall and reed-thin with greasy long hair. He gave her a lecherous smile, showing that his mouth was missing a number of teeth.

"What do you want?" she asked. "I don't have jewelry. The TV's probably the most expensive thing I own and—"

"Shut it, bitch!" Baldy snarled. "You think we're here to fence your stuff?"

Thin Man laughed. "What a stupid bitch!"

"We've got our eye on a bigger prize." He lifted his gun. "Bianchi sends his regards."

Her heart slammed into her ribcage. That *sonofabitch*.

A knock on the door made them all startle. She should have taken a chance and lunged at Baldy, but the voice on the other side made her freeze.

"Sofia!" Lucas called. He rapped on the door insistently. "Sofia! Are you home?"

Baldy's face grew grim. "Who's that?"

"A friend," she said. "Let me get rid of him. Please." Oh, God. *Lucas.* She couldn't let them hurt him. "You don't need him dead, just me. It'll be cleaner."

Baldy pushed her towards the door, the gun pressed to her skull. "Get rid of him."

Relief made tears pool at her eyes. She took a deep breath as they walked to the door. "Lucas," she called, trying to make her voice calm.

"Sofia, sweetheart," he said. "Sorry I didn't buzz. Your neighbor let me inside the building. Are you able to ... let me in?"

"I'm afraid not." She swallowed hard. Lucas's words and calm demeanor made her pause. Did he have an idea what was happening? Surely, he couldn't have heard what was happening inside. Her door was solid steel, one of the reasons she chose this place. "Lucas, you should go home."

"What do you need, sweetheart?"

Tears streaked down her cheeks. She'd always thought that she could face dying in the line of duty, that she would be ready for it. She thought about her mom, wondering what she was thinking about the moment before she died. Because right this moment, all she could think about was Lucas, and how she was never going to see him again. "I need you to leave. Go, Lucas. Please."

This was for the best. Slowly, she turned to face the two men. "Just do it."

Baldy pulled her arm and tugged her to the middle of the room. She stood there, her entire body eerily still and calm. He raised the gun.

She closed her eyes, waiting for the sound of gunfire.

There was a loud boom, and she flinched. But there was no pain in her body.

"What the fuck?" Thin Man cursed.

Her eyes flew open. Her solid steel door was busted down, and Lucas stood in the middle, his face full of rage. Baldy had his gun pointed at him. "No!" she screamed.

"Sofia!" Lucas shouted. "I—"

A loud, deafening roar filled the air, and she felt a strange force knock her off her feet. She hit the floor with a thud. She lifted her head and gasped. "Lucas?" But he was gone. And in his place was a humungous black dog.

No. Not a dog. *A wolf.*

The wolf's head was probably three times the size of her own. Its jaws opened, letting out a deep growl, its hateful gaze directed at the two men.

Baldy was slowly getting up, as was his companion. "Motherfucker ... what is that?" He still had the gun in his hand. He began to raise it toward the wolf.

Big mistake. In a flash, the wolf leapt toward him. As it was in the air, it glanced briefly at Sofia, but it was long enough for her to see its eyes. One blue and one green. Like Lucas's.

The gun went off, and Baldy screamed when the wolf—no, *Lucas*—landed on top of him. On her left, she saw Thin Man reaching into his jacket. Fuck! She leapt to her feet and tackled him before he could fire his weapon, knocking it out of his hand and sending it skidding across the floor. Thin Man fought, his fist reaching out and connecting with her jaw. The pain shot through her, but the adrenaline rushing through her body dulled it. She shoved the heel of her palm into his nose, just as she had been taught in self-defense classes at the Academy. The sickening crack of cartilage and the scream of pain told her she had broken his nose. When she looked down at him, he was curled up in a ball, his hands on his face as blood flowed from his nostrils.

"Sir!"

She looked up and saw Reyes in the doorway, his face pale as he stared at the black wolf. The animal raised its head, blood dripping from its jaws.

Sofia could only describe what was left of Baldy as carnage. She was used to seeing dead bodies and murder scenes, but this made her stomach turn. There was nothing left of Baldy's head.

"Sir, please," Reyes cried out.

The wolf let out a deafening roar, and Sofia felt that shockwave again, sending her staggering back and flat on her ass. Reyes too was knocked down to his knees. What the fuck was going on?

Reyes attempted to stand up, but the wolf's snarl kept him down. The wolf took a step forward. And another. And she realized it was heading toward her.

The wolf stalked toward her, its massive jaw dripping with foamy blood. It was snarling and growling, its blue and green mismatched eyes focused on Thin Man.

Sofia realized what it wanted. Really, she should have stepped aside and let him kill the bastard. But she didn't want that. Not for Lucas.

Slowly, she got to her knees, putting herself between Lucas and Thin Man. "Lucas," she called out. "Are you ... there? Can you hear me?"

"Detective, no!" Reyes cried out. "He can't hear you. Not in this state. He's dangerous!"

This whole thing was absurd, but it was really happening. Lucas had turned into this wolf and now she had to calm him down. "Shhh ... Lucas. It'll be all right. Please. Don't hurt him."

The wolf snapped its jaws at her.

"No, I'm safe, see?" She glanced down at Thin Man, who was still clutching his bleeding nose. "I'm going to arrest him and put him away. It'll be all right."

But it was like the wolf wasn't listening to her. Its focus was on Thin Man. "Lucas!" she shouted, reaching a hand out. "Lucas ..."

Tentatively, she placed a hand on his head. The fur was surprisingly soft and very thick. She rubbed her palm in a soothing manner, all the while her heart beat a mile a minute. *No*, she told herself. *Lucas would never hurt me*. She just knew it.

The wolf went still, then closed its eyes. It let out a soft whine, then lay down. She continued to stroke him, her hands running down its neck and back. She gasped when she felt the fur recede under her fingers.

Slowly, the wolf shrank. Fur disappeared under tanned, muscled skin. She let out a cry of relief and threw her arms around Lucas.

"Detective, please."

She looked up. Reyes stood next to her, offering his hand. But she didn't want to be away from him.

"He needs help, Detective," he said. "Please, let me help him. I know how."

Lucas's skin ran hot under her hands. He was also very still, his breathing shallow. The reality of what happened hit her. *Lucas had turned into a wolf*. It made her head ache, and a wave of nausea passed over her. She took Reyes's offered hand and allowed him to help her up.

"What's going on?" she whispered. "What is he?"

"I'm sorry, Detective."

"Sorry for what?"

She felt a small pinprick in her neck. Her hand immediately went to the spot. "How did you do—" Dizziness buzzed in her head and her legs felt like jelly. Then, the world went dark.

CHAPTER EIGHTEEN

When she woke up, the first thing she thought of was the strange dream she had last night. There were two men threatening to kill her and then Lucas burst through her door and turned into a—

She shot up and glanced around her. Her hands fisted into the unfamiliar scratchy sheets underneath her. A prickle ran up her ramrod-stiff spine. Where the hell was she?

She looked around. The room was like a jail cell. White and sterile. She was sitting on top of a cot, still wearing the same clothes from ... last night? Her head was foggy, and with no windows in this cell, she didn't know what time it was or how long she was out. Fucking Reyes. He'd drugged her.

She got to her feet and took a step forward. Whatever it was he shot into her system was gone now. Of course, now that she was starting to become fully awake, the ache in her jaw bloomed. Yup, yesterday really did happen. Those two men had tried to kill her and Lucas turned into a giant wolf. But what was going on now? And where was Lucas?

"You're awake."

Her body went stiff, and she turned her head toward the door. She didn't even notice there was door until it slid open. A dark-haired man stood in the doorway his arms crossed over his chest. "Sit down, Detective."

"I'd rather stand." She planted her feet apart, her hands flexing at her sides. In her mind, she ran through her options. If she ran fast enough, she could maybe take him by surprise and knock him down, then—

"Don't even think about it." He stepped into the room, and the door slid shut behind him. As he walked closer to her, she gasped.

The man was a little over six feet tall, with broad shoulders and dark hair that had a sprinkling of sliver at the temples. He was handsome, she supposed, but what made her gasp was the familiar features—strong jaw, straight nose, and the dark slashes of his eyebrows, as well as the confident way he conducted himself. His eyes were green, though, and not the same as Lucas's mismatched ones, but this man could be him in a few decades.

"Where am I?" she asked. "And where's Lucas?"

The only reaction she got was a raised brow, and his gaze pierced into her. She felt stripped and naked underneath his gaze, like he was peering into her very soul. "He's none of your concern."

"I want to see him," she insisted. "I want to know he's safe."

The flash of surprise on his face softened his features. "You've been drugged and locked up, and the first thing you want to know is where Lucas is?"

"If you've hurt him—

"Don't be stupid, I would never hurt my son."

Son. But she already knew that. "What's going on? Is he ... sick? He turned into a ..."

"A wolf," he said. "Or as we like to call ourselves, Lycans."

"L-Lycans?"

"I would explain it to you, except you're not going to remember anything."

Not remember anything? "What the fuck are you talking about?" she snarled.

"It really doesn't matter, Detective. We're going to erase your memory and you won't remember a thing."

"This is insane!" she cried. "You can't do that!"

"Oh, yes we can. We've done it lots of times," he said. "You'll forget about what happened last night and you'll never see Lucas again."

His words washed over her. She would never see Lucas again, might even never remember him. She sank down on the cot as her knees turned to jelly. They'd imprisoned her, which meant they weren't concerned at all that they were detaining an officer of the law. Her mind flashed back to those other cases. The ones where the witnesses couldn't recall what happened. *They'd done it lots of times.* And now they were going to do it to her.

The sound of the door sliding open and a gasp made her look up.

"Papa!"

A woman entered the room and approached them. She knelt down in front of her, and Sofia blinked. "Sofia," she began, placing her hands over hers. "I'm Adrianna. Lucas's twin sister."

His twin. Of course. Her features were slightly different

and more feminine, but the eyes were the same. One green and one blue, just like Lucas's, but mirrored.

"Adrianna," the man—Lucas's and Adrianna's dad—barked.

"Papa, no!" she protested. "Sofia ... you care for my brother, right?"

She nodded, unable to speak.

"I think he feels the same way about you," she said. "You wouldn't hurt him, right? Or expose his—our secret?"

"Of course not!" If anyone found out Lucas—and apparently, his family—could turn into wolves, the world would be in chaos. And who knew what the government would do. Probably take them in and conduct experiments. She didn't want Lucas locked up in a cage. "I swear, I won't tell anyone. I just don't want ..." *Don't want to lose him.*

"You calmed him down," Adrianna said. "You stopped him from killing that other man. And brought him back from his bloodlust."

She remained silent, not knowing what to say.

"Adrianna, she already—"

"I said, no, Papa!" Adrianna stood up and poked a finger at his chest. "You don't always know what's best."

"I am Alpha here," he warned. "And what I say is law."

"What about Lucas?" she retorted. "When he gets back, how will he react when he finds out you've erased her memory? Do you think he's just going to back down?"

"He will because he's going to be Alpha soon. Lucas knows his place and his responsibilities to his family and his clan."

The door slid open again. "Stop fighting, both of you."

Sofia's head snapped toward the third visitor. It was

another woman, also dark-haired like Adrianna, but petite. She made a beeline toward Sofia, ignoring the man's death-stare. "You must be Sofia. I'm Frankie. Lucas's mother."

She tried to speak, but couldn't. All she could do was stare at her eyes. Just like Lucas's and Adrianna's. "Oh." She was also drop-dead gorgeous and didn't look like she had two grown children.

"Frankie—"

"Grant," she warned, then turned back to Sofia. "I'm sorry about my husband," she said. "He can be very stubborn."

"Get out of here, both of you." Grant gestured to the two women. "I'm Alpha here."

Despite the fact that she was half a foot shorter than her husband, Frankie Anderson went toe-to-toe with him. She straightened her shoulders and put her hands on her hips. "And I'm his *mother*."

Grant raised his hands in frustration. "Fine, go on. Do as you please."

Frankie turned back to Sofia. "Sofia, I want to believe you, I really do. But what you've seen ... no one can ever know. You understand, right?"

"I do. But Lucas ... he's all right, right?"

She nodded. "He's somewhere safe. What happened last night, that wasn't normal, not for our kind. We know how to control our animals, which is why we've kept our secret for centuries. But Lucas, he wasn't in control. And I think it was because he was protecting you. He must care for you a great deal."

Frankie's words slowly sank into her. Lucas cared for her?

"And I know you care for him too, right?"

"I do." It was the truth. The feelings she had for him she'd never had for anyone else. "If ... if erasing my memory will protect him, then maybe ... maybe you should do it." It wouldn't be so bad. She wouldn't remember him anyway. Not remember all those times together. Of him in the kitchen. Teasing her. Making love until dawn.

Frankie smiled. "Detective, if we take you to him, do you promise you'll keep our secret?"

"Yes." Hope bloomed in her chest.

"Frankie!" Grant protested, which earned him a sharp look from his wife. "We can't trust her."

"We can still erase your memory," Frankie said. "But ... I think you and Lucas should talk first."

"That's a great idea," Adrianna said, her eyes sparkling. "Papa, will you allow Sofia to meet with Lucas first? Then you can decide what to do."

"Do I have a choice?" That earned him a hug from his daughter.

"Can I see him now?" Sofia asked. "Is he here?"

"He's far away, but we can take you to him."

"Frankie, we need to ask permission first," Grant said. "You know she can't just walk into another territory."

"I'll take care of it," Frankie said. "Will you cooperate, Sofia?"

She nodded her head vigorously. "I'll do anything. Please. I need to see Lucas."

Frankie's face shone, her mismatched eyes reminding her so much of Lucas's. "Then you'll see him soon."

CHAPTER NINETEEN

"You finally awake?"

The rough voice was like a saw grating into Lucas's head. For a second, he thought he was seventeen again. The bed he was in was familiar, as well as the scent of the other man in the room. *Sawdust and coffee.*

He opened his eyes, but everything was blurry. After a few blinks, his vision focused into a pair of familiar stark green eyes. "Austin?"

Austin Forrest's mouth turned up at the corners. "It's been a while, Lucas. You never visit anymore."

His head pounded like someone had taken a sledgehammer to it. This whole scenario felt like a dream. Or déjà vu. Of the first time he was here after he had shifted in bloodlust when Kevin Hall—

He shot to his feet, but he overestimated his motor skills and fell forward. Austin caught him and propped him up. "Whoa, slow down. Where's the fire?"

"Sofia," he croaked. His throat felt scratchy and parched. "I have to make sure ... she's okay and—" His wolf was weakened too, but it whined at him, its claws scratching at him and reaching for the surface.

Austin pushed him down on the bed. "Calm down, Lucas. Take a deep breath. Remember what Pa taught you."

Find something to ground you, Jackson Forrest had told him all those years ago. *A memory or a scent can help you stay in control of your body. You need to show your wolf who's in charge.*

It was good thing he and his wolf were both too weak, because the only scent he could think of was Sofia's and it was making him even more anxious. "Austin, I need my phone. Please. Call my father and—"

"He says he's got everything under control." Austin's voice was calm, and so very much like his father's. "Is Sofia your ... the friend who was with you when you shifted in bloodlust?"

Bloodlust. No wonder his head felt like it was splitting in two and he couldn't remember a damn thing. "Yes. Those men were attacking her, and I tried to help her."

"She's fine."

Both of them turned toward the doorway. "Zac." It was strange to see his friend here, but he wasn't hallucinating. "Tell me what—"

"She's safe, Lucas." Zac walked toward them, hands in his pockets. "It's been a couple of hours since Reyes called the security team. Everything was cleaned up, don't worry. No one will know you were there or that anything happened."

"I don't care about that or that bastard," he spat. As far as he was concerned, that man who tried to kill Sofia got what he deserved. "But Sofia—"

"Is still out," he said. "Reyes had to give her a sleeping potion and they took her back to Fenrir."

"To the basement, right?" But it was a rhetorical question. The basement of the Fenrir Corporation building housed a variety of people, but mostly it was those who had sought to harm them. "They haven't given her the forgetting potion, have they?"

"I don't know, I haven't heard from Astrid yet. She's busy helping with the cleanup." Zac said. "But you know what we have to do."

Yes, he did. They would have to make sure she didn't remember seeing him shift into his wolf. Thankfully, the potion they used would only make her forget about the last few hours.

And then what?

Could they go on as they had before? Forever hiding what he was from her, and dosing her with forgetting potion whenever he shifted accidentally?

Then there was his wolf. He had saved her from those guys, but who would save her from *him*? What if he shifted in bloodlust again and he lost control and went after her?

His wolf growled in protest, as if to tell him that it would never do that.

But then again, he never thought he'd ever kill another living creature, not after what happened with Kevin Hall.

"Lucas? Do you need to lie down?" Austin asked.

"No." His mind was clear. Sofia was safe and she could move on with her life, without him. The thought slashed a knife through his chest and made it hard to breathe. "Why am I here?"

"Your parents thought that after what happened, this was

the best place for you," Zac explained. "The Alpha agreed and gave you permission to come. I offered to accompany you in case you had any questions when you woke up."

So, he was back here in the Shenandoah Valley after thirteen years. After what happened to Kevin Hall and Jeffrey Smith, Frankie and Grant Anderson decided that he needed help controlling his animal, and so they sent him here.

And Lucas was glad they did. Jackson Forrest, the Alpha of Shenandoah, ran a special program for Lycans who couldn't control their wolves. He'd been doing it for decades and helped many of their kind, saving them from having to be put down. The months Lucas spent at the ranch had helped him tremendously, and he hadn't shifted in bloodlust after that. At least, not until recently, when the mages had attacked them and tried to hurt Adrianna.

"I need to get up. Stretch my legs and ..." He glanced around. "Is everyone here?"

Austin chuckled. "Of course. Grams and Momma are downstairs with breakfast, and Pa's out with your Grampa Noah checking the fences. Only Jack still lives here, and Katie lives in San Francisco now, finishing up her PhD."

"Oh." It really had been a long time. Katie and Jack had been young pre-teens when he first came here. Now they were both full-grown women.

"C'mon, let's go see Grams and Momma. I'm sure they'd both be thrilled to see you."

As they filed out the room and headed downstairs, that feeling of déjà vu washed over him again. The two-story country-style house hadn't changed a bit, even though it had been over a decade since he'd been here. Even the wooden bannisters felt the same under his fingers, as was the smell.

Wood, grass, earth, mixed with the various scents of its residents. When he walked through the kitchen door, it was like stepping back in time, as it looked exactly like it did thirteen years ago.

"Lucas!" Lily Forrest ran over to him and enveloped him in a big hug. "My, you've grown so much! I can't believe you're here!"

"You're looking good, Lily." She must be in her seventies now, but she looked at least a decade younger, though her hair had gone completely white. "I'm sorry I haven't visited," he said sheepishly.

"Hello, Lucas."

He looked to the other person in the kitchen. Jordan Forrest didn't look like she'd aged at all. She still had the same slim frame, straight dark hair, and laughing hazel eyes. "Jordan," he greeted as he was once again brought in for a hug. "It's nice to see you."

Her smile was warm. "I can't believe you were the same skinny seventeen-year-old kid who first came to us."

"He's definitely all grown up," Austin chuckled.

"I wish I was here under better circumstances," he said.

"You're here, that's all that matters," Lily declared. "Zac told us what happened."

"Don't worry, we're going to help you," Jordan said. "Jackson will make it better."

"All you need is some fresh air and good, hard work," Lily said.

"And for you two to stop coddling him," added a stern voice.

Lucas whipped around to look at the man standing in the doorway. Jackson Forrest looked just as he did all those years ago, the only signs of aging were a new wrinkle or two on his forehead. The tall, hulking man strode forward with the confidence of someone a fraction of his age, and his green eyes were as keen as ever. "Hello, Lucas."

He grabbed the hand his old mentor had offered, gripping it and pulling him forward in a hug. His wolf recognized the scent and bent its head in respect. This was the Alpha of Shenandoah, after all, and even his broken wolf knew not to cross him.

As they released each other, Lucas glanced at the small figure by the doorway. "Jack?"

"Hey, Lucas? What's shaking?"

He could hardly believe this girl—woman, he corrected himself—was Jacqueline Forrest. She'd been barely a teen when he got here, and now she was all grown. He smiled to himself as, she hadn't changed much. She had been a tomboy growing up, preferring the more masculine nickname and wearing pants and sneakers instead of dresses. Now, she was wearing worn overalls, boots, and her long, dark hair was pulled back in a ponytail and hidden under a Stetson hat. A streak of dirt marred her cheek, and she grinned up at him impishly.

"Noah's still outside. Said he's going to finish one more row of posts before he comes in for a break," Jackson said, referring to Lucas's grandfather. Noah was a Lone Wolf but found his way to Shenandoah a few years ago and stayed ever since.

"Jackson," Lucas began. "Thank you for welcoming me into your territory." He'd almost forgotten his manners, though he knew the Alpha of Shenandoah wasn't much for formalities. "However, I can't stay. I need to go back."

Jackson and Jordan looked at each other in surprise. "You know, you're welcome here anytime," Jordan said.

"You're a grown man, Lucas. And soon you'll be Alpha," Jackson added. "I can't stop you from doing what you want. But I hope you'll consider staying."

"At least until you're better," Jordan said.

Better? The word was like a bitter pill, stuck in his throat. Maybe they were right. He should stay here, far away from New York before he could hurt anyone. Before he could hurt Sofia.

"Are you hungry?" Lily asked, breaking the tension in the air.

"I am, actually." He hadn't eaten in almost twenty-four hours.

The older woman's face broke into a smile. "I made your favorites. Biscuits and sausage gravy." His stomach actually growled, which made Lily let out a delighted laugh. "I'll make you a plate now."

He glanced over at Zac, meeting his gaze. His friend gave him a weak smile, and sat down on the table as Lily fussed over him too. Maybe food would be good. A full stomach would help him forge out his next move.

———

"Sitting in an office for eight hours a day turned you back into a greenhorn, Anderson?"

Lucas scowled at Austin, who was grinning at him. "Shut up, Forrest. Or I'll shove this hammer up your—"

"Hold on." The other man held his hands up. "You're the one who wanted to help."

"Yeah, yeah." He tossed the hammer aside. Repairing and building fences had been one of the many chores he did when he had stayed for his own rehabilitation. While most people thought it was just about pounding posts into the ground, there was much more to it than that. If he used too much of his brute Lycan strength, he could bury the entire thing in the ground, but if he didn't use enough, it would fall over and he'd have to start all over again. It was a lesson in patience, one he had learned over a long, hot summer. Really, he should know how to do this, but it had been a long time since he fixed a fence, and the cold, frozen ground wasn't making it easy to gauge how much strength he could use.

"Maybe you need a break," Austin said.

"You need a break, *old man*."

"Old?" Austin said in a mock-hurt voice. "I'm not even forty. And you're the one who's gone all soft."

"Will you two stop yammering and get to work?" Jack waved the metal shears in her hand menacingly at them. "It's almost dark, and I wanna get home."

"So bossy." Austin ruffled his sister's hair, which only seemed to annoy her.

"You heard her." Lucas picked up the discarded hammer.

"Need me to hold your hand, princess?"

Lucas lifted his middle finger toward Austin, which earned him a laugh. Their banter brought back a lot of good memories, and he realized how much he missed this place. It had been his sanctuary, a second home to him when he was troubled. Jackson had been so patient with him, even though Lucas had been resistant to the whole rehabilitation thing. Plus, everyone here felt like family. Austin was like the big brother he never had and was someone who could understand the pressures of what it was like to be heir apparent, since he was next in line to be Alpha after Jackson. He never judged him and shared his owns doubts and apprehensions about the responsibilities that came with being future Alpha and the long shadows their fathers cast.

"You boys done yet?" Noah asked as he approached them.

He was glad his grandfather had found a place here too. Noah was a man of few words, but the look he gave Lucas conveyed love and concern.

"Almost," Austin answered. "Let's finish up and head back."

"Sure."

Lucas tried to take his time doing the work, not just because he wanted to do things right, but because he was almost dreading being idle. The work kept him and his wolf busy, though every moment he had to spare to think was spent on Sofia. He desperately wanted to know how she was. She was alive at least. But what would happen now? If he wanted to keep her safe, he would have to tell her they couldn't see each other anymore. But the more he thought about her, about all the times they'd been together, he wasn't sure if he had the strength to give her up.

When they finished their work, they all headed back to the ranch on foot. Jackson, Noah, and Jack had all hurried ahead, probably eager to get cleaned up and have dinner. He and Austin hung behind.

"So," Austin began as they trudged across the field, "Who's Sofia?"

The sound of her name made him stumble, but he recovered quickly. Putting one foot in front of the other, he just kept walking ahead and remained silent. Maybe Austin would drop it.

"You were calling her name a lot while you were sleeping."

Maybe not.

Austin continued. "And she was the first person you thought of when you woke up."

He kept his stare focused ahead, trying to see if the ranch house was in sight. They were still too far out, and the only thing he could see in the darkness were trees and the rolling hills of the Shenandoah Valley.

"Is she like Caroline?"

The question made him stop walking. Austin knew everything, of course. They all did, save for Katie and Jack. It was one of the conditions of being accepted into the rehab program. "No," he found himself saying. "She's not like Caroline at all." Caroline was beautiful in an ethereal way—unreachable and cool. He thought himself in love with her, but she never saw him as anything other than a childhood friend. Once, he thought she would have been the perfect Lupa, someone who could be a good partner when he became Alpha. Maybe he had been more in love with the thought of her, or having something his own parents had—a perfect partnership, complementing each other's strengths and weaknesses.

"Then what *is* she like?"

"What's the point of this, Austin?" he snarled. Austin was torturing him with all these questions. He didn't want to think about her. What he couldn't have.

"Hey, calm down, Lucas." Austin stopped and pivoted,

facing him and placed a hand on his shoulder. "I just want to talk. To know more about your Sofia."

"She's not my Sofia." *And she never will be.* He pushed Austin's hand away. "She's human, and she can never know about us."

"Now that's just not true and you know it. There are plenty of humans in the know, like those who marry Lycans."

Lucas sidestepped and marched away from him, his teeth grinding together so hard that his jaw hurt. He heard Austin's footsteps behind him, running up to keep pace. Thankfully, the other man didn't say another word, seemingly content to just keep pace. Finally, he saw the ranch up ahead, and all the lights were on, the house like a shining beacon.

"If you care for her so much, then why are you just letting her go?" Austin said in a quiet voice.

God, he just wanted to get inside and lock himself up in his room, away from Austin's nagging. "They've probably already erased her memory."

"Lucas—"

"And the best thing I can do is let her go and let her lead a normal life."

A hand grabbed Lucas's shoulder, spinning him around. "And what about what she wants?"

"She won't want me when she finds out what I am."

Austin's eyes focused somewhere over his shoulder, then turned back to him. "Are you sure about that?"

"Yes."

"In that case, you're an idiot, Lucas."

Before he knew it, Austin whirled him back toward the house. "Wha—"

"Take a good look, dumbass."

"Look where? I—"

His chest squeezed so tight he could hardly breathe. Maybe it was the lack of oxygen that was making him see things. Because standing on the back-porch steps was Sofia. Even in the moonlight, he could see her beautiful face and the myriad of expressions that flashed through them—worry, surprise, apprehension—and finally, as their eyes met, pure happiness.

"Lucas!" She was running toward him, her arms wide open as they crashed into each other. He didn't even realize he'd been running to her too. His arms encircled her, crushing her to him and breathing in that delicious scent of hers as he nuzzled her hair.

"You're safe," she murmured. "You're okay."

He pulled back, brushing the locks of hair away from her face. Her eyes were shiny with tears. "Me? What about you? Those men—" He'd almost forgotten about those two men who broke into her home. The bruise on her jaw, however, was a clear reminder. Anger rose in him—at them, and at himself for failing to protect her from getting hurt in the first place. "Were they trying to rob you?"

"It doesn't matter." She wrapped her arms around him.

He stiffened. "What are you doing here? *How* did you get here? Do you remember what happened? Did—"

"I do," she interrupted. "I remember everything. They tried to take it away but—" She choked and put a hand over her mouth. "We should talk, Lucas."

He agreed. "Austin, I—" But his friend was gone. He must have slipped into the house quietly. "Let's go for a walk." He took her hand and pulled her along. When they were far enough from the house, he spoke first. "What happened? How did you get here?"

"The last thing I remembered was seeing you on the floor of my apartment." And then she relayed the events of what brought her here. As he suspected, they had taken her to the basement of Fenrir. He winced when she described meeting his father and then Adrianna and his mother. He smiled to himself, glad they were there to defend her.

"And then I was on my way here. Your mom even lent me her jet," Sofia continued. "And also, Astrid came with me. She explained everything to me, about ... you guys."

"Lycans."

"Yes." She wrinkled her nose. "It's still confusing to me, about how it all works. Plus, she told me she and her siblings were all different too and that magic exists."

"Yes, witches and the warlocks are real too. And others. We have enemies, too." He wanted to tell her about the mages, but it might be too much for her. Also, he realized that they had been walking for a long time and that she was shivering, despite being bundled up in a thick wool coat. As a Lycan, his body adjusted to the cold easily, which is why he was wearing only a shirt and jeans even though it was late winter. He steered her toward the nearest building—a barn that housed most of the heavy farm equipment used in the spring and summer.

As he opened the door and gestured for her to go first, he asked, "Do you believe what she told you?"

"I watched you turn into a wolf and then back again. How could I not believe it?" She let out a sigh as they entered the warm barn.

He paused, trying to figure out how to phrase the question he wanted to ask her. "And did she tell you about me?"

"Your sister implied that what happened wasn't normal for your kind. When I asked Astrid about it, she said that was your story to tell." She turned to him, her slate gray eyes clear even in the faint light. "Will you tell me, Lucas?"

His throat closed up as the memories began to flood into his mind. He considered shutting down or telling her it was none of her business. That was his knee-jerk reaction whenever anyone tried to bring up the past. But when he stared down at her face, he couldn't stop himself from telling her. "When Lycans shift, we're fully aware of what's happening and we can control our animal, or sometimes let it act on instinct. In the end, we're always the one in charge." He paused. "But not when bloodlust happens."

"Bloodlust?" she echoed.

"No one's really sure what it is or why it happens. It's been described in our records, but never really seen or studied. In fact, it's only been observed in one Lycan in the last few decades."

"Just one?"

"Yes, one. Me." The silence between them echoed as they both contemplated his words. Lucas reached out to brush an imaginary speck of dust on her cheek. "One of our doctors told me that it might be because both my parents are Alphas. Or because of what happened when I was a kid."

Realization swept over her face. "When you were kidnapped."

"The kidnappers—they hurt Adrianna. They hit her when she wouldn't stop crying, and then one of them ... he looked at her in a way that made my flesh crawl."

She swallowed audibly, and her body stiffened. "You saved her, right?"

He nodded. "I shifted into bloodlust. I was ten, and it was virtually unheard of for anyone that young to shift. Whether it was because of trauma or my genes—I don't know, it just happened. I was still small, so I only tore them up."

"And your family covered it up."

"Yes, that's what we do, to protect our secret." He waited for her to ask what he knew what was on her mind. To his surprise, she didn't even say the name. So, he decided to lay it all out for her. "Kevin Hall."

"You don't have to—"

"I do. And if you hate me after this, then I understand."

"Lucas—"

"Let me finish," he pleaded. When she nodded, he continued. "Caroline and I had been friends since childhood. She's one of us. And, well, I followed her around like a puppy throughout high school, but she only had eyes for Kevin Hall. They were together all of senior year. Then the night of the lake cabin party happened. I was inside with everyone else, and Jeffrey Smith, Kevin's best friend, pulled me aside and said I had to come with him. I followed him out back, and that's where I saw them."

The memory of that night was burned into his mind, and he struggled to continue. "She was on the ground, crying, pleading with Kevin to stop hurting her. I tried to get to her but Jeffrey held me back. Then Kevin began to scream at me. He ... he said Caroline was pregnant. And that she had told him about our secret. Even shifted in front of him." Apparently, Caroline thought they were True Mates and she had been excited to let him know. However, she was obviously incorrect as she didn't heal from Kevin's beating right away and their daughter turned out to be fully human. "He called her a disgusting animal and that he could never have gotten her pregnant, and so he thought I was the father. Then he kicked her again, and I lost it. I shifted in bloodlust, and that was the last thing I remember before waking up here. Adrianna and Zac were at the party, but they felt it when I shifted. They described it like a shockwave their wolves couldn't ignore. They found me and saw that Kevin and Jeffrey were ... on the ground. So yes, I did hurt them. I killed Kevin Hall."

He turned around, not wanting to look at her. Not wanting to see the horror in her eyes.

"Lucas." A gentle hand landed on his shoulder. "Lucas, don't turn away. Look at me." When he didn't move, she stepped around and faced him. "You did it to protect Caroline and yourself. It was self-defense." She took a deep breath. "Stop beating yourself up over it. If you didn't know that she would have ... I mean, who knows what would have happened?"

He let out a bitter laugh. "It still doesn't change the fact that I'm dangerous. This place ... this is where my parents brought me after the incident. It's a place where broken wolves are given a last chance."

"And it worked, right?"

"For a while. But then ..." Then the mages came and threatened Adrianna. And those men threatened Sofia. "I'm losing control. I don't know what will happen ... if you ... if something happened to you, I wouldn't be able to forgive myself." Hell, he wouldn't be able to keep living. "We can't ... you shouldn't be around me."

She inhaled a sharp breath. "No. Lucas. You wouldn't hurt me. You didn't last night and you won't ever hurt me."

"But—"

"No, Lucas." She gripped his forearms. "Listen to me. You protected me. Those men, they were going to kill me. But you were there and you saved me." Her eyes, now more blue than gray in the scant light, were full of emotion. "I won't let you take my memories away. I swear to God, if you even try to use that voodoo magic shit on me, I'm going to kick your ass."

The corners of his mouth tugged up. "I believe you would."

"This is who you are, Lucas." She took his hands into hers. "And you're not a bad person. I don't even believe that wolf inside you is bad. The only times you shifted in blood-lust was when you had no other choice and had to protect others. Your sister. Caroline."

"You," he added.

"Yes." She took a step forward and wrapped her arms around his waist. "Please, don't let them take my memories of you away. I can't—"

She choked on her words, and he felt the wetness of her tears on his shirt. "Sofia, no." He pulled her away gently, then brushed the tears away. "Don't cry. Please don't cry. You don't know what it does to me." Unable to bear seeing her like this, he leaned down and kissed her.

He meant for it to be soothing, to comfort her. But when she responded so eagerly and her tongue swiped across his lips, the spark inside him lit into a full-blown flame. God, he'd missed her. Missed the taste of her, smell of her, feel of her in his arms. He lifted her up, wrapping her legs around him.

Carrying her over to a corner, he lay her down on the soft pile of hay.

She giggled against his mouth. "A roll in the hay, Lucas?" But she was already unbuttoning her coat.

He grinned down at her as he whipped his shirt off. "I can't think of a better activity right now."

The rest of their clothes were stripped off, though she kept her coat underneath her as a makeshift blanket. He kissed a path over her flat belly, then spread her legs so he could taste her. Her arousal mixed with her natural scent was a heady combination, and he stroked his hardened cock to ease the pain as he licked and sucked her to orgasm.

"Lucas." Her voice was raspy with need. "Inside me. Now."

He didn't need a second invite. Placing himself between her legs, he nudged at her entrance. She inhaled and her chest rose as he began to fill her, pushing all the way in until he was fully lodged in her. God, she was so tight and hot and perfect. She let out a whimper when he moved his hips and then clenched around him.

"Sofia." He captured her mouth again, this time his lips ravaging hers, seeking her surrender. She opened up to him letting his tongue sweep inside to devour her. He felt her hips pushing up at him and knew what she wanted. He too, wanted that friction, that feeling of sliding in and out of her. But he wanted to take things slow and savor her.

She let out a gasp as he trailed his mouth down her neck, searching for all her sensitive spots, licking and sucking at her soft flesh and moving down to her breast. Slowly, he moved. Teased her by pulling back and then thrusting into her, grinding his hips against her. As his mouth drew in a nipple, he continued his deliberate movements, drawing out gasps and moans and sighs from her.

Her fingers dug into his shoulders as his pleasure built up. "More, Lucas." She raked her nails down his back, her hips urging him to move faster.

"God, you're beautiful," he said as he looked down at her. He kept his gaze on her as he rocked his hips, picking up his pace. He reached down and found her clit, then plucked at the bud. This sent her over the edge, and he watched her face twist in ecstasy as she came, crying his name and squeezed around him. He grunted, trying to get ahold of himself. *Not yet.*

Though she was coming down from her orgasm, her thighs tightened around him, urging him deeper and faster. He obliged, that sweet friction building up his own orgasm. His thrusts became frenzied, pushing harder and deeper. It was all too much—her sweet pussy milking him, her cries of pleasure, and her scent intensifying as she was nearing her peak. When she cried out his name again, he let go, releasing and filling her with his hot come. He gave a few more short thrusts, trying to prolong his pleasure and coaxing another smaller orgasm from her.

He collapsed on top of her, strength draining from his body. He felt spent, but also, at peace. Before he closed his eyes, a lingering thought echoed in his mind. *So this is what it was like to make love.*

CHAPTER TWENTY

WHEN SOFIA WOKE UP THE NEXT DAY, SHE FELT SORE, IN a delicious way. There was an ache between her legs that made her feel wicked. Hell, everything about Lucas made her feel wicked.

They had a quick nap after their little *roll in the hay*, but she didn't want to go back yet. She wanted to have Lucas to herself, just for a little while, but also, she was embarrassed because she didn't even make small talk with the people in the house. The two women in the house greeted her warmly, and Astrid had mentioned she was related to them in some way, which is why she volunteered to come here. She had introduced herself, but when Astrid announced that Lucas was outside, she quickly forgot her manners and rushed out of the back door.

And so, they stayed in the barn, wrapped up in each other's arms, content just to be in each other's company. She had so many questions about them and their kind, and he answered as patiently as he could. When it was late enough, they snuck into the house quietly and crept up to his room.

Lucas tried to get frisky with her again, but she pushed his hands away, afraid that the people inside would hear them. He had laughed and told her that all the rooms were sealed and soundproofed, as many Lycan parents took precautions because of enhanced hearing and smell. Though she felt mollified by his explanation, she did her best to keep quiet the entire night. Lucas, on the other hand, seemed to enjoy coaxing her to scream, and he succeeded in making her moan his name loudly in ecstasy.

"Good morning, sweetheart." Lucas's lips were pressed against her neck. His voice was rough with sleep, sending little vibrations across her skin.

"Hmmmm." She twisted around to face him, her palms immediately going to his jaw. He'd always been clean-shaven, but now he had two days' worth of stubble around his face. "I like this look."

His mismatched eyes danced with mischief as he rubbed his jaw on her cheek, making her shriek. "Like that?"

"Ha!" She pushed at his chest, which only made him hold on to her tighter.

"It's early," she said, looking outside. The sun had just finished rising, bathing the room in early morning light.

"Actually, it's late," he chuckled. "Jackson's probably been out for at least two hours and breakfast will be ready soon."

"I can't believe you spent a couple of months here, doing chores." He had explained to her about his rehabilitation and how the people here helped him.

"Believe it. I hated it at first, you know? But it was good for me."

"I still can't picture it." Lucas steering cattle. Riding

horses. Using a lasso. Wearing a cowboy hat. Or maybe he was shirtless. Yeah, that was good. Lucas, his bare chest and torso, working under the sun. Baling hay or whatever the hell one did with hay. Sweat pouring down his perfect six pack and—

"Stop that." His nostrils flared and his eyes darkened.

"Stop what?" she asked innocently.

"You're thinking about sex."

"What? How the hell—"

"I can smell you." His nostrils flared. "I can always smell you when you get wet."

"You do not!" She sat up, grabbed a pillow and slammed it against his head. He laughed as he batted it away and then grabbed her wrists to pull her on top of him. "Oh, my God, you really can, can't you?"

"I can." He licked at her neck. "And you smell delicious."

"Hmmm ... and so do—"

There was a knock on the door, and they both froze, as if they were teenagers being caught in the act.

"Breakfast!" Astrid's muffled voice sounded cheery, even through the thick wood paneling. "You know Lily doesn't like late risers."

"We'll come down in a minute," Lucas called. He turned to her. "She's not kidding. Lily will put the food away in an hour, and then we'll be hungry till lunch."

They quickly dressed and then made their way down. She didn't bring any clothes with her, though it seemed someone had been kind enough to leave her a shirt and a pair of sweats in the room for her to use. She was a bit apprehensive as they entered the dining room, though Lucas's hand squeezing hers made her relax. When they entered, however, the room was already filled with people, and all heads turned to them.

A woman entered through another doorway, carrying a plate of eggs. "Good morning, you two. Glad to see you're both up." She put the tray down and then walked over to them. "Come and sit down, Lucas, Sofia."

Sofia remembered the younger of the two women she met last night. Jordan. According to Astrid, she was the "Lupa" or head female of this group of wolves. "Thank you, Jordan," she said as they were led to the two empty chairs near the head of the table. Her head snapped toward the man sitting at the end, his intense green eyes boring straight into her.

"You didn't meet everyone else," Jordan began. "You already know Lily, and Zac, and Astrid of course. But that man scowling at you is my husband, Jackson Forrest, Alpha of the Shenandoah clan."

"Jordan," Jackson warned. "You—"

"Don't worry, he doesn't bite." A corner of her mouth quirked up. "Much."

Sofia smothered a nervous laugh.

"That's Austin, my son," she nodded at the man sitting on Jackson's right. He was the spitting image of his father, except for the platinum blond hair. He grinned at her then shot a knowing smile to Lucas.

Jordan continued. "That's Jack, my youngest daughter," she gestured to the young woman at the end of the table, who smiled and waved at her. "We have a middle daughter, Katie, but she lives in California. She won't mind you borrowing her clothes."

Lucas placed a hand on the shoulder of the older white-haired man next to the two empty chairs Jordan led them to. "And this is my grandfather. Noah."

"Nice to meet you, sir."

"Call me Noah," he said in a gruff voice. He didn't look like what a grandfather would look like, certainly not like her *Pappoús*. He was probably Giorgios's age, but he was much bulkier, with wide shoulders and thickly-muscled arms that was covered in tattoos. He looked nothing like Lucas, though he had the same confident air.

"Noah." She repeated, then sat down next to him. The older man gave her a nod, but didn't say anything.

"Well, dig in," Lily said, breaking the silence. "Before the food goes cold."

Breakfast was a surprisingly lively affair. Everyone praised Lily's cooking, and Sofia devoured an embarrassing amount of food, at least for her. But, apparently, Lycans ate their body weight in food, and they demolished the meal in no time.

"Lucas," Jackson began as the plates were being cleared. "Your father and I have been talking about the mages. And the preparations we need to do to stop them."

"Daric's already strengthened the protection wards and spells around the property," Lily said.

"And you know we will be ready, wherever the fight happens."

Sofia frowned. What were they talking about?

As if sensing her confusion, Lucas took her hand and squeezed it. "Remember what I said about enemies? Mages are like witches and warlocks."

"But evil," Astrid added. "Very, very evil. They can do all

sorts of things, like control people and make spells that can harm us."

She gasped. "Harm you? Why?"

"Because they want us dead and they want to rule the world," Zac said. "We, and the witches and warlocks, are the only ones in their way."

"Do you remember that first night in Blood Moon?"

"You mean, your stag party?" she asked in a teasing voice.

He smiled, but it didn't reach his eyes. "Right. They attacked that night and tried to kidnap me and Adrianna."

She sucked in a breath. "That's what you were hiding in the other room? Not some bachelor party debauchery?"

Zac shook his head. "Yeah, sorry. That was the best I could come up with."

Jackson cleared his throat, then turned to Lucas. "Did you decide on what you want to do yet? Like I said, you're welcome to stay until you ... feel better."

"I'd like to go back to New York," he said. "As soon as possible."

The other man's eyes narrowed. "Like I said, you're a grown man, and I can't stop you."

"Can't you stay one more day?" Lily asked.

"I have to check with the security office," Astrid piped up. "And make the arrangements."

"One more day won't make a difference."

Lucas's head whipped to the man beside Sofia. He seemed surprised at his grandfather's words.

Noah grunted. "It's been a while, Lucas. And I could use some help. Fences are almost done, and hopefully we're done with the snow and they'll stay up until the next winter storm knocks them down."

Sofia looked up at Lucas. He seemed conflicted, so she squeezed his hand. "Noah's right. One more day won't make a difference."

"Okay. One more day," he said. "We really do need to mend that fence."

After breakfast, she and Lucas followed Jackson, Austin, Jordan, Jack, and Noah outside. They walked far out to the edges of the property, where the half-constructed fencing was. Sofia wanted to help too, and Jordan came along because she said she was tired of being cooped up in her home office in the attic. Apparently, the Lupa of Shenandoah was also a respected scientist in the field of biochemistry and worked as a consultant for a number of companies, including Fenrir. As the others set out to finish the work, she and Jordan sat on the sidelines.

"I wanted to help," Sofia huffed.

"I know it seems easy," Jordan said. "But it's not. There's much more to it than just pounding sticks in the ground. Believe me, you're helping by keeping out of the way."

"And what are we supposed to do?"

"I don't know. Admire the view?" Jordan's hazel eyes immediately went to her husband. Jackson had taken off his shirt, showing off his lean, muscled frame.

With the exception of Jack, all of them had shucked off their shirts. Her mouth went dry as she watched Lucas, his arms raised as he brought the mallet down on a post. She wanted to lick every inch of Lucas's exposed, sweaty skin and bury her nose in the crook of his neck so she could take in his scent. Jesus, were all Lycan men hot and built? Even Noah was hot, a silver fox, as they say. She found herself admiring the way the muscles on Austin's naked back bunched as he moved, which earned her a disapproving, audible growl from Lucas. She quickly averted her eyes, but not before she saw Lucas toss a shirt toward Austin.

A few hours later, when Jackson called for a break, Lucas strode to her, giving her a possessive kiss before sitting down next to her. They sat in silent contemplation, admiring the rolling hills of the countryside.

"I can see why you like it here." It was so beautiful and quiet. She could imagine that in the spring it would be even more lovely. Out here, she could forget everything. Forget about the grittiness of the city and what was waiting for them. She didn't have to think about her life, about Bianchi and— "Lucas!" She turned to him. "I almost forgot why I called you that night. Back in New York. I have to talk to you about—"

"Shhh." Lucas was frowning at her. "Can we just wait until we get to New York?" He sighed. "I just ... I just need this time."

She stopped. Someone was trying to frame him, and she needed to protect him. But he'd also gone through a traumatic experience shifting in bloodlust, so she wanted to make sure he was better. She decided it could wait. In any case, by now, Bushnell would have checked out Lucas's alibi and then there was nothing to worry about. "All right. We won't talk about it."

They worked along the property line finishing up the fence. By late afternoon it was all done, and they all went back to the house for some leisure time. Sofia and Lucas joined Lily in the kitchen to help prepare for dinner, and they ate another huge meal. Even though she didn't really do any work, Sofia found herself eating a lot of food, almost as much as the hungry Lycans.

Lily and Astrid offered to do cleanup in the kitchen, shooing everyone away as they needed their privacy to catch up and gossip about family matters. They all went to the living room, where there was a nice, warm fire waiting for them.

Sofia cuddled up on the couch with Lucas while Noah and Jackson sat on the recliners, talking softly about what work was left to be done. Jordan, Austin, Jack, and Zac played cards. Austin was grinning maniacally as he kept winning round after round, and Jack kept accusing him of cheating.

"All right, *kids*," Jordan declared, rolling her eyes. "I think it's about time for bed."

"Fine," Jack grumbled. "But I'm not mucking out the stall tomorrow because you cheated." She stuck her tongue out at her brother, then stomped away.

"You're a card cheat," Lucas said to Austin. "I don't know how you do it, but you are."

"What, me?" Austin said innocently, but the sparkle in his eyes told otherwise.

They all said their goodnights, even Noah. He lived in a cabin not far from the house, and before he got on his bike to drive home, promised he'd be here to say goodbye in the morning. Soon, Sofia and Lucas were all alone in the living room, the flames burning down to embers in the fireplace.

"Cold?" he asked, cuddling her closer.

"You're like a furnace," she declared.

"I could keep you warm." His mouth turned up at the corners. "You won't even need a coat next year."

His words were teasing, but she stiffened in his arms at the implication of his words. "Lucas, I—"

"Sofia, I've never felt this way about anyone," he began.

Her heart thudded in her chest. "You're going to be leader of your clan, right?"

"Yes. I'm going to be Alpha of New York."

She swallowed the growing lump in her throat. "And you need ... I mean, you'll need a Lupa. Like Jordan." Who was a *Lycan*.

"It's not a requirement for the position," he said. "Though it's preferable."

She'd always thought that if she and Lucas ever had to part ways, it would be because things would just fizzle out. But she never guessed it would be because she simply wasn't compatible with him, *biologically*. Both Jackson and Zac had called their respective wives "mates", and she guessed that was a Lycan thing. It was something she could never be to Lucas, because she was human. "But you need a Lupa, so you could also have children who are—"

"Sofia, I love you."

His words made her freeze, and the dry tightness in her throat made her it hard to speak. More than that though, she didn't really know what to say.

"You don't have to say it back, not if you don't feel the same way." His tone was patient, but tinged with disappointment.

"Lucas." She placed her hands on his chest. "I do care about you." That's why she was here, wasn't she? "I just ... I just don't know if ... I've never felt that for anyone before and I don't know what it's like." God, why was it so hard? She couldn't even say the *word* out loud. This man had bared himself to her, his feelings and what he was. But she couldn't say it back or admit it. Not when she knew how this would end. She could never be his mate or give him Lycan children. And that felt like a knife stabbing at her chest.

"It's okay," he soothed, pulling her to him. "We'll take things as they go, okay?"

"Okay." She let his scent and presence calm her and pushed all those ugly thoughts away. Like he said earlier, just for now, while they were in this beautiful place, they could forget about the reality that awaited them in New York.

———

Sofia wished they didn't have to go back to New York. During dinner, Astrid had announced that the plane would be picking them up the next day, and so Austin and Jackson offered to drive them to meet the jet.

There was a dreaded feeling in her chest as they made their way to the private airstrip. Lucas didn't say anything after last night's conversation in the living room. In fact, he hardly said anything at all. Sure, they had sex the night before, but there was something different about him. He was almost primal and ruthless about it. How he held on to her a little tighter, moving tirelessly as he coaxed orgasm after orgasm from her before he eventually let go and found his own release.

They had said their goodbyes to everyone and were soon on their way back to New York. In no time at all, they were landing in the small airstrip outside Jersey City. Zac and Astrid took their own car back to Manhattan, while Lucas led her to the waiting town car on the tarmac.

"Hello, Reyes," she greeted the bodyguard as he opened the door for them.

"Hello, Detective. Sorry about the other night," he said sheepishly.

"It's okay, you were only doing your job." She flashed him a smile as she slid into the car, Lucas following her. He moved closer to her and threaded his fingers through hers, though they remained silent even as the car began to move. He didn't feel mad to her, but he certainly had a lot on his mind. She was about to open her mouth when a series of beeps stopped her.

"Sorry," Lucas said, taking his phone out of his pocket. "I just turned it on. I must have a hundred messages." He unlocked his phone and began to scroll through them.

Sofia sat quietly, looking out the window. Lucas was busy tapping out messages on his phone and making short calls. However, he didn't let go of her hand the entire time. That's why, when his fingers suddenly squeezed tight, she let out a pained yelp and yanked her hand away.

"Lucas?" She rubbed her fingers. "What's wrong?"

He had his phone held up to his ear, his face a stony mask. A tick in his jaw pulsed and he slowly put the phone down to his lap. "You talked to Caroline."

The words hung between them like a precarious tightrope walker. What could she say except the truth? "I did."

"How long ago?"

"That night I came to apologize."

"And you didn't think to tell me since then?"

She flinched inwardly but didn't show it on her face. "Does it matter now?"

"You shouldn't have done that." His tone was barely restrained.

"Shouldn't have—" She grit her teeth. "I was doing my job, my due diligence." She sucked in a deep breath, but it didn't calm her. "I already know what happened now, so does it matter? Is there a reason why you didn't want me to talk to your beautiful, perfect Caroline? Was what you told me really the truth?" Yes, Lucas had said he loved her, but in Sofia's mind, he loved Caroline first. And that made jealousy burn through her, despite her logical brain telling her it was unwarranted.

His brows snapped together. "It doesn't matter what I felt for her before. I—" He stopped suddenly. "We're here," he said, nodding at the window. They were outside his townhouse. His eyes darted to Reyes and the driver. "We should continue this inside."

"I will not—"

But he turned toward his door, yanked on the handle, and pushed it open. She should have known. Part of her realized she should have told him about calling Caroline, but so many things had happened since then; that insignificant call seemed like a million years ago. "Lucas!" she called after him as she slid across the leather seats. She scrambled to her feet. He was already halfway to his door. "Lucas! Will you—"

"Lucas Anderson, you're under arrest for the murder of Alfie Fraser."

She froze, unwilling to believe what was happening was real. It was like a horror movie, one she couldn't turn away from. A cop car had pulled in behind them, along with two other unmarked cars. Two uniformed officers were approaching Lucas as he stood on the sidewalk. One of them was already taking out his handcuffs. "Stop!" She rushed over to them, but they blocked her way. "What are you doing?

She turned around and saw Captain Bushnell and Henry Sharpe walking toward her. "Captain! Thank God you're here. Please tell the officers they've made a mistake."

"Detective Selinofoto!" Bushnell's brown eyes were almost gleeful. "Good job on this one."

"Good job?" She looked at Sharpe. His face was drawn into a serious expression. "Detective?"

"Your work was exceptional, as always." Bushnell patted her on the back. "If it wasn't for the way you put all the pieces of the puzzle together, we wouldn't have figured out that Anderson killed Fraser."

It was at that moment, the officers turned Lucas around to face them, his hands cuffed behind him. His mismatched eyes burned with fury and were directed at her.

"No!" she cried. "Lucas, I—"

"No need to be modest," Bushnell said.

Helplessness overwhelmed her as she watched the officers put Lucas in the back of the cop car. "Sir, I told you, I suspected someone is trying to frame him. He has an alibi."

"Not for the night of Frazer's murder."

"What? He was with me."

"Frazer wasn't killed that night," the captain said. "But the night before."

No. She looked at Sharpe. "Detective?"

"Lab confirms it," he said in a gravelly voice. "As did the blood on the shirt we found. We traced the shirt back to Anderson."

"This can't be!"

The cop car roared to life and then drove away. *Lucas.* This wasn't true. She didn't believe it. Whoever was trying to frame Lucas had succeeded. She should have warned him!

"We might also get him for Dixon," Bushnell added. "We have a witness who can destroy both his alibis. He says he was overcome with guilt, and he told us that not only did his security team lie about Anderson staying home that night but also made sure he was alone the night of Fraser's murder."

This was all wrong. Her instinct was telling her it was wrong. Who was this witness? "Sir—"

"I need to get back to the station before Anderson gets booked." Bushnell declared. "Sharpe?"

"I'll follow you, sir," he said. "I have to take care of something."

"All right. I'll see you at the station." He turned and walked toward the car.

Sofia watched the captain drive away, her mind still reeling. They'd arrested Lucas. "This is bullshit!"

"Detective—"

"He didn't do it! Any of it!" Her hands clenched into fists. "I know it."

"Detective—"

"What's this evidence against him? And this witness? Is it—"

"Detective!" The forcefulness of his tone made her stop. "What?"

Sharpe tugged at the tie on his coat. "Detective, please. Hear me out." He looked around, as if he was expecting someone to jump out at them. "I can't believe I'm saying this, but I believe you."

"You do?" She wasn't sure if she'd heard him right.

"Let's take a walk." He gestured for her to follow him as he strode away.

Intrigued, she did and stepped up to keep pace. "You believe me."

He shoved his hands into his pockets. "I don't know Bushnell very well, but his reputation precedes him. That first day I came, I knew it was a well-deserved one. But something changed the other day. It's weird, and I can't wrap my mind around it, but it's like he's a different person."

"A different ..." A chill ran through her. Her mind replayed her conversation with Bushnell, playing it like a movie backward and forward. There *was* something off about the captain. "How?"

"For one thing, he seemed unnaturally obsessed about Lucas Anderson. He said I should focus on him as a suspect." He shook his head. "Twenty years as a detective, and I've never had a superior tell me who my suspects should be."

"That's unethical." And definitely didn't sound like Bushnell. "And what did you tell him?"

"I said I'd be doing my own investigation. But he insisted, and he shared your initial suspicions with me."

"About the connection between Lucas and Dixon? The kidnapping and Kevin Hall?"

"Yes. I have to say, it was fine work on your part. Why did you stop?"

"Because it was all a dead end." She crossed her fingers. That was technically true, but she couldn't tell him the real truth about Lucas and the Lycans. "And then when we found Fraser, it should have all clicked together, but it just felt *wrong*." She looked at him, trying to gauge his reaction. "Bushnell didn't tell you, did he? About my suspicions?"

"No." He stopped and turned to her. "But he did tell me

about your personal involvement and why I had to take over both cases. What suspicions did you have?"

"That someone was trying to frame him. We need to figure out what happened. And why someone seems to want to frame Lucas for these murders. But Bushnell—"

"I don't think we can trust him."

She hated to think it, but Sharpe was right. Maybe someone had gotten to him, was bribing him or something. "We need to look back at all the evidence. And we can't do it at the precinct." Bushnell would be there. And of course, Lucas. She couldn't bear to see him in the cell. The look of hate he gave her before he was taken away ate at her. No, she would make sure he got free and he would never look at her like that again. "We can go to my place."

"I'll grab the case files and meet you there."

CHAPTER TWENTY-ONE

"Detective, you should get some rest."

"Shhh!" She held a hand up. "I need to read this."

"Detective ... Sofia," he said gently. "You've read that autopsy three times."

"I might have missed something."

"If you have, it's because you haven't slept or eaten in hours. Now, stop and take a breather." Sharpe insisted.

"No, there's no time."

"Time is the only thing we have." Sharpe took off his glasses. "We don't have any case."

"Not yet!"

"Sofia." Sharpe looked at her from across the kitchen table strewn with various papers, files, and photographs. "We've been at this since last night. It's five in the morning. Did you even sleep?"

She looked around her. "I closed my eyes for an hour or two."

He stood up and walked over to her, then knelt down to

look her straight in the eye. "I'm sure we'll find something, but you won't be able to if you're tired and hungry."

"But Lucas is counting on us. He's been in that cell all night!" She had called Winters at some point during the night to see how Lucas was doing. It was a Sunday, and no courts were open, so they had to wait until the next day for a judge to grant bail. *If* he gets bail. Lucas had the means to just disappear, so she doubted any smart judge would let him post bail.

"And we'll get him out, but you have to eat and rest."

She sighed, despair slowly creeping up on her. But she refused to fall into that pit. Lucas needed her. "All right."

"Good. Let's go get some breakfast and try to circle back. Maybe if we have full stomachs, we can figure this out."

They walked to a deli not far from her apartment and ordered bagels and coffee. Her stomach growled at the smell of food, and she devoured everything in seconds. Still, she felt ravenous, and she ordered two more egg and bacon bagels.

"This is a disaster," she said. "We haven't accomplished anything."

"You've convinced me that Lucas really is innocent."

She gave him a weak smile. "Thank you." And she meant it. Right now, she could use as many people on her and Lucas's side.

"I really thought it was just me, but now I know what you mean about how everything fell into place too easily. Ready for us to take, wrapped up with a neat little bow. Even that witness who suddenly came forward—"

"The witness!" She searched her mind. "Why didn't I find anything about him in the files?"

"It wasn't in there?" His lips pursed together. "I was pretty sure I got everything from my desk."

Her instincts were telling her now to keep pushing. "Who is it?"

He leaned forward. "David Masters. His assistant. Or former assistant now. Claims he quit because the guilt was too much. Interviewed him myself."

"David Masters." She thought back to that first day she went to Fenrir. Jared had stopped by the desk outside Lucas's office.

"David," Jared greeted.

Damn, she didn't even notice him. She had a vague idea of what he looked like, but never really paid attention to him.

"What's on your mind, Detective?" Sharpe asked.

"Do you know where Masters is?"

"We have an address," he said. "Brooklyn. Red Hook."

"We need to go see him." Masters was the key to proving Lucas's innocence.

"Now?"

She was already getting to her feet. "Something tells me if we don't, we might not find him until it's too late."

———

They took a cab to Brooklyn in Red Hook, the traffic light enough that they made it fairly quickly. On the way, they discussed how they would approach Masters and ask him questions. In the last couple of hours, Sofia realized just how smart Sharpe was. He wasn't just a good detective, but a strategist as well.

Anticipation thrummed in Sofia's veins as well as anxiety

and dread. Masters wouldn't expect them this early in the morning. Unless he wasn't there anymore.

No, Masters would stay where he was. If he really was out to frame Lucas, he wouldn't disappear until the job was done. But was putting Lucas in jail really the endgame? If it was Masters, why frame him for this? Was he somehow connected to the kidnappers?

Masters's neighborhood was one of those places that was on the cusp of being gentrified, but his building was still old and rundown. Good thing for them, because that meant that security was virtually nil. They were able to gain entry by simply waiting for a neighbor to leave and slip in before the front door closed.

"Apartment 2B," Sharpe said.

They climbed up the steps and found themselves in front of Masters's door. Sharpe lifted a hand and knocked. When there was no answer, he did it again, this time louder.

There was a shuffling from inside and then the door opened. "Detective? What are you doing here?"

Sofia blinked. This was David Masters? He looked so young. He was dressed in sweats and a T-shirt, but she supposed if he was in a drab gray suit, no one would notice him. So ... ordinary. Brown hair, brown eyes, straight nose, and a chin on the weak side.

"Good morning, Mr. Masters. Sorry to barge in on you so early. But we just wanted to inform you of Mr. Anderson's arrest."

He breathed a sigh, his hand going to the base of his throat. "Thank goodness. I hope you bring justice to those two dead men."

"We wanted to make sure you were all right and to ask you some questions," Sofia said.

Brown eyes looked straight at her as his fingers stroked his collarbone. "I remember you. You came to visit the office a while ago."

"Yes, I went to interview Mr. Anderson," she said. "About the murder of Thomas Dixon."

"And you left without doing anything. Not even taking him in for questioning."

She didn't miss a beat. "As you know, he can be very convincing."

"Well, thank you so much for stopping by." He made a move to close the door. "I—"

She shoved a hand against the door. "We have a few questions, if you don't mind."

"Just to make sure our case is solid," Sharpe assured him.

Masters hesitated, but pulled the door wider. "All right." He gestured for them to follow him.

Despite being small, the apartment looked tidy and clean. Again, it was so ordinary. There was a couch, a flat-screen TV, some books and magazines laying around. "Can I offer you some water? Tea?"

They declined, but accepted his invitation to sit on the couch, while he sat across from them on the easy chair. "What would you like to know, Detectives?"

"You said that Mr. Anderson was alone that night of Fraser's murder?"

"Yes. His personal bodyguard, Mr. Reyes, had a family emergency that night, and the security team was short-handed. So that night, he went home alone without any detail."

Sofia mustered all her training to try and keep cool. That alone wouldn't have been enough to arrest Lucas, but it was the shirt that tied it all together. "Do you have access to Mr. Anderson's townhouse?"

He shook his head. "Of course not. I'm not a personal assistant. I work strictly at the office."

It was Sharpe who followed up. "And you never handed him any documents at home? Do errands? Or maybe he left his briefcase and you had to run it to him?"

"Never."

They continued to grill Masters, but he was as cool as a cucumber and never wavered in his statements. Sofia was growing frustrated, because she just *knew* Masters was hiding something.

"I think we're done here," Sharpe declared as he got to his feet. "Thank you so much, Mr. Masters."

Sofia took her time getting up. "Yes, thank you." She wanted to wash her mouth after saying that to him.

"Anytime, Detectives." He got up and walked them to the door. "Anything you need from me, just ask. I feel awful about the way those two died. And then those pictures ..."

Sharpe turned around slowly. "Yes, it was terrible, wasn't it?" His gaze turned down to the floor, but before that, it flickered at Sofia so quickly, she could have missed it.

"Yes. All the blood on Fraser. And Mr. Dixon ... his head smashed in like that." His chin trembled. "I still have nightmares."

It took all her strength not to clap at Masters's award-winning performance. Her heart rate picked up, and she prepared herself for what was to come.

"Yes, it was tragic. But," Sharpe's gaze lifted so it met

his, "I didn't show you any pictures. In fact, I never mentioned Dixon until you told me and the captain that he had his security team lie for him about the night of Dixon's murder."

He gave a nervous laugh. "I didn't? I must have read it in the papers or something."

"No, because that was one detail I didn't release," Sofia said. "Just in case."

Masters turned to her. "In case of what?"

"In case the real killer identified himself by slipping up."

The silence in the room was so thick, she could have cut it with a knife. Masters's mouth curled up into a smile. "You think you're so smart, don't you, Detective Selinofoto?"

"I like to think so." She slightly tilted her head in his direction. What she was about to do what a gamble, but she was feeling lucky. "Why did you set him up?"

His ordinary face twisted into a hateful expression. "Why? Because we've been trying to get to him for months. He's so well protected by his damn clan. So, we decided that the best way to get to him was to let the human authorities jail him. Then, once he was trapped, we could finally take what we needed."

Clan. Humans. Sofia's blood ran cold. Masters knew Lucas was a Lycan. Was he one too? "You want to kill him that bad that you would frame him for murder?"

"Do you have any idea what he is? The abomination that is their kind?" Masters's voice grew distorted from anger. "You know," he spat. "And still, you whored your body to that filthy animal!"

"David Masters, you're under arrest." She relished those words.

"It took you long enough to figure it out." Venom dripped from his words. "Too bad I'm going to have to kill you."

She would have laughed if he wasn't so pathetic. "With what weapon?" He definitely wasn't hiding anything under his clothes.

His hand went to his throat, his fingers stroking his shirt— no, there was something under the fabric. Little sharp bumps, like he was wearing jewelry. He stretched his other hand out. "With this."

The sound of a gun cocking made her freeze. Her gaze darted to Sharpe, who had raised his arm and his weapon pointed at her. "Sharpe," she said in a low voice. "You don't want to do that."

"Probably not."

She jumped as both Sharpe and Masters said the words in unison. "What the—" Astrid's words came back to her. *They can do all sorts of things, like control people and make spells that can harm us.* What were they called? "You're a ... mage."

Masters laughed. "Correct. It's too bad Lucas Anderson hates your guts, otherwise I might have used you as bait."

"How did you—" And then she realized the truth. Sharpe's hazel eyes had turned a deep brown, just like Masters'. And yesterday, the Captain's eyes were the same shade. "You can control Bushnell. And see what he sees."

"Yes." He slipped a finger under his collar and took out something gold stuck around his neck. It was a thick chain that had a large disk hanging from it. In the middle of the disk was a large red gem. "Thanks to this, I can control anyone. Well, any human. But once we have taken Lucas's blood, I will be able to control Lycans and other magical beings."

"You bastard!" She wanted to do something—like kick his fucking teeth in—but Sharpe's gun was still trained on her. "Sharpe," she pleaded. "Henry ... you have to fight it."

"He can't!" Masters spat. As if to prove a point, he twisted his hand and made Sharpe point the gun at his own head.

"No!" she cried. "Kill me. But let him live. Can't you ... erase his memories instead?"

"I don't think so. We can't leave witnesses, can we? No, after he kills you, he will turn the gun on himself. We're covering our bases so even your captain has to go. Unfortunately for the poor captain, he's about to die in a terrible car crash, care of my associates."

"Fuck you!"

"I wouldn't even touch you with someone else's dick, you whore." His grin turned evil. "Maybe I should make your death slow. A shot to the stomach so you can bleed out." Sharpe trained the gun back at her.

This was it. She swallowed the lump forming in her throat. This was how she was going to die. Her gaze went back to Sharpe. Hopefully, he wouldn't have to remember anything.

But just as she was about to resign herself to her fate, she saw something that made her grasp at the last threads of hope. Sharpe's eyes went back to their hazel depths, just for the briefest of seconds. A bead of sweat rolled down the side of his temple. He was fighting for control! She didn't know how, but she knew.

"Goodbye, Detective," Masters sneered.

A split second before the gunshot rang out, Sharpe pulled his hand back, sending the bullet ricocheting just over her left shoulder. The ringing in her ear was painful, but she didn't have time to contemplate how close the bullet had gotten to her because she threw her body at Masters.

He screamed in surprise, his hands going up to cover his face. This was her chance. Her fingers targeted his neck—to the necklace—and ripped it off him, making him wail in pain. *Good.*

"Freeze, motherfucker!"

Sofia rolled off Masters, and when she looked up, Sharpe stood above Masters, his gun pointed at the mage. She nearly wept in relief. "I'll call 911."

CHAPTER TWENTY-TWO

"Is that it?" Sofia asked as they watched the uniformed police officers put the handcuffed Masters into the cop car. The mage's face was stony, and he was silent the entire time, from the moment they restrained him until the officers arrived to read him his rights.

Sharpe held his hand up, as he was listening to whoever was on the other line of his phone conversation. "Thank you, ma'am. Yes, we're headed back now." He put the phone back in his pocket. "Yes. They're releasing Anderson now."

Relief washed over her like a wave. *Thank God.* Masters's confession in front of two detectives was enough for the DA to drop the charges against Lucas. "And the captain?"

"Critical condition, but the doctors are positive he'll make a recovery." It seemed Bushnell had been in an accident, and had lost control of his car while he was driving into the city. But she knew better. Speaking of which, she and Sharpe had yet to discuss what Masters was.

"Sharpe," she began. "About what happened in there—"

"What is he?" he asked in a contemplative voice. "And what is Anderson?"

She couldn't tell him about Lycans, since she promised Frankie Anderson to keep their secret. But she supposed she didn't say anything about mages. "I know this will be hard to wrap your head around, but magic exists. And Masters, he used dark magic to control you. Like he controlled Bushnell, which is why he was acting weird."

He rubbed the bridge of his nose. "If I didn't experience it myself, I wouldn't have believed it."

"How did you break free of his control?" Even Masters had been surprised.

"I ... I don't know exactly. Even though he controlled me, I could see everything that was happening. It was like a rope was wrapped around me and I just imagined peeling it off me." He shrugged. "I thought my head was going to burst."

"We can't put the truth in our report," she said. "We already know Masters is guilty. But if we expose what he is—"

"His lawyer could plead insanity or say *we* were the crazy ones," he finished. "We'll keep that part to ourselves. If he does expose himself, then it's our words against his, and no judge will believe magic exists."

"I—Oh, shit! The necklace!" She had been so preoccupied that she just tossed it aside. She and Sharpe ran back to the apartment. Crawling to where she last saw it, she searched for the necklace, but didn't find it. They turned over the entire room, but there was no trace of it. "Motherfucking hell! Where could it have gone?"

"Maybe someone snuck in and got it," Sharpe guessed.

"Anyway, it doesn't matter now. It's not like it's going to help our case against Masters."

True, but that evil necklace was out there, somewhere. She had to tell Lucas. *Lucas!* He would be out any moment, and she wanted to be there to see him. "Let's go back to the station. We can get our stories in order on the way."

As they drove back to the precinct, they decided on a modified version of the story. Masters exposed himself by slipping up about Dixon's head injury and had no choice but to confess. He tried to escape and Sharpe drew his gun, but the shot went wild. Sofia then tackled him, and they subdued him together.

As they approached the station, she saw the familiar town car waiting outside, Reyes already by the door. Sharpe had barely stopped his car when she flew out. Lucas was already out the door, surrounded by two men in suits, Zac, and Astrid. His clothes were rumpled, and his stubble was now thicker and covered half his face.

"Lucas!" she called, her heart bursting with emotion at the sight of him. "Thank God—"

His mismatched eyes went dark, like a sudden storm forming over the ocean. "Did you come here to stop them from releasing me?"

She skidded to a stop, as if an invisible barrier stood between them. "Lucas? What's the matter?"

"What's the matter?" he snarled. "Was this your plan all along? Were you building your case, hoping to entice me to confess by sleeping with me?"

His words were like a thousand knives, cutting into her skin. "No," she croaked. "You can't believe—"

"I heard every word your captain said." His mouth pulled

back into a tight line. "About how you did a good job gathering the evidence."

"No! I swear I didn't do anything!" She managed to grab onto his lapels, but he pulled her hands away, his fingers digging into her wrists so hard she knew they would bruise. "Lucas, you're hurting me."

"You deceitful bitch," he spat. "I never want to see you again."

"Lucas, please! I didn't do it, I swear. I love—"

"Don't you dare!" His voice thundered, and she flinched visibly. "Don't you even try to say those words." He pulled her closer and whispered low. "And if you tell anyone about us, I'm going to crush you. I'll make sure you won't even find work as a meter maid, then destroy your grandfather's restaurant."

His threats had their desired effect, and she nodded meekly. He let go of her wrists, then turned away and marched into the car. Reyes scowled at her as he held the door open. She could feel the tears burning behind her eyes, but she refused to let them form.

Despite the fact that her heart felt like it was being crushed under an eighteen-wheeler, she still wanted to protect him. The mages might still be out there, and they had the necklace. "Astrid!" she called out as the young woman was about to enter the town car after Lucas.

Zac stepped protectively in front of his mate, his blue eyes like shards of ice. A snarl left his lips and she wanted to cower back. "You have to listen to me," she began, very voice shaky.

She whispered something to Zac. "Go to Lucas," she said.

He looked like he wanted to argue, but when his wife flashed him a meaningful look, he held his tongue.

"Two minutes," he warned before walking away from them.

When they were alone, the Lycan spoke. "You heard Lucas." Whiskey brown eyes were flashing with barely contained anger. "I won't let you hurt him."

"I'm trying to protect him!" She fisted her hands at her side. "I swear I wasn't investigating him for Fraser's murder. I already suspected he was being framed." But that didn't matter because Lucas really believed she lied. "It was David Masters. He was trying to frame Lucas. Masters is a mage."

Astrid's expression turned from anger to shock. "His assistant?"

She relayed to Astrid what happened with Masters. "He used a necklace to control my partner and my captain." Hopefully she wouldn't ask about Sharpe, as she would hate for him to lose his memory.

She looked like she was processing the information, but finally, she spoke. "I'll relay it to the appropriate party."

"Astrid ... please." She was grasping for words, her emotions in turmoil making it hard to form a thought. "Just ... take care of him."

An inscrutable look passed over the other woman's face. She nodded and then turned on her heel.

Sofia stood there frozen in her spot as she watched the town car drive away. Her heart felt like it was ripping in two, and she couldn't breathe. He thought she had betrayed him. They had been arguing about Caroline before he was arrested. And then those words Bushnell—no, it was Masters —said had been the last nail in the coffin.

She stumbled back, her knees like jelly. Lucas's expression of pure hate would be forever burned in her mind. She had tried to tell him she loved him, and he rejected it. And then he threatened her family ...

"Easy, Detective." Sharpe's lanky arms caught her before she fell back.

The words were stuck in her throat and she let out a pathetic cry.

"You should get some rest," Sharpe whispered gently. "Do you want me to take you home?"

She nodded weakly. "Yes, but not to my apartment."

He guided her back to the car, helping her into the passenger seat. She murmured the address she knew by heart, and he didn't protest at the distance or the traffic building up at the Queensboro bridge, but just drove her to where she wanted to go.

They stopped outside the familiar building, the cheerful mural of blue domes greeting her. But she didn't feel anything. She grew numb on the ride over, her heart's defense mechanism so she wouldn't feel anything. Just like when her mother died.

She didn't even know how she had gotten out of the car or trudged into the restaurant. *Pappoús* looked up as he wiped up a table, his face turning bright as he saw her. "Sofia! What a nice surprise." He put down the rag and walked over to her. "Where have you been? I've been calling you, and you haven't been answering."

And then, the dam of emotions broke. "*Pappoús*," she bawled as tears poured down her cheeks, and she collapsed into his arms.

"When will you stop moping like this, Sofia?" George Selinofoto asked. "Isn't it about time you go back to work?"

She raised her head to look at her father from where she was lying facedown on the mattress. "Are you kicking me out?"

"No, Sofia." George let out a deep sigh as he sat down on his daughter's bed. "You know you are always welcome here." He placed a large hand on her shoulder. "But you've been here for a week. You haven't left the house, gone to work, talked to anyone." When she arrived at the restaurant, she gave them an annotated version of what happened with Lucas.

"I don't want to do any of those things." She pressed her face to the pillow. "I just want to be left alone."

"I know, baby. And I'm sorry." He tipped her chin to the side to face him. "But you have to at least get out of this bed."

She didn't know if that was possible. Her bed was safe and warm, and anything outside of it was ... not. After what happened with Lucas that day, she just didn't want to face the world anymore. Even taking a step out of bed to go to the bathroom felt like a chore. All she wanted to do was sleep and forget. Forget about Lucas and his mismatched eyes. And all the times they made love. And the hateful expression on his face when he called her a deceitful bi—

"At least you haven't lost your appetite." She could hear the smile in his voice. "In fact, you've eaten so much lately, you might eat me out of house and home."

"Dad," she whined.

"It's okay, I'm just glad you're still enjoying food." He

chuckled. "Though with your appetite, you'd think you were pregnant or something. Your mother was the same." The mattress rose when he took his weight off. "I'll bring you some food from the restaurant tonight, okay?"

"Thanks, Dad," she said. As soon as the door closed behind him, she flopped onto her back. Of course, her mind began to drift to Lucas, so she quickly shut it down. Instead, she thought about her job. She had cashed in as much vacation time as she could, but she knew she would have to go back on Monday.

Sharpe had been nice enough to keep her updated on what was happening at the station. Bushnell was recovering but would be out of commission for a couple of weeks while he healed from the injuries from the accident. One of the more senior lieutenants, Jameson, was acting captain for now, and according to Sharpe, was doing a decent job at least.

Winters also called her once over the week and relayed some messages from the D.A.'s office. The attorney assigned to Bianchi's case was freaking out because she hadn't been answering her messages when the trial was coming up in two weeks. She asked Winters to relay to them that she was still going to testify. However, she didn't tell the D.A. or anyone about the two men who had attacked her in her home. The crime scene had been cleaned up, and she would have to make a report and expose the Lycans. Attempted murder of a police detective would have been a nice addition to the charges, but she already knew Bianchi would be going away for a long time.

She didn't ask about Masters, but Sharpe assured her that their case was solid, and he was currently still locked up. However, he refused to talk about what happened, not even to defend himself or deny the charges, but it looked like he would be pleading guilty to avoid a long trial. She wondered if his associates had anything to do with that, but she didn't really give a shit as long as he rotted in jail.

It was almost ironic now. Her job was her life, and she always thought she would feel unfulfilled if she wasn't a detective. But right now, it didn't seem to matter. She felt empty and hollow, and so broken, but she just didn't know how to fix it.

Her stomach growled. Apparently, her body thought food was the best way to fill her emptiness. And to think she'd just had lunch. God, she would get fat if she kept eating this way. Her hand went down to her stomach. Dad would have to roll her out of—

"Oh. No." She sat up so fast, a wave of dizziness passed over her. It couldn't be. They had been careful. Except those last couple of times at the ranch. *All it takes is one time,* her high school health teacher had said. But surely, it was too early for her to be showing signs of pregnancy?

Hopping to her feet, she began to pace. Only one way to find out. She grabbed her coat and put her shoes on, then went to the pharmacy around the corner. Thank God her dad was at the restaurant, because then he didn't see her zipping up the stairs with a bag full of pregnancy tests.

She tried reading the instructions or figuring out what the day of conception could be and when her next period would be, but she just got so confused that she bought a bunch of them.

She ran straight to the bathroom, not wanting to wait much longer to take the tests. She took all five brands. And each one of them had the same results.

Pregnant.

A calmness came over her. Frankly, she thought she'd freak out more at the news. She was having a baby. Lucas's and hers. A million thoughts ran through her mind. Would it be a boy or a girl? What name should she pick? Would it look like her or him? Maybe a dark-haired little boy with blue and green eyes.

Tears prickled at her eyes—whether they were sad or happy tears, she wasn't sure. Maybe neither, and this was just her being hormonal. Oh, God, she was going to have a baby. Her hand crept down to her stomach. Still flat, but it was incredible to think there was life growing inside her.

She fell back on the bed. *Lucas.* She wanted to get over him as soon as possible, and the only way to do that was to never see him again. But now she would be forever linked to this man who despised her. He had to know about the baby, of course. That was the right thing to do. But would he even want to see her?

There was still time yet. For now, she couldn't stay in her old bedroom and mope all day. There was so much to do and plan, and she certainly had no plans of getting fired. It was time to rejoin the world, for her baby's sake.

———

Sofia went back to work that following Monday, determined to get her life back to normal. A week had passed, and so far, so good. Well, as normal as she could, anyway, in her condition. She must have only been two weeks along when she took the tests. Maybe there was something in Lucas's Lycan biology that made the pregnancy easier to detect. Not that her baby was going to be Lycan. But still, it shared 50 percent of Lucas's DNA. All the more reason to tell him.

But the thought of approaching him right now made her stomach clench. For one thing, she wouldn't be able to stop from bawling. She had tried earlier that week. Gathering up as much of her courage as she could, she drove down to Fenrir to wait for him to come out. And when he did ... she couldn't stop the tears from flowing at her first glance at Lucas. It was funny, she almost didn't recognize him. The dark stubble he didn't shave off in Shenandoah had grown into a full-grown beard. His eyebrows slashed together in what seemed like a permanent scowl. Her heart leapt out and felt like it had been broken again. There was no way she was going to approach him, not when she couldn't control her emotions. When she told him about the baby, she wanted to be calm and business-like. They were adults, and they could deal with this like grown-ups.

"You feeling okay?" Sharpe asked as he stared at her from his desk. They were now officially partners, and she was happy about that. He was a good detective, and she knew she could learn a lot from him.

"Yeah, I'm fine." She grabbed a protein bar from her desk drawer. God, she was always so hungry. Dad was right about eating him out of house and home; she still went home to Queens because she didn't want to be alone, plus she wasn't sure what the state of her apartment was after the Lycans cleaned it up. She didn't get any angry phone calls from her super, so it must be okay.

"I need to check on a source." Sharpe stood up and put his coat on. "Wanna come along?"

"Nah, I need to finish up some stuff."

"If you need to talk—"

"I know," she said in an impatient voice. "Sorry." She didn't mean to snap at him, it just came out. She was tired. So fucking tired of her life being in chaos. "Go on, you don't want to keep your source waiting."

The hours crawled by, and Sharpe hadn't returned. She didn't really notice, seeing as she was busy with her own workload. She was getting ready to leave for a late lunch when the phone rang. With an annoyed grunt, she picked it up. "Selinofoto."

"Is this Detective Selinofoto?"

"Yes, this is she. Who is this?"

"I ... I can't tell you." The woman on the other line sounded scared. "But I have a tip for you."

"Ma'am, we have a tip line for things like this."

"Please! I was told you could help me. It's for a case you were working on. Prelevic."

She searched her memories. It rang a bell ... human trafficking case? That had been at least a year ago, and Johan Prelevic was still awaiting trial. "What about Prelevic?"

"He still has girls locked up. New ones," the woman said. "I have the address."

Sofia really wanted to go to the burger place around the corner and have a double cheeseburger, chili fries, and a strawberry milkshake. But if this tip had any merit, then it might mean saving a lot of girls. Just an initial look around couldn't hurt. "All right." She grabbed a pad of paper and a pen. "Where is it?"

The woman rattled off an address, and she wrote it down on a notepad. It was in Rockaway Beach, which was out of the way, but at least she would be in Queens. Maybe she could just take the rest of the day off and go home. After shoving the note in her pocket, she went to her car to make the long drive.

It took her over an hour by the time she got to the address. Pulling up, she saw it was an abandoned building at the edge of a commercial area. She got out of the car for a closer look. It was only two stories tall, and the red bricks outside were dirty and overrun with growing vines. The gate was boarded up and had a large "Keep Out" sign on it.

"*Fuck*." This was a goddamn wild goose chase. Obviously, someone was playing a prank on her. Angry, she whirled around to walk back to her car, then froze. Her mouth went dry and her every single muscle in her body tensed.

A man was standing behind her, a gun pointed right at her chest. "Hello, Detective." He smiled at her, showing a mouthful of teeth, reminding her of a shark. "Don't try anything stupid. Now, be a good detective and do as I say."

Her body tensed as adrenaline began to pump in her veins. She was trained to deal with situations like this, but she knew there was no way she could disarm him before he pulled the trigger.

Scared for her life and that of her unborn child, she nodded obediently.

CHAPTER TWENTY-THREE

LUCAS STARED OUT OF THE WINDOW OF HIS OFFICE ON the sixty-eighth floor watching New York bloom before him. In the last week, the signs of early spring were everywhere; the snow was gone, children were out and about playing outside, and people seemingly were much more cheerful about the warming temperatures, dressing in bright colors. But wherever he turned, Lucas could only see only harsh and gray gloom. And emptiness.

His wolf whined pathetically, but he ignored it. Right after that *incident* outside the police station, the damn animal had been raging at him, clawing him up and trying to take control. He knew what it wanted. It wanted *her*.

In his rage, he had screamed at his wolf. *She didn't say it back! She was a scheming bitch who used us to further her career. She never loved us!*

And that had sent his animal into a deep depression. It backed down and cowered from him, its presence barely felt. He told himself this was better, that at least now, he didn't have to fight his wolf all the time.

"Mr. Anderson," came Jared's cool voice through the intercom. "Are you ready for your next meeting?"

He turned back to his desk, checking his calendar. It seemed like his life the past two weeks had been nothing but Fenrir business. In fact, it was the only thing keeping him occupied these days, and working from sunup to sundown ensured he didn't have time to think about anything else.

"All right, let them in."

He prepared himself by taking his seat, folding his hands on top of his desk. The door opened, and his father, Nick Vrost, Zac, Astrid—and to his surprise—Daric and Cross Jonasson walked inside. He hadn't seen the warlock or his hybrid son since the attack at Blood Moon. "I didn't know you were bringing more people," he said to his father.

Grant folded his arms over his chest. "Daric and Cross have uncovered something about the mages, and we need to act now. There have been some more developments."

Lucas tensed. He'd been so occupied with keeping himself occupied, he'd ignored Lycan affairs. There were much bigger and more important things happening right now. "What have you—"

A buzz from the intercom interrupted him. With an apologetic look at everyone, he pressed the call button. "Jared, you know this is an important meeting."

"Yes, Mr. Anderson, but I think this is just as important."

"What is it?"

"There's a detective downstairs. A Detective Henry Sharpe."

"What does he want?" Lucas didn't have time for this. He'd been out of jail for two weeks and a detective from the NYPD was the last person he wanted to talk to.

"He says he has information about the mages."

Lucas's head snapped up and met his father's gaze. "Send him up."

"A detective who knows about mages?" Nick said. "How?"

"I don't know." Grant's eyes narrowed. "But we should be prepared. Daric?"

"I can take him away if necessary," the warlock said.

They made a quick plan of action and positioned themselves strategically around the room. When Jared announced the detective was here, Lucas instructed him to let the detective in.

The door opened, and the man barely stepped inside when Nick grabbed him by the arms and twisted him around, pushing him down to his knees. Astrid searched him and removed the gun strapped under his jacket.

"What do you know about mages?" Grant asked as he stared down at Detective Sharpe. They had decided to take the direct approach, and if it turned out to be a fluke or hoax, they could always erase his memory.

Sharpe looked up, strangely calm. "I know they exist." Then he turned his head and looked straight at Lucas. "But I'm not here about them. Mr. Anderson, I need to talk to you about Sofia."

The sound of her name, one that no one had dared say around him the past two weeks, made him shoot up to his feet. "I don't want to talk about her."

"Well too bad, because I won't tell you what I know about mages unless you hear me out and what I have to say about her." Nick tightened his hold, and he winced in pain, but continued. "I promise, I'll tell you what I know. It has something to do about that day you were released from jail."

Grant turned to Lucas. "Son? Why don't you listen to what the detective has to say?"

He gritted his teeth, knowing what his father wanted. It was a simple exchange. All he had to do was listen to what this man had to say about that bitch. "Fine. Say what you need to say."

"I was there that day you were released, Mr. Anderson, and you've read the situation wrong." Sharpe took a deep breath. "You know that David Masters was the one who framed you, right?"

Lucas's grip on his temper was slipping. He'd been surrounded by traitors all this time and he didn't even know. "He's dead, right? Shanked in prison?" His lawyer had told him earlier that day. It happened just last night.

Sharpe nodded. "Did you know he was a mage?"

Everyone in the room went still. "No," Lucas said. "We did not."

"Actually," Astrid spoke up. "Sofia told me, and I told my father."

Lucas pinned his future Beta with his gaze. "And you didn't think to tell me?"

"Would you have believed her?" she shot back. "You didn't even want anyone speaking her name. Anyway, right after you were released, she told me about Masters being a mage, and I told Dad. He said he was going to look into it."

"And we have confirmed it," Daric added. "Which is the reason why we are here now."

Lucas huffed and turned to Sharpe. "Well? Go on," he barked.

"While you were in jail, Sofia and I tracked him down," the detective continued. "Actually, she'd been working all night, trying to find a way to prove you were innocent and that someone was framing you." Sharpe looked him straight in the eyes. "She believed you. From the beginning, when we found Fraser. She even told the captain and that she had a relationship with you. Bushnell put her on paid leave and passed the case on to me."

Lucas refused to let Sharpe's words get to him. "And so, you found me guilty?"

"Actually, I was still trying to wrap my case up when Bushnell pushed me to have you arrested. When I refused, he went ahead and did it anyway. Sofia had nothing to do with it; she hadn't even been around."

Because she'd been with him at Shenandoah. "But why did your captain have me arrested?"

"It was Masters. He'd been controlling the captain the entire time. With a necklace he was wearing. If he hadn't used it on me, I wouldn't have believed it."

Astrid, Cross, and Daric all looked at each other. Lucas was starting to get annoyed. What else was the trio hiding from him?

"A necklace?" This time, it was Cross who spoke. "What did it look like?"

"I don't know. I didn't see it. But the moment Masters used it on me, I couldn't control my own body. He made me point a gun at Sofia and tried to kill her. But I broke free, and we took him down."

"This is what I was afraid of," Daric said. "Alpha, Lucas, the reason we called for this meeting is because Cross has uncovered something very important about the mages, including some information about a necklace."

"There is such an artifact that can be used to control humans," Cross said. "And—"

Grant cleared his throat and glanced at Sharpe. "We can talk about this later." He turned his gaze to Lucas. "Son?"

A pit began to form in Lucas's stomach. He was still processing Sharpe's words, trying to figure it out. Sofia had nothing to do with his arrest and worked to set him free. Could he believe the detective?

The intercom buzzed again, and he marched to his desk to answer it. "What now?"

Jared sounded apprehensive. "Er, Mr. Anderson, sorry, there are two gentlemen who are causing a ruckus downstairs. They are demanding to see you, refusing to leave. They're threatening to call the press on you."

Why the fuck was this his concern? "Who the hell are they?"

"It's a Giorgios and George Selinofoto, sir."

Sofia's grandfather and father. For a brief second, guilt overcame him as he remembered his words to Sofia. He wouldn't have done anything to harm her grandfather's restaurant; that was petty of him. He was talking out of anger, and it had obviously worked because she did stay away.

"I'll have our men escort them out," Nick said.

"No." The two men had been kind to him that night, and he wouldn't let them suffer the indignity of being thrown out of the building. "Let them up and I'll speak to them in the waiting room."

"We don't have time for this, Lucas," Grant said in an exasperated voice. "The mages—"

"This will just be a second." He didn't bother to explain further, but instead, walked out to the waiting area. A few minutes later, the elevator doors opened, and he walked over to greet Sofia's dad and grandfather as they stepped out of the car.

"Sir, I—" But he didn't get a chance to say anything as a meaty fist connected with his jaw. It didn't knock him down, though he did stagger back in surprise.

"You bastard!" George Selinofoto's voice was filled with rage. "You fucking asshole! If I had a shotgun, I would shoot you in the fucking balls!'

"Excuse me?" Lucas rubbed his aching jaw. "What the fuck are you talking about?" He looked at the older Selinofoto, who just stood there, his expression fierce.

George's face was red with anger. "Sofia, that's who we're talking about."

"I haven't seen or talked to your daughter in two weeks," he said.

"Well maybe you should have!" George's face went nuclear. "Because then maybe you would know that's she's pregnant!"

He understood the words, but his brain had a hard time processing it.

"Pregnant?"

Lucas turned around. It was his father who said the words. Everyone had filed out from his office and was in the waiting room.

"Yes, pregnant," George spat. "She told me about what happened between the two of you. What you did and that you didn't believe her even though she worked her tail off trying to get you free! And now, I'm cleaning up her room, and I find five pregnancy tests! All positive. She should have left your sorry ass in jail!"

All he could do was stare at George. Pregnant. Sofia was pregnant. With his—

"Mr. Ander—I mean Lucas! I've been trying to reach you for days!"

His head whipped toward the second elevator. He didn't even hear the chime announcing its arrival or the person who had hopped out.

"Who the fuck are you? And how the hell did you get up here?" The private elevators could only be accessed by authorized personnel.

The petite, red-haired girl rolled her eyes and pulled what looked like a cherry lollipop from her mouth. The t-shirt emblazoned with a cute cartoon character and the short, checkered skirt she wore made her look like she was fifteen years old. "Duh, I cracked it. My dad always said the security on it was pathetic. I like the updates you made, but really, you need to make them better. A 356-bit encryption would—"

"Lizzie!" Astrid strode over to them. "What are you doing here?"

So, this was Lizzie Martin. Arctic blue eyes stared up at Lucas. "Like I said, I have to talk to you!"

"Me?"

"Hello? You hired me, remember?" she said with exasperation, her curly strawberry blonde hair bouncing as she shook her head. "I've been trying to reach you for days! You haven't been picking up your private line."

In truth, he hadn't looked at his private number in a while because it was too hard. He would be tempted to look at his messages with Sofia and torture himself with all the memories. "Well, what is it?"

"Remember the names you asked me to cross-reference? Bianchi and Selinofoto?"

"What about them?"

"I didn't find anything about them that wasn't on public record already. But, when I checked the chatter on the dark web, I did find out one thing." She paused, her pretty face suddenly turning serious. "Bianchi put out a hit on a Detective Selinofoto. Seven figures if done by the end of today."

A fit of rage surged through him, and his wolf let out a deep, angry growl. He dashed back into his office and grabbed his personal cellphone. He dialed Sofia's number and waited. It rang but no answer, so it went to voicemail. He tried again, but it was the same.

"She's not answering her phone," he said to no one in particular.

"I'll call the station." It was Sharpe. He was standing in front of his desk, already fishing his cell phone from his pocket.

Lucas dialed again. And again. Straight to voicemail, the robotic voice seemingly mocking him.

Dread and anger filled him at the same time. He'd been blind. His anger at her supposed betrayal stopped him from seeing what was right in front of him. All he could think about was that she was a human, not to be trusted. He was also angry at her for not saying the words back. For not loving him.

But she did love him. Tried to tell him that day outside the police station. Then he threw it back in her face and threatened to hurt her family. And she was pregnant, to boot.

The thought of Sofia being pregnant with his child should have elated him. But, with her out of reach and the threat of Bianchi out there, he felt real terror and dread.

Please, let them be okay, he pleaded to any god or deity who could hear him. *I don't want to lose them.* He wanted to hold her in his arms again, watch her grow with his child in her belly, and be with her forever.

"She's not there?" Sharpe said, his brows furrowing together as he spoke on the phone. "When did she leave ... that was a while ago. Did she say where? No?" The detective was pacing back and forth now. "Tell me what you saw ... yeah ... wait!" He stopped in his tracks. "Yes, go to her desk. Grab the notepad and use a pencil and rub it on the top—yes, you know how to do it." He nodded and paused. "Good job Sergeant Winters. I'll let you know when I find her."

Anticipation made him impatient. "Where is she?"

"One of the sergeants saw her scribbling down on a notepad and then she left. I have the address she wrote down."

"Where?"

"Forty-five Bonnet street in Rockaway."

Pure panic set into him. "I have to get there. Now." But how? Traffic would be terrible. It might take them over two hours to get there and by then, it might be too late. Or it might even be too late now.

"I'll take you."

Daric! How could he have forgotten they had a warlock who could travel through space in an instant?

Astrid was already looking up the address on her phone and showing it to her father. Daric nodded, then trained his blue-green eyes on him. "Come." He held out his hand.

Without a second thought, he grabbed it.

———

Lucas had never traveled using magic before, and to say it was disconcerting was putting it mildly. There was a cold, clammy feeling that crawled over his skin, then penetrated deep into his bones. It took longer than he thought, but at the same time, it was too quick. He only blinked once, and when his vision focused, he found himself outdoors.

"We are here," Daric declared.

There was a soft *pop* behind them, and when he turned around, Cross, Grant, Zac, and Astrid had appeared.

"There!" Astrid cried out pointing to the warehouse across the street. It looked abandoned and derelict, however the gate that guarded it was open. But the state of the structure wasn't what distressed Astrid. It was the thick smoke curling out from the roof windows and the flames licking at the walls, threatening to devour the entire place.

"She's in there," Lucas said. He didn't know how, but he just did. Panic and rage coursed through his veins, and his wolf which had been silent for days was now on full alert, its hackles raised. "I need to—" A loud, deafening boom drowned out his words as part of the building collapsed. "I said—let go, Papa!"

Grant held him back, using all his strength to keep him in place. "Son, you can't! You'll get yourself killed."

"I don't care!" he growled. "I need to go to her!"

"Son, you're—"

"Do you think she is still in there and alive?" Daric asked.

"Yes." He knew it. She had to be, because he couldn't

imagine living in a world without her in it. "Daric, I—"

"Go." It was Cross who spoke. He was already unbuttoning his shirt. "I'll be right behind you."

Daric nodded at Grant who let go of Lucas reluctantly.

Lucas didn't even wait. He let his wolf out, his clothes shredding to bits, and headed straight toward the building as soon as all four paws landed on the ground.

He pushed his wolf, but it really didn't need any more encouragement. It was sprinting toward the front of the building, focused on getting inside. However, it skidded to a halt. The front door was ablaze and the heat from the flames made it too dangerous to get any closer.

No! He had to get inside. The wolf took a few steps back. Maybe if they could knock it down—

A growl made the wolf turn its head. A large, white albino wolf stood behind, its red eyes staring straight at them. *Cross.*

The albino wolf focused its stare on the door. Lucas wasn't sure what happened, but suddenly, the panels flew off its hinges, leaving the doorway clear.

He didn't waste any more time. His wolf sprinted inside, not caring if the smoke was burning its eyes and lungs or if the flames singed the tips of its fur. The inside of the warehouse was huge, but thankfully, it was gutted out so there was only one main space. Setting down low on its paws to avoid the smoke, Lucas glanced around.

There.

A figure lay on the floor, about ten feet from him. *Sofia!* The wolf scrambled toward her. She lay on her side, her face on the dirty floor. The wolf sniffed at her and licked her hand.

I need to get her out of here, he pleaded to his wolf. *Let me come back.*

The wolf growled, keeping its claws tight on their shared body. *Please*, he begged. *I promise I won't let her go, ever again.*

He felt the wolf rear back and then tuck itself deep inside them. The change was so quick, he felt dizzy, but he quickly recovered and scooped Sofia into his arms. *I love you*, he said silently. *Please don't die.* She was soft in his arms, and he felt her labored breath. He had to get her out of here.

Something brushed against his thigh. *Cross!* He was still in wolf form, and was brushing his flank against him. "Cross, shift back. I need you to—"

The air whooshed out of his lungs as a coldness crawled over his skin. He wasn't sure what was happening until he looked around and saw that they weren't inside the burning building. They were across the street in the abandoned lot, surrounded by the people they had left earlier. Twice now, Cross had used his warlock powers in wolf form. He didn't even know that was possible.

"Lucas!" Astrid came running straight at them. "Is she ..."

He looked down at the woman in his arms. Her eyes were closed, and soot covered her face. Quickly, he lay her on the ground, opened her mouth, pressed his lips to hers, and then pushed air into her lungs. "Sofia," he said. "Please." He brushed her face with his fingers, and he felt the trickle of tears down his face. "Don't die." He did it again, willing every atom of his being to fight. "I need you," he said between breaths. "I need you and our baby." When he felt her body jerk and cough, his heart soared with hope. "Sofia."

Sofia hacked and coughed as she continued to dispel the

smoke from her lungs, and he lightly tapped at her back to help her. When she looked up, her eyes were unfocused, but after a few seconds, they became clear with recognition. "Lucas?" she rasped.

He let out a cry of relief and gathered her into his arms. He kissed her hair, moving to her temple and then down her cheeks. "I love you," he murmured before he captured her mouth with his. She went still, unmoving, and he moved his lips away, peppering her cheeks and forehead with his kisses instead.

"Lucas," she gasped when he pulled away. "What happened? I was—"

"It doesn't matter," he said. "None of it matters."

"But—" She ran a hand down her face. "I ... you ... you hate me," she choked out. "You said you would ... that ... *Pappoús* and ..."

Fear and sadness clouded her beautiful slate-colored eyes. At that moment, Lucas swore to God that he would do everything in his power to never see that expression on her face again. "I was wrong. I made a mistake. I should have listened to you and believed you and ..." He took her hand and kissed it. "I'm sorry. Please forgive me. I love you so much."

She stared at him, her mouth parted. "I ... I'm sorry I didn't say it back right away. I just wasn't sure at that time."

"And now?" *Please*, he thought. *Please love me.* It would crush him if she didn't, but he would understand, especially after what he did and the names he called her.

"Now, I'm sure." She reached out to cup his jaw. "I love you too."

Incredible lightness, happiness, and joy filled him at

those words. He kissed her and wrapped his hands around her, never wanting to let go. However, the sound of someone clearing their throat made them pull away. Sofia looked up, then blushed.

Grant stood in front of them, arms crossed over his chest. Behind him was everyone else, waiting for them to say something.

Lucas got to his feet and helped Sofia up. "She's fine," he said, pulling her to his side.

"And she's yours," Daric added, a smile on his face.

"What?"

"If you haven't guessed it by now, Sofia is your True Mate."

"My—" He looked down at Sofia, who looked even more confused than he felt. "Sofia. The baby."

Her cheeks went pink, and her hand immediately went down to her stomach. "How did you know?"

"Er, well your dad told me—"

"Dad?"

"I'll tell you later. But, it's true, right?"

She bit her lip and nodded.

Lucas didn't think he could be happier after hearing her say that she loved him, but he was wrong. Sofia was going to have his baby. His Lycan baby. Though that didn't matter to him, because he would have been happy with a human baby, as long as it was with her.

"Wait, how did you know?" he asked Daric.

"When I touched her wrist in Blood Moon, I saw it in a vision," the warlock said. "Which is why I didn't dose her with the forgetting potion."

"Why didn't you tell me?" Lucas said. "Did you see all

this happening?"

"I cannot tell you what I saw," Daric said. "I can only say that I saw your futures intertwined. It has always been my policy not to reveal my visions to anyone. Besides, she is human. You would have resisted her."

Daric was probably right, Lucas mused.

"Wait, what's going on?" A wrinkle between Sofia's brows appeared. "I'm your what? Mate? But I'm not Lycan."

"No, but you're a True Mate. And that's special."

"Special?"

"It means you're mine." The words sounded so right, and his wolf preened. The damned thing knew it all this time. "We're meant for each other. And that any child we have will be pure Lycan."

Her jaw dropped open. "Lycan? I'm carrying your Lycan baby?"

He nodded. "You're also invulnerable. That's probably how you survived all that smoke inhalation. Our son or daughter was protecting you."

"I ..."

He could see that she was still in a state of shock. "I'll explain everything later, sweetheart." He covered the hand over her belly with his. "All that matters is that you're alive. And that we're going to have a healthy, happy baby."

She blinked as tears filled her eyes. "Lucas ... Lucas ..."

He wrapped his arms around her and allowed her to sob against his chest. Everyone around them moved away, giving them privacy. "I'll never leave you or push you away again. You're a much bigger person than I am. Thank you for believing me and forgiving me."

"I love you," she whispered, wiping her tears away with

the back of her hand. "I'm just sorry I didn't get to say it back right away."

"You don't have to apologize for that. And I'm the one who wronged you. I'm sorry, and I'm going to make it up to you in any way I can."

"In any way?"

"How would you like me to do it?" he asked. "I'll give you anything you want. A nice apartment by Central Park? A new car? Jewelry? How about a trip to Greece? Or I can invest in Giorgios' and open chains all over the country? Or maybe—"

"Stop," she said playfully. "I don't need all that. I don't *want* any of that."

"Then what do you want, sweetheart?" He could give her the world on a silver platter if she asked.

Slate-colored eyes looked up at him, and he was struck by the expression of pure love in her eyes. "You. I just want you. And our baby."

He tightened his hold on her, his heart bursting from joy and love. His entire life was going to be turned upside down because of this human, this woman that he loved and would do anything for. Some Lycans would be resistant at the thought of a human Lupa. And then there was the brewing war with the mages.

For now, he would enjoy this moment of having his mate in his arms. Of Sofia's orange blossom and olive scent surrounding him, comforting him. And of his wolf, finally content and deliriously happy at the prospect of a pup. He had everything he could ever want, and more than he deserved. And now, he was even more determined to fight their enemies, for the sake of his mate and their pup.

CHAPTER TWENTY-FOUR

One month later ...

Spring had finally arrived, and New York was in full bloom. Everyone was out and about enjoying the weather, from the office workers on their way to Friday night happy hour to the tourists snapping selfies in front of the Upper West Side's iconic Art Deco buildings. The trees were lush and green, and the flowers were in full bloom. The air smelled of grass and—

"Achooo!"

Sofia took out a tissue from her pocket and blew her nose, though she didn't stop walking, her steps keeping pace with the other New Yorkers around her as they crossed Central Park West. With an unhappy grunt, she looked down at her flat stomach. "You can protect me from fire and smoke inhalation, but you can't do anything about allergies? Some magical baby you are."

A woman rushing by jostled her as she stepped up to the sidewalk. "I'm in a hurry too, lady!" she shouted. "You don't see me trying to run over other people!" Ugh. Sometimes she didn't know if she loved or hated this city. With a determined shrug, she continued walking. She was already late as it is. Driving would have been faster, but when she heard about the gridlock on fifty-ninth on the police scanner, she decided against taking her car and rode the subway home instead.

Even as she rushed ahead, it was hard to ignore her surroundings. New York really was beautiful and vibrant in the springtime. The changing seasons was something Sofia had always loved about the city. How did people who lived in places with the same season notice the time passing?

Still, she couldn't believe it had been over a month since her life changed. It seemed like only yesterday she had just met Lucas. And in a couple of months, she would be giving birth to their baby. She had never felt happier in her life knowing she would always be with Lucas. Now that they had discovered they were True Mates, things had changed, though that didn't mean she put her old life behind her.

She was able to testify at the Bianchi trial, and with the additional proof of the mob's contract on her life, helped put him away for life with no chance of parole. Many of her colleagues at the precinct still hated her, but not as openly as before, especially after they found out about the attempt on her life. Bushnell was still in the hospital, recovering, and he didn't have the faintest idea that he had been controlled by a mage.

Although she knew Lucas didn't like that she put her life in danger every day, he never asked her to stop being a detective. How could she? This was what she was born to do, and it was part of her. She did concede on one thing: moving into The Enclave with him. With the mages out to get them and knowing about her existence, it was the safest place for her and the baby.

She picked up her pace as she continued walking uptown. Only a few more blocks and she would be home. Fuck, why did she have to be late, tonight of all nights, during Lucas's ascension ceremony? Frankie and Grant would not be happy if she caused the delay. Of course, they would probably forgive her and somehow find a way to make it Lucas's fault. His parents, after learning the truth of who she was and what she did for Lucas, came to love her. Frankie, especially was thrilled when she found out about her grandfather's restaurant. They all went to dinner there one night, and she was very happy to hear about the story of Dad and Mom's engagement at Muccino's.

Finally, she reached her destination. It was really funny how the mini-city where the New York Lycans lived was hidden in plain sight, right under everyone's noses. Lucas had explained that there was some kind of magic protecting it, not only to prevent their enemies from going in, but to compel humans to ignore its existence.

She stopped at the front door, holding her key fob in her hand. Only residents had the little electronic key that would open the door into the main entrance. As she was about to touch it to the pad, she heard a woeful *ruff* behind her.

"Oh," she said as she turned around. "Have we met before?"

The wolf—no, the Lycan—blinked at her, its tongue lolling out of its giant maw, as if it was smiling. She had met so many Lycans in the past month that she really couldn't remember them all, much less know who they were in wolf form.

"Are you trapped out here?" Lycans ripped their clothes when they shifted. Maybe this one lost his keys as well. "Well, come on then." She unlocked the door with her key fob, and as soon as she opened the door, the wolf slipped in, nearly knocking her down. "Hey!" The wolf darted down one of the hallways. *Oh, well.* Maybe he or she was in a hurry to get home.

There was no time to stop at her and Lucas's place, so she went straight to Frankie and Grant's penthouse apartment in Center Court, the middle of the three main buildings at the Enclave. The Lupa had sent her a message telling her she had to come there as soon as she arrived.

"You're late," Frankie said as she yanked open the door.

"Traffic. Took the subway," she quickly explained. "Hey, what—"

"I have everything ready for you." There was a hint of mischievousness in Frankie's mismatched eyes.

"Ready?"

"Yes, come on." Frankie tugged at her, dragging her into the spacious guest room. There were three people waiting inside. "They're here to help you."

"Help me what?"

They descended on her, like vultures on carrion. There wasn't any time to explain and they prodded at her and whipped her into shape. After thirty minutes, the hairstylist, makeup artist, and clothes stylist had her all ready.

Sofia gasped as she looked at herself. She was wearing the most gorgeous, off the shoulder floor-length blue-gray dress. Her hair was piled up on top of her head in a sophisticated French twist, and her makeup was applied perfectly. "Is that me?"

Frankie laughed. "Yes. Now, come on, the ceremony's starting soon."

They left the apartment and took the elevator all the way down, then dashed down the hallway that led to the outside courtyard. In their hurry, they nearly collided into someone running into the building.

Frankie staggered back, but caught herself before she fell. "Lara! How nice to see you. I love that dress." She pointed toward the courtyard. "The ceremony's that way."

The pretty redhead composed herself quickly. "Frankie! Sorry I didn't get to see you earlier." She was older, probably about Frankie's age, and was dressed in a cute vintage-style dress.

"This is Sofia," Frankie introduced. "Lucas's mate. Sofia, this is Lara Henney, Lupa of San Francisco."

"Nice to meet you, Lupa," she said.

"Oh. That's fantastic. Nice to meet you, Sofia." Her eyes darted around. "I was actually looking for Elise. Have you seen her?"

"Sorry, I've been at home the whole afternoon," Frankie said. "I'm sure she just went to the bathroom or something. The ceremony's probably about to begin, though."

"I should go check anyway." Lara frowned. "It's just ... never mind, I'll go check the ladies' room." With a quick wave, she headed down the hallway.

"Hmmm," Sofia muttered. "Should we help her?"

"No!" Frankie was pushing her out of the courtyard. "We're already late."

Apparently, becoming the Alpha of New York was a big thing, and lots of people were coming to this party. She'd already met all of Lucas's immediate family and some of his extended ones. As she walked through the crowd, she saw a few familiar faces—Jackson, Jordan, Noah, Astrid, and Zac. In the front row was Adrianna and her mate, Darius—whom she recognized as the silver-haired man outside the French restaurant. Next to them were Lucas's two younger sisters—Julianna so serious and business-like, dressed in a dark suit and her hair chopped down to her chin; Isabella, wearing designer clothes from head to toe, her hair in glossy curls down her back and makeup applied to enhance her already perfect features. She had gotten to know the two younger women in the past month and liked them both immensely, despite the fact that they were so different from each other.

Frankie ushered her forward toward the dais set up in the courtyard in the middle of the Enclave. Lucas was already up there, as well as Grant. Five people stood across from them— the Lycan High Council—as she had been told. One of them was holding a large, mother-of-pearl inlaid box. Lucas was looking at her, and he was not happy.

Sorry, she mouthed at him.

He shook his head and then began to walk toward her, much to the confusion of the council members.

"I said I'm sorry," she hissed. "What are you—"

"You're late," he said. "Very late."

"I know! We can talk about this later. You have some very important people waiting for you."

His frown turned into a smile. "I really wanted you here earlier because there's something very important I need to ask you."

"What is it?"

He glanced up on stage. "Usually, at ascension ceremonies, the future Lupa stands at her mate's side."

"Oh." She glanced around. Everyone was looking at them, and she blushed.

"I really wanted to make it official before we went through with it, so," he got down on one knee and then took something out of his pocket. "Sofia Selinofoto, will you marry me?"

She didn't know what to say so she let out a loud gasp. The beautiful solitaire diamond winked up at her. "I ... yes!" He slipped it on her finger.

Lucas whooped happily, then got up. Everyone was clapping and cheering as he took Sofia by the hand and pulled her up to the dais with him.

She watched by his side as he went through the ceremony, her chest bursting with pride. She did feel squeamish about him gripping the dagger with his hand and cutting himself so he could seal the vows with blood, but she expected it and understood it was part of tradition. When he said the final words and was declared Alpha, he turned to her immediately and mouthed the words, *I love you.* She mouthed them back as she beamed at him, feeling pride surge in her.

Everyone was still cheering and clapping, but a loud crack of thunder stunned them into silence. The atmosphere instantly changed, and she felt something dark and foreboding in the air.

"Lucas?"

His eyes glowed. "Danger."

There was a gasp and someone said, "Up there!"

Sofia looked up, and she too let out a gasp. A glass dome-like structure appeared right above them, glowing with a strange yellow light.

"The protection spell," Lucas whispered.

Another crack of thunder struck, this one so strong that the ground shook. There was a loud crash, and the dome shimmered, then began to fade away.

"Fuck!" Grant cursed. "Get everyone to safety." He stopped, then turned to Lucas. "Alpha ..."

Lucas nodded with understanding. He was Alpha now. "Into the basement shelters." His hand sought Sofia's. "You need to go with my mother. She'll keep you safe."

"I won't leave you! I—"

A strange ripple in the air made the hairs on her arms raise. She blinked, not sure if she was seeing things, because two figures appeared in front of them.

"No one move or she dies."

A tall, thin man wearing a dark red robe held a young woman against him, his deathly-pale fingers wrapped around her neck. Her electric blue eyes were frozen in fear and her face was drained of color.

A mage.

"Elise!" someone shouted. When Sofia looked to the source, she realized it was Lara Henney. She rushed forward, her hands raised. Her eyes burned with determination as wind swirled around her body, whipping her skirt and hair.

Sofia inhaled a sharp breath. Lucas had told her about a witch who could control air currents, but she didn't realize it was Lara.

"I said don't move!" he tightened his grip and the woman —Elise—choked and sputtered. Lara dropped her hands to her side, her face twisted in agony.

With the mage distracted, two figures dashed onto the

dais—Cross Jonasson and Julianna—putting themselves between the mage and Lucas and Sofia.

"Don't hurt her," Lucas said in a calm voice. "What do you want, mage?"

The mage laughed. "I want *that*." His gaze was directed on the ceremonial dagger Lucas still held, his blood flowing down the blade.

"You can have it." Slowly, he held it up in his hands. "Just let her go."

"You!" the mage sneered at Julianna. "Bring it here."

Lucas nodded at his sister, who took the bloody dagger and then held it up toward the mage.

The mage snatched it up with glee. "You stupid dogs! Using the dagger in your idiotic rituals. You have no idea what you've had all this time."

"Elise," Cross said in a calm voice. "Elise, do it."

The young woman's eyes widened. "No. Please, Cross, don't make me."

The mage's demeanor suddenly shifted, and his attention turned to the young woman he held.

"Do it," Cross shouted. "Elise, NOW."

A scream ripped from the mage's mouth as what seemed like white hot currents of electricity burst across his body. He let go of Elise, the threads of current still crackling between them and keeping them connected. Julianna and Cross leapt toward them at the same time, then all of a sudden, a bright, blinding light flashed. Lucas immediately pulled Sofia behind him, shielding her with his body.

She shut her eyes, and she heard a loud, deafening ringing sound. When it went silent all around her, she opened her eyes slowly. "Lucas?"

They both turned together, and Lucas let out a growl as she felt his wolf come to the surface, ready to go to battle. But there was no one there. The mage, Elise, Julianna, and Cross were gone. Like they'd disappeared into thin air.

Her logical detective's mind tried to grasp for an explanation but couldn't find one. "Where did they go?"

Lucas's jaw tensed. "The mage must have taken them." He looked behind her, his mouth settling into a firm line. Turning her head, she saw Daric, his wife Meredith, and Grant approaching them. Grant looked like he wanted to destroy something with his bare hands. She shivered, though she could feel that Lucas probably wanted to as well knowing Julianna was in the hands of their enemy.

"Alpha," Daric bowed his head deeply in respect. "Are you all right?" He seemed oddly calm for a man whose son just disappear into thin air. Beside him, his wife looked like she was fighting tears threatening to spill while trying to keep her anger in check.

"We're fine," he said. "But Julianna, Elise, and Cross ... did the mage take them away?"

"I don't believe he meant to take them." The warlock's expression turned pensive. "I think it's time we tell you about Cross's missions and what he has uncovered. He did not want to reveal everything until he was sure his research was accurate, but now, I am more convinced he is right."

"What did he uncover?" Lucas asked in an impatient voice. "As your Alpha, I demand you tell me."

"He found out that the three artifacts of Magus Aurelius really do exist."

"The three artifacts of—"

Before Lucas could continue, they were once again

surrounded by a bright light and the same ringing sound from earlier pierced the air. She shut her eyes, but the dazzling glow was so bright, it penetrated behind her lids, so she covered them with her hands. When the ringing sound stopped, she dropped her hands to her sides.

"Elise!"

Sofia blinked, still not quite sure what was happening. Cross, Julianna, and Elise had materialized in the same spot where they'd disappeared minutes before. Lara, who was being comforted by Frankie, cried in relief and immediately ran to her daughter.

"Cross!" Meredith threw herself at her son, her body wracking with sobs. "What are you wearing? Wait, what are you *all* wearing? And Julianna—your hair!"

"What happened?" Lucas's voice was calm, but the power in his tone was unmistakable. He really, truly was Alpha now. Sofia stepped up beside him and took his hand in hers. Though his gaze remained in front of him, he squeezed her hand. In that moment, she knew, this was her fight now too. She was his Lupa, and these were her people to protect. She may be human, but she would fight for Lucas, their child, and every single one of the Lycans under their protection.

"It's a long story," Julianna said with a sigh. "A very long story." She glanced over at Elise; her expression sympathetic.

"But you were only gone a minute or two," Grant said as he pulled his daughter to him in a hug.

Cross's blue-green eyes turned stormy, like a tempest brewing over the ocean. "Like she said. It's a very long story."

———

I hope you enjoyed Sofia and Lucas's story!

The next book is out! You can get A Witch in Time on Amazon now.

I have some extra HOT bonus scenes for you - just join my newsletter here to get access:

http://aliciamontgomeryauthor.com/mailing-list/

You'll get access to ALL the bonus materials from all my books and my **FREE** novella **The Last Blackstone Dragon.**

ABOUT THE AUTHOR

Alicia Montgomery has always dreamed of becoming a romance novel writer. She started writing down her stories in now long-forgotten diaries and notebooks, never thinking that her dream would come true. After taking the well-worn path to a stable career, she is now plunging into the world of self-publishing.

facebook.com/aliciamontgomeryauthor

twitter.com/amontromance

bookbub.com/authors/alicia-montgomery

CPSIA information can be obtained
at www.ICGtesting.com
Printed in the USA
BVHW040600210523
664489BV00005B/64